STORMHAVEN

Also by Jordan L. Hawk

<u>Whyborne & Griffin</u>
Widdershins
Threshold
Stormhaven

<u>SPECTR series</u>
Hunter of Demons
Master of Ghouls
Reaper of Souls
Eater of Lives
Destroyer of Worlds (2014)
Summoner of Storms (2014)

Heart of the Dragon (short story)

STORMHAVEN

(Whyborne & Griffin No. 3)

JORDAN L. HAWK

Stormhaven © 2013 Jordan L. Hawk
ISBN: 978-1493759255

All rights reserved.

Cover art © 2016 Lou Harper

This book is a work of fiction. Names, characters, places, and incidents are products of the author's imagination or are used fictitiously. Any resemblance to actual events or locales or persons, living or dead, is entirely coincidental.

Edited by Annetta Ribken

I wrote this book for you.

CHAPTER 1

NEWLY INSTALLED ELECTRIC lights blazed from atop the department store, theater, and even the street corners where ordinary gas lamps had burned just a month ago. An ugly tangle of wires cut across the night sky like the weaving of some huge, and quite demented, spider. The harsh light revealed the cracks in the sidewalk and threw sharp-edged shadows, far less kind than the radiance of either sun or moon.

I'd not seen the lights in operation before, as I didn't generally stray outside after sundown without reason. Christine had wished to observe them, however, as had Griffin, and so here I stood on the sidewalk, just past sunset on a mild August night.

I'd rather have remained home.

"Very impressive," Christine said, as we strolled down River Street. Christine, or more properly, Dr. Christine Putnam, was my colleague at the Nathaniel R. Ladysmith Museum and one of two people I truly called friend.

"Electric lights have been in use in Chicago for a while, although of course the battle between the electric and gas companies still rages on," said my other friend, Mr. Griffin Flaherty. At least, the rest of the world considered us to be good friends who lived in the same house because we found one another's company congenial. Which we did, although our relationship consisted of a more romantic nature than most would imagine.

Griffin touched the brim of his hat to a group of laughing young women who passed us on the street. One or two took a lingering look at his overlong curls and trim form. I did my best not to glare at them. "Still, I feel certain this is the way of the future," he went on. "I've been thinking about having electricity installed at the house."

"Absolutely not!" I exclaimed. Had the man gone completely mad?

Griffin gave me a surprised look. "Why ever not?"

"Well…" I flailed for a moment, trying to put my objection into words, "for one thing, these electric lights are too steady. Sterile, one might say. Not like *real* light from a candle or gas lamp."

"Weren't you just complaining about the dimness and flickering in the study last week?"

I ignored his absurd question and forged ahead. "They have no warmth. And they lack the aroma of gas lighting."

"This summer, you claimed to be dying first from the heat, then from the fumes."

"I don't see what that has to do with anything," I said crossly. "These lights are far too modern for Widdershins, or anywhere else, for that matter. They will never catch on."

Griffin's green eyes flashed with amusement, and a dimple appeared on one cheek when he grinned. "My dear Whyborne, things do change, even here in Widdershins." He gestured to the garish lights above the department store. "And once they do, nothing ever goes back to the way it was before."

"Hmph."

"Well I, for one, rather like them," Christine put in. She walked with her arms swinging at her sides, rather than holding onto either of our elbows, as a woman might normally be expected to do when in the company of two men. But normal didn't really describe any of us. "Can you imagine having electric lights to use in a tomb during a dig?"

"When do you leave for Egypt?" Griffin asked, diverting the conversation from the lights with a skill which no doubt served him well in his occupation as a private detective. Of course he would be in favor of these hideous new lights: they diminished the shadows in which criminals might hide their secrets from him.

We turned away from River Street and meandered through the side lanes, which would eventually return us to Christine's boarding house. Griffin and Christine discussed plans for her excavations in Egypt, once the field season began anew. The stars shone out thickly above. Moths clustered around the gas lamps, which, in my opinion, gave more than adequate illumination. A friendly cat on a doorstep meowed at me, and I stopped to give it a scratch between the ears.

A shriek of horror shattered the night.

The cat bolted. I spun around, searching frantically for the source of the cry. Ahead of me, Griffin gripped his silver-headed sword cane, while Christine swore in Arabic and dug through her purse for her pistol.

The shriek came again, from another street over, high and fearful as that of someone trapped in a nightmare. Griffin bolted down an alley between homes, and I followed, with Christine at my heels.

A man stood in the street outside one of the houses, staring down at his hands. In the dim light, they looked to be coated with some black substance although, as we drew closer, I realized from the rusty smell it must be blood.

He raised his head as we approached. The light from the nearest streetlamp fell across his face, his features startling me with their familiarity.

"What's going on here?" Griffin asked, the same instant I said, "Allan? Allan Tambling?"

He stared at us in confusion, his bloody hands still held out before him. "Dr. Whyborne? Dr. Putnam? What...what's going on?"

I hadn't the slightest idea. Allan Tambling was a quiet young man, hired to restore any damaged but valuable paintings which entered the museum's collection. What little I knew of him suggested he was unusually focused and sober for an artist and certainly not the sort I expected to find staggering about in the street, bloody as if he'd just come from apprenticing at a butcher's.

Christine stopped just out of Allan's reach, gripping something in her purse—her pistol, no doubt. "Good Gad, man, what happened to you? Are you hurt?"

Tambling blinked slowly, before shaking his head. "I...I don't know. I had dinner with my uncle, we went to his study...and I found myself outside, with blood all over! I don't know how I got here. I thought I saw someone running away..."

"Which direction?" Griffin asked instantly. When Tambling pointed a shaking hand, Griffin immediately dashed in pursuit, although I doubted he'd catch anyone at this point.

"Here," I said, pulling out my handkerchief and passing it to Tambling. "Where is your uncle's house?" Perhaps if we convinced him to go inside, we could discover if he'd been injured or at least calm him down.

"Th-there," he said, pointing to the house behind him. The door stood open, and a warm scarf of light lay across the front stoop.

Before we took a single step toward the house, however, a woman's scream came from within. A moment later, a maid appeared at the doorway.

"Police!" she shrieked at the top of her lungs. "Help! Mr. Bixby's been murdered!"

Some time later, Allan Tambling sat on the stoop, his face buried in his now clean hands. Police milled about, bustling in and out of the house. As the body had already been taken away, I couldn't imagine what business so many of them had within, outside of the desire to gawk at the spot a man had died.

The maid had left, swearing never to return. I'd remained out of some sense of loyalty to a fellow employee of the museum although, so far, my presence hadn't proved at all useful, except to answer one or two questions for the police.

"Is there anything I can get you, Mr. Tambling?" I asked awkwardly. What I would do if he requested something, I hadn't the slightest idea. I couldn't exactly boil him a cup of tea or procure a stiff brandy here on the street.

He took a deep breath, as if to master himself. "No, I...no. Thank you, Dr. Whyborne. I've sent for my older brother, but otherwise I don't think there is anything to be d-done."

"Yes. My condolences," I added. "I'm certain the police will catch whoever is behind this very soon."

"Thank you, sir."

Feeling utterly useless, I turned away and looked for my companions. Christine waited on another stoop, ignoring a policeman's attempts to escort her from the scene. Griffin, however, seemed engaged in lively argument with a man I recognized as Detective Tilton.

I wandered close enough to listen in. "But you didn't see anyone," Tilton said.

"No," Griffin replied, "but I'm only one man. If your men conducted a thorough search—"

Tilton's eyes narrowed, and his mustache quivered. "I don't need you telling me how to do my job, Flaherty. You believe you know something about investigation just because you were a Pinkerton thug, but I assure you, I've forgotten more than one of your ilk will learn in a lifetime."

I bridled at the insult. "Mr. Flaherty isn't some heavy-handed strike-breaker," I snapped. "I daresay he knows as much about investigation as anyone in this town."

Tilton gazed at me coolly, and my anger drained away abruptly. What was I thinking, drawing the attention of the police? Although Griffin claimed they weren't trained to somehow spot men like us without any other signal being passed, my stomach turned over queasily nevertheless. In the eyes of the law, Griffin and I were criminals many times over by the very nature of our relationship.

"Dr. Whyborne," Tilton said neutrally. "I'm sorry to see you're still keeping company with this lout."

"A sad state of affairs," Griffin agreed cheerfully. "Very well, Tilton, I see you won't listen to reason. I will keep my advice to myself from now on."

"See that you do."

We collected Christine and started back the way we had come. As we passed Allan, I slowed my steps, intending to give him some look of sympathy or encouragement. But he sat on the stoop, staring fixedly down at his hands with a dazed expression, as if my presence couldn't penetrate the fog of grief and fear around him.

"Why can't I remember?" he whispered to himself. Although he'd wiped off his hands, blood still caked beneath the nails. "Why?"

His words sent a little shiver down my spine, and I hastened to catch up with my companions.

In the small hours before dawn, I opened my eyes and found myself drowning.

Water pressed down upon me with palpable force: cold and dark, as if I had sunk to the very bottom of the sea. I thrashed madly, struggling for the surface, but I might as well have been swimming through treacle. Some force held me in my watery grave, until my burning lungs gave up the fight, and I inhaled sharply.

I breathed.

A blink, and the darkness receded, my eyes mysteriously able to penetrate the blackness of the abyss. A great city rose up around me, its cyclopean architecture humbling even the mighty pyramids of Egypt. A single block of barnacle-encrusted granite loomed larger than a house. But I found the architecture oddly repellent. None of the lines seemed to meet quite as one expected, so perspective became distorted, angles which appeared acute one moment seeming obtuse another.

The ghastly place showed no signs of inhabitants, but life filled it nonetheless. Barnacles clung to every surface, corals sprouted, and a thousand fish swarmed high above my head, like flocks of birds. Thin, shell-like tubes projected from many surfaces, their fan-shaped inhabitants stretching out delicate tendrils in a thousand colors, resembling living flowers. I reached out to touch the nearest, and it ducked back into its cylindrical home.

How had I come here? I struggled to remember, but found nothing to explain the city or my presence in it. Where was Griffin? Was I alone?

The ocean current stirred against my cheek, bringing with it a scent both noxious and strangely familiar.

No, I wasn't alone.

My heart jerked against my ribs at the sudden, overwhelming conviction something else occupied this Tartarean city. And whatever it was, it knew I was here...and it wanted to find me.

I tried to run, but the heavy water clutched at me, slowing my steps. A slot between buildings offered a place to hide, but as I rushed toward it, an abnormal eel lunged out, snapping teeth like glass needles.

I fell back from the misshapen thing, casting about frantically. I had to hide! Whatever searched for me was almost here, and if it found me, something terrible would happen. It was getting close; fish fled before its coming, and even the monstrous eel darted off into the murky distance. The fan-like worms shut themselves into their tube homes, and the muck beneath my feet came alive as even the foul, crawling things of the ocean floor sought to escape.

Oh God. It was behind me now. I knew it with an unshakeable certainty. Every muscle locked into place, and I struggled to breathe through the blind, animal instinct which equated movement with death.

It saw me. I couldn't just stand here and wait for it to seize me. I had to turn and face it.

With a sense of unspeakable dread, I slowly forced myself to turn and see what hunted me. When I did, my paralysis broke, and I screamed.

~ * ~

"Whyborne! Steady on; you're having a bad dream."

I dragged in a great breath, every muscle locked in terror. Sheets, damp with sweat, pressed against my back. The moonlight filtering through the open window revealed the familiar ceiling of our bedroom. Griffin's scent, of sandalwood and male skin, enveloped me, his warm hand resting on my shoulder. My head pounded as if someone had attempted to drive a nail into my skull.

"Oh," I said. I intertwined my fingers with his, and he gave them a reassuring squeeze. "It seemed so real."

Griffin's lips brushed the bare flesh of my shoulder. "Poor love. Would you like to tell me about it?"

I tried to recall what had horrified me, but the dream had already begun to unravel into fog. "I don't quite remember," I admitted. "Something about a city, and the ocean…something hunted me…"

Perhaps I'd had the disturbing dream on account of the murder we'd happened across. After seeing poor Tambling so deeply shaken, no wonder I'd had a nightmare.

Griffin stroked my shoulder. "You're safe," he said. "There's nothing hunting you."

"I know. It just seemed extraordinarily real at the time."

A breeze stirred the curtains, bringing with it Widdershins's fishy smell. Our cat, Saul, sat in the window, peering out at the lawn below, apparently fascinated by the movements of some nocturnal creature. Crickets chirped. I heard a nightjar loose its lonely cry.

"Night terrors often do." Griffin's hand drifted along my chest, tracing across my heart, down to my belly. My skin pebbled in response, nipples drawing tight. "Shall I distract you from the memory of it?"

My length twitched against his thigh, clearly approving of the suggestion. Griffin chuckled and bent to kiss me, his hand resting just below my navel. In the moonlit dark, he was nothing more than a half-glimpsed silhouette, best understood through the touch of his warm skin, his thigh sliding across mine, fingers twining in my hair.

I returned his kiss, exploring the contours of his mouth. He let out a little muffled moan and sucked on my tongue, which action stiffened my member entirely.

When we'd first met, I'd never even kissed anyone before. I spent my life successfully denying my urges, yet something about Griffin rendered him irresistible. His touch inflamed my every passion; my skin ached for the feel of his pressed against it.

"Yes," I whispered against his lips.

His hand dipped lower, fingers trailing lightly along my cock from base to tip, making it jump and bob with need. His hard length pressed against my thigh, and he pushed his hip against mine, rubbing slowly. My arms encircled him, shaping the muscles of his back and side. He murmured encouragement.

Griffin nudged my thighs with his hand, and I spread my legs eagerly, baring myself to whatever he wished to do. I had no shame with him, my need too great to allow it. Warm fingers cupped my sack, rolling and tugging gently. I gasped at the pleasure. His teeth closed lightly around a nipple, worrying at it, and my hips jerked up, a bolt of ecstasy going straight from nipple to balls. "Griffin," I said, but his name came out more of a moan.

He shifted lower on my body, his fingers finally encircling the base of my cock. A moment later, his lips closed around the head. I groaned with the desire to push into the wet heat of his mouth. I kept still, though, while he slid lower then back up, tongue worrying at the slit until I whimpered.

"I love how you taste," he said, lips brushing the sensitive skin.

"Let me taste you, too, please," I begged.

"Gladly." We shifted position on the bed, until his legs bracketed my head, his cock pointed at my mouth.

I gripped the base with one hand, tugging him down eagerly. I rubbed the tip over my lips, spreading the salty, slick dew across them. In response, he groaned and sucked at me harder.

God! How I loved this, and him. Difficult to believe I'd known him for less than a year, so thoroughly had he become entwined with my life. My heart craved his presence, and my body craved his touch, like an opium addict reaching for the pipe again and again.

I took him into my mouth, concentrating on the feel of his thick shaft, the ridged veins against my tongue. Since my hands were now free, I gripped his taut buttocks, spreading him and getting a growl in response, which vibrated through my shaft.

I paused in my ministrations long enough to thoroughly wet a finger with my spit, before taking him in my mouth again. I slid my finger along his crease, probing the tight ring of his passage.

He moaned around me and redoubled his efforts, sucking on my cock and tugging my sack, as if he wished to push me over the edge first. I took it as a challenge, if an unintentional one, teasing his hole before pushing in, searching for the spot inside him which would give him the greatest pleasure.

The muscles of his thighs went tight, and his member stiffened further against my tongue, warning me of his release. I swallowed the hot, bitter spend, taking him into me. He moaned as he spent himself, never pausing in his attentions to my organ, and his passion inflamed mine further. I closed my eyes and thrust up into the heat of his mouth, until my need eclipsed all control. I gave myself over to the blinding pleasure.

He pulled away, my softening member sliding from his lips. With a happy sigh, he collapsed on the bed beside me, head on my shoulder. "Well, my dear, did I distract you?" he asked, his voice ragged still as his breathing slowed.

"Distract me from what?" I mumbled, wrapping my arms around his broad shoulders.

He chuckled. "I'm glad to have been of service."

I meant to make some reply, but languor gripped me as I slid away into a deep and mercifully dreamless sleep.

CHAPTER 2

THE FOLLOWING FRIDAY, I carefully set a bowl of water in the center of my desk then shut the door behind me. Located in the windowless basement of the Nathaniel R. Ladysmith Museum, my office was quiet and out of the way, which kept potential interruptions to a minimum. Indeed, if Christine were in the field, I might go weeks without speaking to anyone but the secretarial staff. A situation I quite preferred, in all honesty. The privacy allowed me to conduct my research without interruption.

And that's all this was. Research. Outside the bounds of my job as the museum's comparative philologist, but research of a sort.

Ignoring the guilt squirming in my chest, I took my seat behind the desk. I had cleared it off—well, shoved the piles of paper and journals to the side and relocated the cuneiform tablet I was in the process of piecing together to an out-of-the-way corner of the floor.

While I waited for the water in the bowl to still, I once again checked the book I carried in my coat pocket. I didn't speculate too closely on the strange, fine-grained leather of its cover or on what hand had filled its pages with encrypted writing, alchemical symbols, and disturbing sketches.

When the *Liber Arcanorum* first came into my possession, I'd assumed the spells and sorcerous incantations inscribed within to be the ravings of a medieval madman, the sort of thing embraced by occultists of only the most gullible sort. Much to my surprise, I'd soon discovered the spells not only worked, but I could perform them.

Griffin wished me to restrict my use of the book. He didn't understand it was just a tool, no different than his revolver or sword cane. All my attempts to convince him of his error had fallen on stubborn ears, even when I pointed out, quite rightly, the spells within had saved our lives on more than one occasion.

Having no desire to quarrel unnecessarily, I simply conducted my experiments where he wouldn't have to see them. This way, we could both be happy.

When the water stilled, I leaned forward, careful not to stir the surface with my breath. This was a bit more complicated than lighting fire with a word, or summoning wind with a drawn sigil and an incantation. Air and fire were the elements most easily changed, at least according to the *Arcanorum,* and thus even the will of a novice might have some effect on them. Water was thicker, more resistant, which took more sorcerous skill.

Of course, I was no sorcerer. Just a dabbler in a branch of science not fully understood.

Focusing my will, I concentrated on the water in the bowl. All else faded from my consciousness. I recalled its weight, the cool drops which splashed onto my hand when I filled the bowl, the taste when I touched my lips to the surface.

Moving slowly, so as not to jostle the desk, I raised my hand a few inches above the bowl and pointed a finger. Holding the result I wished very clearly in my mind, I moved my finger in a slow, counter-clockwise motion.

The water stirred. Slow at first, then faster, responding to the speed of my movements, far more easily than I had expected.

Elation filled me as the little bowl turned into a whirlpool, the water swirling almost to the rim—

"Whyborne, have you heard?" Christine demanded, flinging open the door to my office without knocking.

My concentration broke. Water went everywhere, cascading across the table and drenching my chest and lap.

I leapt to my feet, groping in my pocket for a handkerchief. "Christine! Knock!"

Her dark brows drew down over her eyes. "What the devil are you getting up to in here?"

"Keep your voice down!" I admonished, wiping ineffectually at my dripping clothes. At least the *Arcanorum* had escaped a soaking. "You interrupted an experiment with a spell."

Having rendered assistance to Griffin and I on several occasions, Christine was quite familiar with my secrets. "What, here at work? Why on earth didn't you lock your door?"

"Perhaps I expected my colleagues to knock first?"

"There you have it. Really, you ought to know better by now."

As if to prove her point, Bradley Osborne strolled inside. "Have you heard —oh." He took in my wet clothing, and a condescending smile settled onto his lips. "Had a bit of an accident, eh, Percy?"

"Er, yes," I muttered, feeling the tips of my ears go hot. No doubt Bradley would spread the tale to the rest of the museum the moment he left.

"Whatever do you want, Mr. Osborne?" asked Christine, not bothering to conceal her impatience.

"The same thing you do, I suspect, Miss Putnam."

"Doctor Putnam," Christine and I said at the same moment.

Bradley, as usual, ignored us both. "It's all over the museum, of course, but I imagined Percy hiding down here in his monk's cell wouldn't know yet."

I clenched my sodden handkerchief in my hands. "Know what?"

"Tambling," Christine said hurriedly, before Bradley had the chance to respond. "They've arrested him for the murder of his uncle."

"Wh-what?" The strength seemed to leave my legs, and I sank into my chair. It squelched under me. Now my backside would be as wet as my front.

"Tambling, the painting restorer," Bradley said, as if I didn't know. "Did away with his uncle in a most gruesome fashion, according to the papers. Stabbed him with an obsidian blade from the man's own collection."

"Tambling's been jailed?"

"Even worse!" Bradley said with relish. "The doctors and judge think he's violently insane and have sent him to the Stormhaven Lunatic Asylum."

"How horrible," I said. Poor Allan. Surely, it couldn't be true, could it? He'd seemed confused and grief stricken on Saturday, but hardly the picture of a dangerous madman.

"You and your womanish sympathy," Bradley said. "If you ask me, he always seemed prone to nerves. Dr. Hart should have fired him before he had the chance to go insane."

"If the director fired everyone here who might go mad, half the museum would be depopulated," Christine replied. She exaggerated, of course—I felt fairly confident less than a quarter of those who worked here could reasonably be said to have taken leave of their sanity at some point or another. The library staff would be rather decimated, though.

"Oh, really?" Bradley said, turning a patronizing smirk on Christine. "Afraid for your own position? You women have delicate nerves, after all—one of the many reasons the sciences should be the sole province of men."

Christine drew in a deep breath, her eyes widening and her shoulders squaring. Knowing the signs well, I slipped around my desk and out of the office. As I left to get a towel from the washroom, I heard her shouts echoing down the hallway. Bradley responded in kind, yelling something about hysteria.

The man had no sense of self-preservation whatsoever.

As I dried off my clothing as best I might in the men's washroom, my thoughts went back to Tambling. Had he really killed his uncle? Yes, he'd been covered in blood, but he'd also been standing in the road shrieking, which didn't strike me as the act of a murderer. And afterward, he'd seemed overcome with grief. Although perhaps what I'd mistaken for sorrow had, in fact, been remorse.

I was no expert in human behavior; quite the opposite. Perhaps he'd done exactly what he'd been accused of. At any rate, the question of his guilt or innocence was entirely out of my hands.

Or so I believed.

Later in the afternoon, I bent over the fragments of the cuneiform tablet, attempting to piece them into a coherent whole. A knock from Miss Parkhurst on my open door interrupted me. "Dr. Whyborne? You have a visitor."

"Oh. Er, come in," I said. I hadn't been expecting any visitors. I didn't recognize the man in the doorway, twisting his hat in his hands, although he seemed vaguely familiar. Perhaps I had seen him around town?

"Forgive me for the intrusion, Dr. Whyborne," he said, extending his hand. "I'm Ernest Tambling. Allan's brother."

"Oh," I said. I saw the resemblance now. "A pleasure to meet you, Mr. Tambling. Can I, er, offer you a seat? Some coffee?"

"I'll fetch it," Miss Parkhurst said, hurrying off before we had the opportunity to either accept or decline.

Mr. Tambling lowered himself into the chair. Dark circles shadowed his eyes, and the knot on his tie hung askew. I couldn't imagine how much stress the poor fellow must be under. Should I offer him condolences on his uncle's death, or would such a reminder be too painful?

Fortunately, he spared me the decision. "You must be wondering why I've called upon you," he said. "But I didn't know where else to turn. Allan speaks very highly of you."

"He does?" I wouldn't have imagined Allan had ever given me a passing thought before Saturday night. "That is, how may I be of assistance?"

"You saw him Saturday night, yes? Immediately after the…incident? Gave your testimony to the police?"

"Oh. Yes." My heart sank. If he wished me to declare his brother either guilty or innocent based on our encounter, I wouldn't be of much use. "He seemed, er, confused."

Ernest Tambling leaned forward, his eyes intent and a little wild. "I don't know what happened, Dr. Whyborne, but I'm sure Allan didn't kill our uncle."

"Oh," I said again, unsure how else to respond. "Were they, ah, close?"

"Our parents died some years ago," Ernest said. "Uncle Victor had no children of his own—a confirmed bachelor, as they say—and took on the role of father to us both. Allan is the sort of man to carry a beetle outside rather than smash it with his heel, let alone murder someone who showed us nothing but kindness!"

Miss Parkhurst returned with the coffee. "One sugar, just as you like it, Dr. Whyborne," she said, placing it in front of me with a smile. Her floral perfume enveloped me, and I struggled not to sneeze as I thanked her.

By the time she left, Mr. Tambling seemed to have regained control of his emotions. Picking up his coffee, he held it in his hands without drinking. "I have evidence," he said. "My uncle is—was—a collector of antiquities. He had a rather large ceremonial bowl in his study. It's gone missing. Surely, whoever killed him must have stolen it."

Although I knew the antiquities trade had a reputation for viciousness—Christine had a near-infinite supply of tales concerning tomb robbers and murderous thieves—killing a man here in Widdershins seemed rather extreme. "Are you certain he didn't simply sell it?"

"The maid said she dusted it earlier. I've told the police, but they refuse to listen, and the doctors at the madhouse are no better. They say the fact Allan can't remember Uncle Victor's death is proof of his lunacy. Even Dr. Zeiler, whom we've met socially from time to time, considers the matter to be closed. But how could a man lapse into complete insanity for ten minutes or less, brutally murder his own uncle, make off with a large bowl, which is yet to be found, then revert to perfect sanity afterward? It makes no sense!"

I remembered the fleeing figure Allan claimed to have seen. Griffin had found no trace, so it could have simply been a madman's fancy. "It would seem impossible," I agreed cautiously. "But I fear I know little of medicine, and still less of the alienist's arts."

"Allan is my younger brother, Dr. Whyborne. With our uncle gone, we're one another's only family. I must render whatever aid possible." Mr. Tambling leaned forward, his eyes fixed hopefully on my face. "Allan said you helped a private detective recover the scroll stolen from the museum during the Egyptian Gala. I fear I can't recall the man's name, if I ever knew it. I wonder if you might arrange an introduction?"

Ah. Now his visit made sense. As far as I knew, Griffin was the only private detective in Widdershins. He did not advertise, however, relying on a good word from previous clients and a reputation for discretion to bring him new business. "Oh, er, of course. I'll speak with Griffin—Mr. Flaherty—as soon as can be arranged."

"Thank you. I'm not a wealthy man, but my position at the bank has allowed me to put aside some money, and I would spend every cent to clear my brother's name." Ernest rose to his feet, discovered he still held his coffee, and downed it in a single gulp. "I eagerly await word."

He left me with his card. Once he departed, I sat down and sipped from my own rapidly cooling cup. Although I'd given my promise, I could not honestly say I was eager to bring the case to Griffin. Under any other circumstances, I would have no hesitation. However, with the connection to the asylum…

But if Allan's confinement proved as unwarranted as his had been, Griffin would never forgive me for not bringing it to his attention.

"Blast," I muttered. "I knew we should never have gone to look at those accursed electric lights."

When I arrived home in the evening, I found Griffin sitting in the downstairs parlor, a pensive look on his face. As he normally used the parlor for meetings with clients, I allowed myself a moment to hope he'd just taken on a new case and would be unable to investigate Allan Tambling's guilt or innocence. Or sanity and insanity, as the case might be.

"Is everything all right?" I asked, hanging up my hat in the hall. I kept on my suit coat, as was my habit, at least until we retired upstairs for the evening. Saul trotted down the stairs and wound about my ankles, mewing piteously in an unsuccessful attempt to convince me Griffin had neither fed nor petted him all day.

Griffin let out a sigh and rose to his feet. Rather than answer, however, he came and slipped his arms around my waist, tipping up his face for a kiss, which I gladly granted. In some ways, it still seemed strange to spend the evenings in the company of another, let alone a handsome man who wished both physical and emotional intimacy from me. How many years had I trudged up flights of stairs to a lonely apartment, with nothing to occupy me but the ciphers I solved for amusement and a cold bed at the end of the evening?

Too many for my body, which reacted as it usually did to his proximity. "Did you miss me?" he asked, pressing against me.

"Always." I nuzzled his hair, breathing deeply of his scent before reluctantly drawing away.

"What shall we have for dinner?" he asked, heading for the kitchen. "I believe we have the ingredients for a fish stew, if you'd like."

"That would be lovely," I said, following him.

"Good. You can help me make it."

I sighed loudly enough for him to hear. "I don't know why you're so determined to teach me to cook."

He went to the pantry and began to take out various vegetables. "Because every time I have to leave town on a case for a few days, I come home to discover you subsisting on canned beans and bread, or cheese sandwiches from the lunch counter."

"I lived on my own for quite some time, you know," I replied, a bit stung by his implication. "I'm in no danger of starving just because you occasionally leave for a few days."

"Then it is because I enjoy torturing you." He cast me a devilish grin as he put an onion on the cutting board and handed me a knife.

"That I can believe." I took the blade from him. "Very well, if it pleases you, I will go along with this ridiculous notion of yours. When my cooking kills us both, I hope you recall this conversation."

He stole a kiss, before walking to the sink, where he set to filling a large pot with water. "I shall. I trust you had a pleasant day?"

I sliced into the onion. A minute later, its fumes blew into my eyes, and I blinked back stinging tears. Curse the man; couldn't he have given me potatoes to cut instead?

"Er, well, I suppose. I might have a case for you. Maybe. Or, rather, *I* don't. You recall Allan Tambling from Saturday night?" What an idiotic question. Who forgot a man covered in blood, screaming in the middle of a street? "His brother, Ernest, came by my office. He doesn't believe Allan is guilty, and he, uh, wishes to retain you."

Griffin stilled. "Ah."

"Allan is... Well, he's..."

"In the lunatic asylum," Griffin finished for me, his voice flat. "I read it in the papers this morning."

I hated to be the one to bring this to him. "Ernest disagrees with the doctors and the police and swears up and down his brother is innocent. I don't know Tambling terribly well, but I would never have thought him a murderer."

"You would be amazed how many people say as much about acquaintances who prove to have committed all sorts of atrocities," Griffin said wryly.

"I didn't answer for you, of course. Perhaps you should speak to him face-to-face? Ernest, I mean."

Griffin let out a long sigh. "I suppose I should."

"I'm sorry."

"For bringing the case to me? There's no need to apologize."

I groped about for a happier subject. "And your day? Did anything interesting happen?"

"In a matter of speaking." Setting the pot on the stove, he turned to me with a rueful expression. "I received a telegram from my parents. They're coming to visit."

CHAPTER 3

GRIFFIN ARRANGED TO MEET me for lunch the next day, after he'd had the opportunity to speak with Ernest Tambling and learn the particulars of the case. Christine invited herself along as well, on the basis of having been present when we encountered the bloodstained Allan.

We soon found ourselves seated in a booth at Marsh's Diner. A group of clerks laughed over their sandwiches at a nearby table, and a pair of salesmen gossiped in another booth, their sample cases on the seats beside them. Like most of the restaurants in Widdershins, Marsh's specialized in seafood. I ordered the poached fish, while Griffin and Christine opted for sandwiches.

"I've decided to take the case," Griffin said briskly, while we waited for our meal. My heart sank a bit at his declaration, but in truth, I'd expected he would. "The asylum superintendent was a friend of the dead uncle and, more casually, of the Tamblings. Ernest has written him to arrange a meeting first thing Monday morning."

"At Stormhaven?" I asked.

"Of course." Griffin took a sip from his coffee cup, looking a bit white around the mouth.

"I'll accompany you."

"You have work—"

"No one save Christine will even notice I'm gone," I said firmly. "But I'll send in a note pleading illness if necessary." I would no sooner let Griffin go alone to such a place than I would allow him to chop off his own arm. How could he think otherwise?

Some of the color crept back into his face. "Very well. And…thank you."

The arrival of our food temporarily halted our conversation. Once the waiter had departed again, I asked, "Will your parents' visit hamper your investigation?"

"No. When I replied to their telegram, I let them know I had an urgent case and would most likely be unavailable for parts of their visit."

"Your parents are coming to Widdershins?" Christine asked. "Why on earth would they want to do that?"

"Really, Christine!" I exclaimed.

"Well, Kansas surely isn't so benighted they don't have post. I should think a letter would be satisfactory enough for most people."

"Not everyone is happy to go decades without seeing their family."

"As if you wouldn't do the same if you had the option."

Griffin hid his grin behind his sandwich. When he had swallowed, he said, "I've been here a year now, or I will have in September. They wish to see I'm as settled and happy as I claim to be in my letters."

"Hmm." Christine glanced at me. "And what of Whyborne? I assume your parents know you have a boarder?"

A trace of heat warmed my cheeks. I stared down at my poached fish. Griffin and I had discussed things the night before, of course, but leave it to Christine to drag everything out into the open.

"Well…no," Griffin admitted. "I left Kansas after an indiscretion, shall we say. As far as they know, I never repeated the act, but I don't wish to give them any reason to doubt. They do know Whyborne and I are friends. In fact, they were beside themselves with joy to learn I'd made the acquaintance of a man of quality."

My face burned hotter. Christine cast a glance at me then scowled at Griffin. "So what is poor Whyborne to do—go to a hotel?"

"Not at all," Griffin said. "My parents have declared their intention to stay in a hotel, in fact."

"Why?"

"I don't know, and I certainly have no wish to pursue the matter, since it's to my benefit. When they come to see the house, I'll lock the door to Whyborne's room and come up with some excuse as to why it is unused. As for the rest of the house, it should be easy enough to make it appear as if I live alone. The rest of the time, I'll take them about Widdershins and show them the sights. Being from a tiny farming community in Kansas, I should have no trouble finding things to dazzle them with until they leave. Then life will return to normal."

"And what do you think of this, Whyborne?"

I picked at my half-eaten fish. "It seems a good plan."

"What other choice do we have?" Griffin asked irritably, glaring at Christine. "If they knew…well, they wouldn't go to the police, but they'd be terribly hurt. They've always wanted nothing more than an ordinary life for me."

"My mother wanted an ordinary life for me," she shot back. "If I'd acceded to her wishes, I'd be sitting at home someplace with a husband and a bunch of squalling brats."

"I owe them," Griffin replied doggedly. "Has Whyborne told you of my history?"

"Of course not," I said, a bit hurt he would think such a thing of me. "I'm not in the habit of repeating confidences."

"Forgive me, my dear. But I didn't mean it to be a great secret." Griffin set aside the remains of his sandwich. "James and Nella Kerr are my adoptive parents. My true mother and father died when I was quite young; I don't remember anything about them. My sister died with them. The Children's Aid Society placed my brothers and me on an orphan train to the west."

"Oh," Christine said, a bit stiffly. "I'm terribly sorry, Griffin. I didn't realize."

"No need to apologize. The Kerrs adopted me in Kansas. They had no children of their own, you see, and decided to take in an orphan to raise as a son. I was very lucky. Some of the children ended up no better than slaves…or worse."

"What became of your brothers?" she asked tentatively.

Griffin's expression grew sad. "I never saw either of them again, nor heard any word. Many families changed the names of their new wards, so it would do me no good to search for other Flahertys. I can only hope they found a home, as I did. But you see why I feel I owe it to my parents to…to live up to their expectations. I can't stand the thought they would regret the choice they made that day on the platform."

I could picture it clearly: a train depot in some small town, the raw wind sending shivers through the children lined up on the platform, while adults inspected them like heads of cattle. A young Griffin among them, his brothers gone, alone and at the mercy of these complete strangers. How frightened he must have been.

Christine sighed. "I can understand how you might feel so," she said grudgingly. "Although I think it's a damnable shame they can't simply be content to know whether or not you're happy, whatever form such happiness takes. But they are hardly alone in their attitude, as I believe Whyborne and I can easily attest. How may I assist?"

Griffin smiled. "Thank you for the offer. I won't trouble you save, perhaps, if we should dine out, to ask you allow Whyborne to escort you."

To make our deception more convincing, I supposed. The arrangement didn't please me, of course, but Griffin thought it necessary. Christine pursed her lips and eyed him, before shaking her head with a sigh. "Very well. For Whyborne's sake. But you owe me a favor, Griffin Flaherty."

"Whatever you wish," he agreed quickly.

"Ha! You will regret not forcing me to specify," she said, pushing her plate away. "Come along, Whyborne. If you won't be about on Monday, you should put in a few more hours at the museum today."

We parted from Griffin in front of the diner. As Christine and I turned back toward the museum, I said, "Thank you for your offer of help."

The line between her brows deepened. "Against my better judgment. Griffin is taking things too far, in my opinion, trying to construct some elaborate charade for their benefit. However, if he is determined to do this, there should at least be someone sensible involved."

"And I take it I don't qualify?"

She snorted. "*You* are far too love-stricken to do anything besides agree to whatever preposterous plan he comes up with."

"Christine!" I hissed, the tips of my ears burning. "That isn't true!"

"I suppose it's a good thing for me he saw fit to return your affections," she went on, ignoring my protest. "I shudder to think all the moping about I would have had to endure from you had he been content to remain mere acquaintances."

I wished to sink through the sidewalk. I didn't know a spell to open the earth beneath me, so instead I said, "You are being entirely unfair. I do not 'mope about,' as you put it."

"Not unless it comes to Griffin." She shook her head. "Ah well. I only hope when the house of cards he is building falls, it doesn't come down on your head as well."

That night, I again wandered the lanes of the sunken city.

I found myself in a vast plaza, surrounded by the alien architecture. Segmented creatures, which seemed half worm, half centipede, wriggled through the black slime under my feet. Jellyfish drifted in the water above me like animate clouds, their long tentacles waving gently in the currents.

I froze, feeling hideously exposed. Where was the thing which hunted me earlier? Was it still looking for me? Or did it know exactly where I was?

In the distance, someone—something—began to sing.

If the song came from a human throat, I couldn't make out the words. And if it came from some alien organ, did I really want to see what produced it?

The song seemed to emanate from a temple, which loomed at one end of the noisome plaza. It reminded me simultaneously of a stepped pyramid, a ziggurat, and the stone temples of South America, only unfathomably larger. Gargantuan statues flanked what seemed to be a door, and I found myself oddly glad barnacles and coral obscured the details of their faces.

The song shifted and became more urgent. Although I still couldn't understand its content, I realized the voice belonged to my mother.

Which made no sense. Mother was confined to her bed—what would she possibly be doing here in this nameless city befitting Poseidon?

The song grew stronger, and I felt its alien harmonies tugging at me, almost like a physical thing. I had to go to mother. I had to save her.

No. Whatever this thing was, it wasn't—couldn't be—Mother.

It was a trap, set by the thing that hunted me before.

I fled the plaza, seeking the streets. If I could only escape the city, perhaps

I could save myself.

The cloud of jellyfish descended, blocking my path. Their stinging arms wrapped stickily around me, and I cried out—

And found myself sweating and gasping in bed, Griffin curled against my side.

Early Monday morning, Griffin and I hired a carriage to take us to the lunatic asylum. Low gray clouds blocked out the August sun, and a stiff breeze blew in from the ocean, carrying with it the scent of salt, rotting seaweed, and dead fish. The narrow road followed the coast out of Widdershins proper.

The town clustered around the mouth of the Cranch River where it entered the bay, but to the north the land rose sharply into a series of bluffs overlooking the ocean. One of these jutted out from the rest, its leeward side forming a small cove where, legend had it, the smugglers of old took refuge from inclement weather. Although Stormhaven Cove was no longer used for such purposes, the name still lingered, and the asylum built on the cliff above had taken its moniker rather than that of the town.

A dreary landscape surrounded Stormhaven, consisting mainly of rock, tough grasses, and trees stunted on the windward side. Apparently the asylum had fallen victim to the new electricity craze, because poles strung with ugly wires marched alongside the road, providing perches to a flock of bedraggled crows.

As we rode, I watched Griffin out of the corner of my eye. How would he react to the sight of the asylum? Could he truly bring himself to go inside? I longed to take his hand, but of course the presence of our driver made such a gesture impossible. So I merely watched his knuckles grow whiter and whiter as he gripped his silver-headed cane.

"Unless I am much mistaken, the lunatic asylum is run by the city, is it not?" he asked after we had ridden for a while.

"Yes." I would distract him if at all possible. "Construction began in 1864, using the Kirkbride plan."

"I wouldn't have thought a city of Widdershins's size would have enough patients to supply such a place."

"Is this going to be one of those conversations where you tell me everything you think wrong with our town? You chose to move here, may I remind you." I sat back and folded my arms over my chest. "Besides, I'll have you know the only person in *my* family to go mad was my maternal grandfather, Isaiah Endicott. Nor did he ever set foot in Widdershins, so far as I know. He lived near Ipswich, on Essex Bay."

"You've never spoken of this before," Griffin said. "What happened? If you don't mind my asking."

"I don't mind." Not with him, anyway, although it wasn't precisely the sort of thing the family wanted widely known. "Apparently, Isaiah went mad about two months before my mother was born. He tried to kill his pregnant wife—

attacked her with a knife, I believe, screaming something about cutting 'it' out of her."

Griffin shuddered. "How horrible."

"Quite. Mother was their first child. Perhaps the stress of impending fatherhood brought forth some hidden delirium. Fortunately, the servants intervened in time. Grandfather Endicott went off to a private hospital and died shortly thereafter. Grandmother relocated permanently to Boston and eventually remarried, to a kind man who treated my mother as his own daughter. So I suppose the story has something of a happy ending, at least."

He smiled at me warmly. "Indeed. Especially happy for me, since you would not have existed, had your grandfather succeeded."

We rounded a bend, and his gaze went past me. Focused as I was on his face, I saw his complexion go ashen, while beads of sweat sprang up across his brow. His hands tightened on his cane, and he swallowed convulsively.

I turned to look out the window on my side, even though I already knew what I would see. We had rounded the headland, and the cliff overlooking the ocean and cove unfolded before us, the lunatic asylum perched atop it.

We had come to Stormhaven.

My first impression was one of shock at the building's truly massive size. From the end of one wing to the other, I judged it to stretch nearly a quarter mile. Fully four stories tall and built of dark stone, Stormhaven dominated the headland. Spires jutted out from the corners of the central part of the building as well as from each wing, and a clock tower clawed at the underbelly of the low clouds.

We came to a high stone wall, the carriage pausing at the iron gates while our driver conferred with the guard. After a few words, the gates swung open.

Beyond the wall, a great lawn stretched out before us, its grass rather bare and patchy. A fountain played in the center of the carriage drive, and although only badly stunted trees grew on this wind-blasted height, a few beds of flowers added a splash of cheerful color near the main doors.

A young woman wearing a misshapen dress crouched in the carriage drive, watching our approach. The driver yelled and waved his whip, but she failed to move.

"What the devil?" I asked.

Griffin frowned. "One of the patients? But there should be a nurse with her."

The carriage rolled to a halt, and the woman immediately rose to her feet and came to my window. "For you," she said, holding out a single yellow daisy.

"I, er…" What on earth was the proper etiquette when a madwoman offered one a flower? I began to think my upbringing had been sorely lacking in a number of necessary points. "Thank you," I said finally, and took the somewhat bedraggled flower.

Clearly my acceptance pleased her; her big eyes all but glowed, and she gave me a happy smile. "You hear it too, don't you?"

I heard nothing but the wind, whistling over the rocks of the bluff and shaking the leaves of the stunted trees. "Er, no."

"Yes, you do," she said impatiently. "At night. In your dreams. You hear it singing."

The hair on the back of my neck tried to stand up. The dream of the temple…but no, I would be as mad as she if I believed she knew my dreams. It must be a coincidence, nothing more. "I don't know what you mean."

"Amelie!"

A woman in a nurse's uniform emerged from one of the side doors, making her way toward us. "Amelie, get back here this instant! I don't know how you keep getting out, but I'll see you punished for it!"

The madwoman took a step back from our carriage. "Help me," she said, staring at me through a curtain of red-gold hair. "Help. Me."

Spinning on her heel, she ran back toward the asylum, forcing the nurse to take off in pursuit.

I sat back uneasily as the driver got the horses moving again. "Well. That was strange. And unpleasant."

"Yes," Griffin agreed, looking as disturbed by the incident as I felt.

A few moments later, the carriage came to a halt in front of the portico. Griffin stared at the asylum with an expression of rising dread, and for a moment, I considered ordering the driver to take us away with all haste. Then Griffin's jaw firmed, and he flung open the door and climbed out. I followed, not at all certain this had been a good idea.

As we ascended the steps, the asylum's door swung open and two men emerged. One dressed in an ordinary sack suit, but the other wore the fine coat of a professional.

"How may I help you, sirs?" he asked.

I glanced at Griffin, only to see he'd gone deathly pale. His eyes widened, as if at some vision of utmost horror, and beads of sweat sprang out on his brow and lip. For a terrible moment, I thought he would collapse into a fit right there on the very steps of the madhouse.

I had to do something to distract the men. "Allow me to introduce myself," I said, extending my hand. "I'm Dr. Percival Endicott Whyborne."

"Dr. Wilhelm Zeiler, the superintendent of this facility. I've met your father and older brother on occasion, and it's a pleasure to make your acquaintance at last."

"I'll give them your regards," I lied. I had nothing to do with either of them if I could at all help it.

"Please do." He glanced at Griffin, brow raised in a question.

Thank goodness, Griffin had recovered himself somewhat. "Dr. Zeiler, Mr. Griffin Flaherty," I said. "Ernest Tambling said he'd sent word we'd be visiting his brother?"

"Ah, yes, of course," Zeiler said. They shook hands, but Griffin snatched his back so quickly as to border on rudeness. "I was a friend to the deceased, and had met Ernest and poor Allan on occasion." The superintendent turned to the other man. He must be an attendant or some sort of employee, one who didn't rate an introduction, in Dr. Zeiler's estimation. "Jones, summon Dr. Peck, won't you?"

"Dr. Peck?" I asked.

"My duties seldom allow me to interact personally with the patients," Dr. Zeiler explained. "Dr. Peck is the physician overseeing Allan's case. If you'll come with me, we'll wait on him in my office."

Chapter 4

I watched Griffin carefully as we followed Zeiler inside. Usually his acting skills were worthy of the stage, but nothing could hide the unnatural pallor of his face, the tightness of his shoulders, the way he held his cane more like the weapon it actually was, rather than a fashionable prop. He seemed to expect Dr. Zeiler to attack us or, perhaps, slam the doors shut and, laughing maniacally, declare us inmates.

"Forgive me," Zeiler said, frowning at Griffin slightly. "You seem very familiar. Have we met?"

"Is there a washroom?" Griffin asked hoarsely.

"Yes, of course. Down the hall and through the door," Zeiler said. Griffin departed with alacrity.

"Forgive my friend," I said, trying desperately to think of some excuse for his behavior. We should never have come here. "He, ah, had oysters with dinner last night. It isn't a month with an 'r' in it, and, as the saying warns, they proved unhealthy."

"Oh, of course, of course. Not from the coast and so didn't know to avoid them?" Zeiler asked with a sympathetic nod. "I can tell from his accent. I'll have my secretary mix up a glass of Bromo-Seltzer for the poor fellow."

"Most kind of you."

The entryway was quite large, with dark wooden floors and lovely rounded arches of rococo plaster. Leaded glass let in the watery light of the day. Dr. Zeiler led me through a door immediately to the right, with his name etched on a brass plaque. The room was no different than what one might expect to find in a fashionable home: burgundy paper on the walls, a cheerful ceiling lamp whose glass sported designs of blue and orange flowers, and dark paneling around the hearth and windows. Indicating I should sit in one of the comfortable chairs drawn up near a couch, he asked, "Would you care for any refreshment? Coffee? Tea? Something stronger?"

"Er, no thank you," I replied.

Zeiler opened a side door and spoke briefly with his secretary, who scurried off to fetch the tonic.

"How is your father?" the doctor asked, seating himself across from me.

"Well," I said neutrally. I'd thought most of Widdershins society knew of our estrangement, but perhaps Zeiler imagined the rumors to be exaggerated.

A wooden box sat on a low table near my chair, its open lid revealing odd gauges and coils of wire. Seeing my gaze fall upon it, Zeiler said, "A Faradic battery. The application of electricity to various organs is one of the newest advancements in medical science. Our facility can boast several electrotherapeutic cabinets, in additions to smaller devices such as this. Do you know much of batteries, Dr. Whyborne?"

"No," I said shortly. Fortunately, Griffin returned before Zeiler could expound on the wonders of electricity. Although still ghost-pale, he seemed more composed. The damp ends of his hair betrayed where he'd splashed water on his face.

"I explained the oysters to Dr. Zeiler," I said, before Griffin could invent some conflicting excuse.

"Thank you." Griffin sank down on the very edge of a chair, as if ready to spring to his feet at any moment.

The secretary returned with the glass of Bromo-Seltzer. A moment later, another man entered behind her. I thought the newcomer quite attractive, with dark hair and impressive muttonchops, a sensitive mouth, and gold-rimmed spectacles, which leant him a scholarly look. He wore a somber, fairly fashionable suit, although not of expensive materials, and the body beneath moved with vigor. I guessed him close to my age, perhaps a year or two older, despite the tiny fan of gray hair at each temple.

Dr. Zeiler introduced us. "Mr. Griffin Flaherty, Dr. Percival Endicott Whyborne, allow me to present Dr. Solomon Peck. Solomon, these gentlemen have come to see your newest patient."

"A pleasure to meet you," Dr. Peck said. His hand felt cool and dry, the skin soft. A little line of concern creased his brow. "Dr. Whyborne, if you're here to examine Allan, I assure you we have made a thorough study of him already."

"Oh! Er, no. I'm not that sort of doctor," I said hastily. "I'm a student of languages, actually. I work with Allan Tambling at the Ladysmith Museum."

"Of course, of course. He'll be pleased to have a friend visit," Dr. Peck said with a smile.

"This isn't a pleasure jaunt, I'm afraid," Griffin said tightly. "His brother hired me to prove his innocence."

"Oh." Peck's expression fell.

Zeiler folded his hands behind his back and rocked forward on his heels. "I suppose Mr. Tambling told you I'm acquainted with the family? As a friend, I would prefer to believe Allan would never have killed his uncle. But I fear no doubt exists as to his guilt."

"Clearly, his brother doubts a great deal."

"Ernest is a fine man, who feels himself responsible for his younger brother. Having looked after Allan for so many years after their parents died, of course he can't bring himself to believe Allan could do such a thing, even in the grip of some awful delusion." Zeiler offered a pitying smile. "I fear the unbiased eye of medicine sees things differently."

Griffin's expression didn't waver. "I'd like to speak with Allan Tambling and decide for myself."

Zeiler's lips thinned slightly. "I know you do not mean it as an insult, Mr. Flaherty, but please let me set your mind at rest. Despite the sensationalism of the press, we do not lock away sane men within our walls. If our doctors have said a man is mad, trust it is so."

The smile on Griffin's face resembled the grimace of a skull. "I am well aware of your practices, Dr. Zeiler."

"If it will help put Mr. Tambling's mind at ease, then by all means." Peck gestured to the hall behind him. "Let us visit Allan, shall we?"

Dr. Peck led us through the wide corridor, past a huge staircase of dark oak, to a short hall. At the end of the hall lay a steel door.

"Allan has been very quiet since he was brought in," Dr. Peck said, pausing in front of the door and taking out his keys. "So we've allowed him to stay in the lower ward, for the less-troublesome patients."

"Despite the violence of his supposed crime?" I asked in surprise.

"He came quietly and has not caused the slightest bit of bother since arriving," Peck replied as he unlocked the door. "I think it possible his mania was confined to the person of his uncle. Time will show whether or not I am right, or if it will reoccur in a new form."

The door swung open, revealing a wide, long hall lined with more doors, though these were of wood rather than steel. Cheerful yellow paint struggled to liven up the place, even with the gloomy day outside. Sturdy rails ran along each side of the hall, between the doors, no doubt for the use of the more debilitated patients.

Peck went inside, but I paused and waited for Griffin to come up beside me. Putting a hand to his shoulder, I murmured, "Steady on, old fellow. We can turn around and leave this instant, if you wish."

He licked his lips, as if they had gone dry. "No. No, we're here to see Tambling. I won't leave without speaking to him."

I squeezed his shoulder and let go. "I'm very proud of you."

He looked at me in surprise, as if it had never occurred to him I might feel thus. How could I not? Had I been required to come here, having endured an unjust confinement, and Zeiler spoke to me so, my nerve would have broken already.

Peck waited for us, looking a bit quizzical, but I didn't feel up to repeating the lie about the oysters. Fortunately, he didn't ask, only shut the door behind us once we were inside. A nurse sat in a little room to one side, which looked out onto the hallway through a row of glass windows. To keep an eye on who entered and left through the locked door? She greeted Dr. Peck politely, peering at us with undisguised curiosity as we passed by and into the ward proper.

Despite the open windows and the constant sea breeze, the air stank of urine. Patients sat or stood in the hall, all of them dressed in shabby, ill-fitting clothes. Some smiled at us with a child-like simplicity of expression, while others only stared blankly. As we passed one of the open doors, I saw no less than three beds crammed into the tiny room. Heavy iron bars over the window turned the view of the wide lawn into a bleak reminder those within were not free men.

Peck led us to what appeared to be a small sitting room near the center of the ward. It looked out over the lawn as well, simply furnished with rocking chairs and a small table, on which two patients played cards.

An attendant joined us there, leading a man by the elbow. It took me a moment to recognize Allan. Normally, he dressed in a good suit and tie, with his face neatly shaved. Now, he wore the same poor-fitting, shabbily made clothes as the other inmates, and stubble shadowed his jaw.

"Dr. Whyborne!" He made as if to rush forward, but the attendant pulled him roughly back.

"It's all right," I said, giving the attendant a startled look. "Aren't the patients allowed to greet their visitors?"

The man ignored me, instead looking to Dr. Peck. "Let him go," Peck said. Turning to me, he added, "I'll leave you to speak in private. If you need anything, I'll remain within earshot. Summon me when you're ready to depart."

We watched him go, Tambling rubbing his arm where the attendant had gripped him. With a shake of his head, he turned back to me and clasped my hand. "Thank you for coming," he said sincerely. "You cannot know what this means to me."

I might not, but I rather suspected Griffin did. "Of course. Mr. Tambling, this is Mr. Griffin Flaherty…I'm not sure if you remember him?" I added awkwardly. Given Griffin had last seen Allan covered in blood and suffering from a memory lapse, should I consider them previously introduced or not?

"I remember that much, at least. Call me Allan, please," Tambling said, indicating we should sit in a small group of chairs away from the other patients. "You are my very lifeline at the moment, along with my brother."

"We intend to prove your innocence, if we can." Griffin took out a notebook and pencil. "Tell us everything you can recall, up until the point we met you on the street."

"Very well." Allan took a deep, trembling breath. "I went to visit Uncle

Victor in the evening. We had a pleasant dinner, and after, we went into his study for cigars and brandy. There came a knock at the door, and I went to answer it, as the maid was occupied in the kitchen and the other servants out for the night."

The younger man closed his eyes and pressed his fingers against his lids. "I remember nothing further, until I found myself standing in the street, covered in blood!"

Griffin stared intently at Allan. "And you had nothing in your hands at the time?"

"No. But I thought I saw someone running away, if you recall."

Griffin nodded. "I do. Did they tell you a ceremonial bowl is missing from your uncle's study?"

"Ernest mentioned it. I'm certain I saw it there when we went in after dinner. Perhaps I let in some thief, who then attacked us and took the bowl?" He let his hands fall limply to his lap. "But why can't I remember? I suggested a blow to the head might have caused me to forget. The doctors insist there is no evidence of such…but what else could have happened?"

"Let us retrace your steps further back in the day," Griffin said soothingly. "What did you do earlier, before dining with your uncle?"

Allan looked at a loss. "How could it matter?"

"Indulge me."

"Well, I worked at the museum for the first half of the day, of course," he said, glancing at me. "After leaving, I had lunch and a few drinks at the Barndoor Skate Saloon."

"How much did you drink?" Griffin asked.

Allan flushed. "One or two beers only, I assure you. Afterward, I went home to change, and thence to Uncle's for dinner." He stared at us both helplessly. "I don't see what assistance that could possibly be."

"One never knows," Griffin said cryptically. He stared off into nothingness for a moment, tapping his lips with a forefinger in a sure sign of deep thought. Then he shook himself. "Well, I believe I've no more questions for now."

"You think me innocent?"

Griffin's expression softened. Focusing his gaze on Allan, he leaned over and gripped the younger man's hand. "I swear I will do everything in my power to clear your name and show you didn't commit this hideous crime," he said gravely. "It may take some time, but I beg you, don't despair. Your plight hasn't been forgotten. We *will* free you."

Allan offered him a tremulous smile. "Thank you, sir." The smile slipped. "But…if you can…please, hurry. Since the crime I'm accused of was dreadful, I fear I'll be sent to the fourth floor before long."

A chill fell over me. "The fourth floor?" I asked. "What does that mean?"

"I'm not sure," Allan confessed. "The second floor contains the children's wards, and the third is for what they term 'troublesome' patients." Griffin flinched at the word, although I didn't think Allan noticed. "The fourth is only whispered about. But the other inmates are terrified, and I've already heard one of the nurses use the threat of it to force a patient to behave."

"I see." Griffin's face had taken on its previous pallor, but he summoned up a smile. "There's no need to worry, Allan. We'll have you out long before it becomes an issue, never fear."

The look in Griffin's eyes told me he feared, very much. But Allan didn't know him as I did, and so only nodded in relief. "Thank you, sir. Thank you."

We took our leave soon after. As our carriage departed back through the high wall, Griffin said, "We have to get Allan out of there as quickly as possible."

"Because of this fourth floor business?" I asked. "Dr. Peck mentioned nothing of it. Perhaps Allan is mistaken."

Griffin's mouth pressed into a tight line, as if he struggled to hold back some outburst. "I cannot speak of it now," he grated out at last. "But there's something else going on; there must be."

"What do you mean?"

"Dr. Zeiler. I didn't know his name until today, but I recognized him. God, how could I forget him?"

My heart began to beat faster with worry. "Griffin? What do you mean?"

His face ashen gray, he whispered, "Zeiler was the doctor who certified me insane and condemned me to the madhouse."

CHAPTER 5

I HAD NO opportunity to question Griffin further. Not only due to the presence of the driver, but also because we had to go directly from our appointment to the railway station, in order to meet the train bringing Griffin's parents to Widdershins.

We arrived at the station as the first passengers began to disembark. I'd visited the depot only a few times previously, not being inclined to leave Widdershins if at all possible. The place was generally chaotic, with persons rushing to and fro, many of them shoving carts piled with baggage or crates or even live chickens ahead of them. The platform was a great, swirling mass of skirts, hats, running children, dogs, baggage, and a lone cage with a live parrot inside, screaming its head off.

Its shrieks were joined by those of a young girl, red faced and crying, apparently having lost sight of her mother. Perhaps reminded of another young child standing alone on another train platform, Griffin stopped and went down on his knee beside her.

"Are you lost?" he asked kindly.

She nodded and kept howling.

Griffin looked up at me, and perhaps saw the expression of horror on my face. "Whyborne, would you be so kind as to find my parents? I shall help this little one."

"Of course," I said hastily. I had no experience dealing with children, and hadn't the slightest notion what to do when confronted with one.

I hastened to the crowd of disembarking passengers, only to realize I hadn't any idea what his parents looked like. What on earth was I doing here, anyway? My inclinations meant many drawbacks in terms of society, but surely one positive was not having to receive the approval of my lover's family. And yet here I was, stumbling about like a fool, while Griffin played hero.

A number of people—porters, perhaps, or hired drivers—shouted the names of new arrivals. Perhaps I should do the same? "Kerr?" I called tentatively. "Er, Kerr?"

A diminutive older woman popped out of one of the compartments, almost on top of me. I barely had time to register a seamed face, simple dress, and plain bonnet before she shouted "Kerr?" back at me.

"Yes?" I said helplessly.

The next thing I knew, she shoved a small trunk into my arms. "Look, Pa! Griffin hired us a porter to carry our things!"

A man with an impressive white beard exited behind her. "That boy always was thoughtful," he said, grinning happily as he swung an even larger trunk into my arms atop the first. The weight staggered me; what on earth had they brought with them, bricks? Stones from the fields of Kansas? "Seems a bit on the scrawny side, though."

"I'm, er—" I tried to object.

"Now, now, don't you listen to him," Mrs. Kerr said, piling a hatbox and carpetbag on top of the lot. My back let out a twinge of protest. "Carry these quick, and there'll be a nice tip in it for you."

"But, I'm not..."

"Come on now, Ruth, don't be shy."

I peered around the pile of baggage as best I could to catch a glimpse of a young woman following them off the train. Griffin hadn't mentioned anyone else, so who could she be?

Whoever she was, she looked mortified. Curls of blond hair protruded from her bonnet. She wore a neat, though not terribly in-fashion, dress. I was no judge of women's beauty, but I thought she resembled at least in general what most men seemed to consider attractive.

"I'm sorry," she whispered, a light blush pinking her cheeks. She reached to take the hatbox, but Mrs. Kerr cut her off with a call to come at once. "S-sorry," she mumbled at me. "Coming, Aunt Nella!"

Aunt Nella? Griffin had some explaining to do.

I somehow navigated the platform without dropping everything, although the pile of baggage blocked my sight, so I bumped into several people and barely managed not to fall onto the tracks. That would be quite the headline: NILES WHYBORNE'S SON RUN OVER BY OWN TRAIN. Father would probably raise me from the dead just so he could kill me himself.

"Oh, Griffin, it's wonderful to see you!" I heard from somewhere in front of me, so I aimed in that direction. "And sending a porter to take our things—you *must* be doing well!"

"A porter? I—oh!"

Thankfully, Griffin rescued me just as my arms were about to give out. Together we lowered their possessions to the platform; I resisted the urge to collapse into a heap on top of them, but only because I felt my dignity had already suffered enough for one day. As for Griffin, his expression teetered between laughter and horror.

"Mother, Father," he said. "Allow me to present my friend, Dr. Percival Endicott Whyborne."

For a moment, all three of them stared at me in confusion. Then Mrs. Kerr's eyes went to the train, with the gaudy, stylized W on the side of every car. "No, he's not...oh heavens! I am so sorry, Dr. Whyborne!"

"Quite all right," I wheezed. "I was happy to help."

"Now there's some manners, right enough!" Mr. Kerr beamed and clapped me on the back, nearly sending me flying. "I'm James Kerr, and this here is my other half and helpmeet, Nella."

Griffin had by now noticed the third member of the party, and had assumed a rather fixed expression on his face. "Mother? Father? Are you not going to introduce the young lady?"

"Well, it's Ruth, of course," Nella said, as if Griffin should have guessed. "Your cousin, you know. You've been corresponding for months!"

Ruth's face turned scarlet, and she stared at the platform as if she wished to sink through it. I rather understood the sentiment. "It's a pleasure to meet you, Mr. Flaherty," she mumbled at the ground.

Griffin, of course, was ever the gentleman. Bowing over her hand, he said, "And a pleasure—if an unexpected one—to meet you, Miss Kerr."

Ah. His parents hadn't mentioned her presence to him either. At least it explained why they'd wished to stay in the hotel. Technically, it would be proper for Miss Kerr to stay with them under Griffin's roof, as his adopted cousin... unless his parents had some other role in mind for her.

No, no, such a thought was absurd. Wasn't it?

We found an actual porter and soon had their luggage loaded on a cart. At the cabstand outside, Griffin hailed a cab to take them all to the hotel. "Thank you for accompanying me this morning, Whyborne," he said, shaking my hand. "Will you be at the museum tomorrow?"

"Yes, I should be," I said, feeling like an idiot. After spending my whole life keeping my thoughts and emotions carefully concealed, the months with Griffin had rusted my skills. Had I come off as friendly or aloof?

"I hope to see you there," he said, releasing my hand before even the most suspicious mind could think our touch overly long or familiar.

"I, uh, yes. So do I." Now I sounded like an idiot as well.

He followed his parents and Ruth into the carriage. They waved at me, and I waved back. When they vanished into the general traffic around the depot, I turned my attention to the vacant hansoms. I'd get at least a few hours of work in at the museum, and it might take my mind off any number of things, not least of which was the unexpected presence of Griffin's cousin and what it might portend.

~ * ~

I spent the evening tidying the house, removing any trace of my presence to the safety of what was ostensibly my bedroom, although in reality Griffin and I never slept apart. He'd said he intended to bring his family by tomorrow, after their visit to the museum, but I kept a careful ear out for any approaching carriages nonetheless. I could all too easily imagine them insisting on coming here this evening, forcing me to hide in a closet like an actor in a French farce.

Fortunately, Griffin returned alone. "How was dinner?" I asked as he hung up his hat and coat in the front hall.

"Well enough. I took them to Marsh's, and they were all very impressed by the variety of seafood."

I waited for him to say something more, but instead he went into the parlor and began to sift through the papers on his desk. "Er, Griffin?" I said from the doorway. "Can we talk about the case?"

"What about it?" he asked without turning around.

Surely, he must know. "You said you recognized Dr. Zeiler."

His hands stilled. "I don't wish to speak of it."

"I know, but I think we must anyway," I said carefully. "I don't wish to upset you, but it doesn't seem possible. I don't know a great deal about Stormhaven, but I'm under the impression Dr. Zeiler has been the superintendent for some time. Why would he have been admitting patients to a hospital in Illinois?"

Griffin straightened, his hands curling into fists at his sides. "How the hell should I know? It isn't as if we sat down together for coffee and pleasant conversation! I never even knew his name until today. And you heard him—he recognized me."

"He said he thought you familiar. Surely, he would have recalled a man he consigned to a madhouse not his own."

"Why should he remember my face?" Griffin turned on his heel, and the savage look on his features caused me to take a step back in alarm. "Perhaps he would have better remembered me were I naked, bent over at the waist with my hands about my ankles so he and his lackeys could probe me!"

"Wh-what?" I asked, or tried to. There was no air left in my lungs, in the room, in the world.

His lips twisted with disgust, perhaps aimed at Zeiler, perhaps aimed at himself. "As part of the 'inspection' for certifying me a lunatic. Somehow they found out. Elliot wouldn't have told them, so I've no idea who did. They admitted me for 'violent delusions,' but someone added a note about 'sexual deviance.' Do you know the 'cures' they inflict on us?" His voice rose steadily into a shout. "Do you know what the attendants do, when there are no doctors about, laughing and asking if we like it when they—"

He spun suddenly, sweeping a pile of books off his desk and onto the floor. A forgotten teacup went flying, to shatter against the hearth. Then, with a low cry, he buried his face in his hands.

Horror froze my blood, nausea roiling in my stomach, while some little voice inside said *no, this could not be true. These things happened, yes, but not to Griffin. Not to my love.*

Had I not held him through his fits, though, when he screamed in the clutches of nightmare? I knew terrible things had happened to him, even if he'd always refused to speak of them. Why had I not been better prepared for this moment?

What should I do? Go to him? Stay away? God, what if I made things worse, somehow?

But I couldn't just stand here like a fool, not when he needed me. I crossed the room in three strides and put my hands to his shoulders. "I…I'm here," I said, feeling more helpless than I ever had in my life.

He turned to me, pressing his face in my shoulder, so I slipped my arms around him. I meant to hold him lightly, but when he asked, "How can you bear to touch me?" in a low, grating voice, I instead clung to him with all my strength.

"Because I love you," I whispered into his hair. He shuddered and pressed against me more tightly, and I held him while he wept into my coat.

"Here," I said, placing the tea service on the small table in the upstairs study. "Allow me to pour for us."

Griffin sat at one end of the couch, the loudly purring Saul ensconced in his lap. Griffin's eyes were red rimmed, but he seemed a bit more himself when he said, "I didn't realize you were of the 'a cup of tea cures all ills' school of thought."

"I'm not, but Miss Emily would serve me up one as a child, whenever I needed comfort," I said, stirring a bit of sugar into his tea. "Or a cup of cocoa in the winter. It always stood me in good stead."

"I'd like to meet her some day," he said, taking the cup from me and cradling in his hands. "Thank you, my dear."

I prepared a cup for myself as well then sat beside him. What was he feeling? I could barely identify my own emotions. Grief, and anger, and even fear. Not to mention a deep desire to do violence to Dr. Zeiler. "Is there anything else I can do?" I asked awkwardly.

He sighed and leaned his head against my shoulder. "You've already done it."

I didn't know what he meant. "If I've ever made you feel uncomfortable, or hurt you," I began uncertainly.

"Ival, no." He lifted his head to fix me with a stern look. "You must not think such things."

"I don't mean to, I just…I only want whatever is best for you."

He took a sip of his tea, redirecting his gaze to Saul's ears. "When Pa—Father—rescued me from the asylum, I couldn't imagine ever feeling anything again, other than exhaustion and fear. Desire seemed like a foreign land I had once visited but existed only in my memories. I could no more picture wanting to be touched than I could laughing or singing or feeling safe."

His words wrung my heart like a sodden rag. I leaned my head against his shoulder, because it brought us into contact, and I hoped he might find comfort in the gesture.

"Time passed, as it is wont to do," he went on, "and eventually I began to come back to myself. To stop jumping at every sound, to no longer expect a blow for speaking, or looking directly at someone, or…or anything else. One evening I stood at the window of my room, gazing out over the fields, and I saw one of the farmhands washing up before dinner. The day had been hot, and he'd stripped off his shirt to better clean himself at the pump in the yard. The sight of his tanned body aroused me, I admit. And perhaps I should have been disappointed the cure hadn't taken. But instead I felt the most overwhelming sense of relief."

Had he truly wished for his inclinations to be altered? Certainly it would make life easier. Perhaps he could imagine a version of himself who didn't love other men.

He pressed his lips lightly to my hair. "So I came here, to Widdershins. I considered visiting the bathhouse, but I didn't quite know what my reactions might be. Better to wait and be sure, I thought." His voice deepened to a growl. "Then I saw you."

I put my tea aside, to give my hands something to do, and to hide my blush. "The day in the Ladysmith…"

"Oh, no, my dear, that wasn't the first time." He set aside his tea as well, dislodging Saul from his lap. "I did not entirely trust you weren't part of the Brotherhood yourself, if you recall. I watched you for a while before approaching the museum to ask for your assistance. The first time I saw you, I loitered about the newsstand across the street, pretending to read the morning paper. You hurried up the stairs, your arms full of books, your hair looking as mussed as if you'd just tumbled out of bed, and I found myself *very* keen to meet you as soon as possible."

My cheeks felt hot enough to fry an egg. "I'm not…"

"Oh, you are." His fingers twined around my tie, tugging me closer. "By the time I finally got you into bed with me, all I could think of was how badly I wanted to do anything and everything with you."

My member stiffened in response. "Griffin…"

Hot breath ghosted across my cheek. "What is between us is fire, and passion, and a need I have never felt before for anyone. I am not some flower, bruised if you touch me the wrong way. I want everything you have to give me."

I swallowed against the tightness of my throat. "I'm yours," I whispered.

"Come to bed and show me."

Did he feel some need to prove himself? To assert he was still a man, and a whole one, no matter what they had done to him?

Perhaps. I knew he wanted me, maybe even needed me, and I would happily do anything for him. Christine called me love stricken, deservedly so, but was it such a bad thing?

Griffin kissed me, hard and deep, and I opened for him with an eager moan. He could set my blood afire with a look, let alone a touch, and my skin ached for contact with his. His fingers slid through my messy, spiky hair, tugging gently, then more insistently.

"God," he gasped, when we broke apart. "Do you know the moment I fell in love with you?"

I found it difficult to believe he had in the first place. "No."

"The night we went to the warehouse and encountered the Guardian."

"I remember." As if I'd forget my first encounter with otherworldly forces beyond anything I'd ever imagined. "What of it?"

He chuckled softly against my mouth. "You were so damned brave. Anyone else would have run screaming when confronted with such a thing, but you stayed and fought. And after, you were so certain, no matter what we had seen in the warehouse, or what secrets the *Arcanorum* revealed, it could all be explained by some rational system, even if we didn't yet understand it." He kissed me again. "And I sat here in this very room and fell completely and utterly and irrevocably in love with you."

I didn't understand. What was lovable about the simple application of logic to a system? "I'm not brave," I protested against his lips.

"Ival?"

"Yes?"

"Stop arguing, accept what I say, and let me drag you to bed and make you scream my name."

CHAPTER 6

It was an order I had no wish to refuse. His hands folded over mine, pulling me to my feet and after him to the bedroom. My heart galloped in my chest, and I felt as though all the air had left the room. As soon as he let go of my hands, I slid my arms around him, burying my fingers in his chestnut curls.

He kissed me hungrily, before shoving my coat from my shoulders. As I shook it the rest of the way off, he undid the buttons of my vest, then seized my tie again to drag me closer.

"Tell me what you want," I gasped, pressing tight against him. My member ached, and I ground against his hip, shuddering with pleasure.

"Mmm." He drew back, licking his lips. "Suck me."

I dropped to my knees immediately, fumbling at the buttons of his trousers. His shirt and vest hit the floor beside me, and I pulled his trousers down over his narrow hips, leaning in to kiss the skin of his belly, the fine trail of hair leading down from his navel. He tasted of sweat and salt when I traced the line with my tongue. His erect cock strained against his drawers, and I mouthed it through the cloth, receiving a soft hiss of anticipation in response.

"Yes." His fingers curled in my hair, tightening when I peeled away his underclothes.

I caught his length in my mouth when it sprang free. The velvety skin felt hot against my lips, and his musky flavor spread over my tongue. I gripped the base of his shaft with one hand and sucked teasingly on the tip. He whimpered slightly, and I took pity, sliding my lips further down, savoring the taste and feel of him.

He groaned and shivered, breaths growing faster and more heated. I closed my eyes and concentrated on giving him pleasure, using tongue and teeth and lips. Nothing mattered but this, but him.

After a few minutes, he gasped and pushed me away. "Not yet. Take off your clothes."

I stood up and divested myself quickly while he watched, green eyes dark with lust, his hand stroking his length idly. "I love to have you look at me so," I confessed.

"And I love to look at you."

I lay down on the bed, wondering eagerly what he wanted from me. I would give anything, do anything, and enjoy every moment of it. He crawled on top of me, kissing his way from belly to nipples to mouth, until I writhed under him. He was heat and home and every good thing, and the thought of anyone hurting him made me want to weep.

He distracted me from such thoughts by straddling my hips and bringing our lengths into contact. I gasped and arched against him, loving the feel of his cock against mine, hard and wanting. "Hold us together," he ordered, and I hastily wrapped a hand around our members.

He leaned over me, bracing his hands on my shoulders. His eyes were intent, but a wicked grin played around his mouth. "Do you want me to move?" he teased.

"Please!"

"Tell me what you want me to do to you."

He loved making me say such things as to make me blush. "R-rub yourself against me," I stammered. "Until you come all over my stomach."

He murmured wordlessly, rocking his hips against me. I gathered the dew at our slits, using it to slick our organs. He gasped and shuddered at my touch and thrust harder.

I watched him, his face, needing to know he found this good, that he wanted it. His gaze met mine, stripped raw and vulnerable in this moment of intimacy.

"Say you enjoy this," I begged.

His parted lips curved into a grin. "I *love* this," he growled. I ran my free hand up his arms, feeling the tension in the muscles braced against me. "I love rubbing against you, and sucking you, and fucking you, and I love it when you suck and fuck me. I cannot get enough of you."

My fingers tightened on his shoulder, and my hips jerked instinctively, although his weight held me in place. He looked so handsome above me, his curls tumbled over his forehead, his muscles tight across his broad shoulders, his lips parted with passion. Every stroke of his member against mine generated a new wave of pleasure, each building on the next, my balls tightening and drawing up. "Griffin," I gasped.

"Yes, Ival," he growled, "let go, let me take you there, come with me, come—"

I didn't hear what he said after, words lost beneath the raw cry dragged from my throat, my body arching like a bow under his. Heat and pleasure built in my cock until I could stand it no longer, tumbling over into ecstasy, my spend hot on the skin of my belly.

Griffin followed close after, his body shaking, grinding frantically against me until our sensitized skin forced him to stop. He collapsed against me, face pressed into my neck as his breath slowly evened out. "God," he mumbled in my ear. "You amaze me, my dear."

He drew back and kissed the tip of my nose. I framed his face with my hands and drew him down for a more sensual kiss. "I love you," I whispered. "Nothing will ever change my feelings for you."

He smiled, but it had a pensive air. "Perhaps we should sleep apart tonight," he said, regret lacing the words. "I'm almost certain to have a fit, and there's no reason for you to suffer."

I wrapped my arms tightly around him. "You're reason enough."

I lay on the ocean floor, starfish crawling across my face, their tube-like feet sucking my skin and tangling in my hair. Opening my eyes, I beheld the blackness of the abyss above me. Unnamable detritus sifted down like foul snow, slowly covering me.

I sat up, peeling off some of the starfish. They covered the vast plain of the great plaza in a crawling, undulating blanket. A fish swam past, its face a nest of jagged, misshapen teeth so long its mouth wouldn't close. Its flat, insensate eye stared at me, as if wondering at my intrusion.

The song I'd heard before slithered through my brain, whispering to me of warmth and comfort and home, even in this terrible place. My mother was here —or perhaps Griffin? The thing which had hunted me had caught her—him— and now kept them prisoner within the massive temple.

I had to go inside.

Choking on fear, I stumbled to my feet. I tried not to step on the heaving mass of starfish as I crossed the plaza, but there were too many to avoid. It seemed to take hours, days, to cross the vast square, but at last I stood between the barnacle-covered statues flanking the door. Were their faces more distinct, the mass of growth over them less? I looked away quickly, certain I didn't want to see.

The door to the temple swung slowly open, dislodging a great drift of sediment. Something gelatinous squirmed out of the way, blundering into the starfish, which wrapped their arms about it before I could clearly make out its form. Whatever it was twitched beneath the marauding starfish as they tore it to pieces and devoured it still alive.

I stepped into the tremendous antechamber. A figure stood across from me, shrouded in shadow. Was it masculine? Feminine? I couldn't tell.

"Hello?" I asked, my voice breaking. How I spoke within the depths of the ocean I questioned no more than how I mysteriously breathed. "Who's there?"

I thought it spoke—or perhaps it sang? Either way, I couldn't make out the words. "I can't hear you," I said.

I moved hesitantly closer, yet its form became no more distinct. My heart beat in my throat as I reached out to touch its face.

My fingers encountered nothing but a drift of black ink.

The next morning, after an uncomfortable night's sleep, we went to view the murder scene.

Griffin wished Christine and I to accompany him, in the hopes one of us might shed some light on the artifact, which had disappeared so mysteriously the night of Victor Bixby's death. Christine excused us from work by telling the director we needed to examine some items which might be of interest to our collection.

Ernest Tambling met us at the door to his uncle's house, which had been shut up since the night of the murder. He looked even more careworn than when I'd last seen him.

"You spoke to Allan?" he asked, as he led us into the foyer. The house was a newer one, the Bixbys and Tamblings having only been residents of Widdershins for a generation or two, and lacking both the money and the ancestry to secure a place amongst the old families. Having been closed up for a few days, it had taken on a musty odor, and I wondered if Ernest would object to my opening some of the windows. "How is he holding up?"

Griffin's mouth had set into a taut line. We'd agreed not to alarm Ernest unduly, since he could do nothing about Allan's situation. I'd told Christine only the barest of facts, of course, and hinted nothing about Zeiler's possible role in Griffin's confinement.

"As well as can be expected." Griffin said neutrally. "It is of the utmost importance to secure his freedom as soon as we may, however."

The study lay at the back of the house. All was silent, save for our steps and the buzzing of flies; with the servants gone, the clocks had all wound down. The acrid, rusty smell of old blood drifted even into the corridor, overwhelming the mustiness I'd noticed earlier. Griffin entered the room ahead of us, pausing just inside the door, and I followed his example.

The carpet near the desk bore a dark stain. It was here the flies had gathered, drawn by the repulsive scent. If one could overlook the bloodstained carpet, the rest of the study was quite impressive. The blank eyes of various idols stared at me, cast in bronze or hewn from marble. A curio cabinet proudly displayed a human skull topped with a hank of blank hair. With it I saw a fragment of a marble Grecian frieze, an Egyptian necklace dripping with gold and lapis-lazuli, and a mounted monkey. A mummy case stood in one corner, accompanied by fragments of bas-relief, and a delicate gold cosmetics pot had been turned into an inkwell on the desk.

Christine's eyes narrowed, and she glared at the mummy case. "That case is from the Nineteenth Dynasty! A priceless artifact—or it would have been, had some wretched tomb robber not stolen it from God knows where, no doubt destroying half the site in the process. All so it could sit here, collect dust, and be of no use but to awe simple-minded fools!"

Ernest looked shocked, which well he might, considered she slandered his murdered loved one. "Er, what Dr. Putnam means," I said hastily, "is to ask if you've thought about honoring your uncle's memory by donating any pieces to the museum?"

"Bah!" Christine said.

"I-I haven't thought of it," Ernest replied, eyeing Christine as if he feared she might attack him at any moment.

Griffin cleared his throat. "What can you tell us about the stolen piece?" he asked our host.

Tambling pointed to an open cabinet on one wall. It contained ivory miniatures from China, a medieval censor, and a row of stone spear points. The largest compartment was conspicuously empty. "It was a large ceremonial bowl of some sort. I don't know anything about it, other than it was…well, hideous, in my opinion. Uncle kept an inventory where he described all his pieces—would you care to see it?"

"Please," I said.

He went around the desk and removed a ledger from a drawer. As I took it, Griffin said, "You understand I will have to search the entire room—perhaps the house—if we're to discover who wanted the artifact badly enough to kill for it. This includes his private papers."

"Whatever it takes to free Allan." Ernest handed Griffin the key to the desk. "If you'll excuse me. I'll wait for you in the fresh air outside."

He fled the room, no doubt fearing Christine would begin to harangue him again. "Well, I suppose he's out of our way, at least," Griffin observed.

I hefted the book in my hand. "Do you wish me to look through this now?"

"Yes. Find another room, if you would; it's a bit tight in here already."

I'd happily get away from the smell of blood and sound of buzzing flies. "Very well."

"In the meantime, I'll examine the room, and Christine can answer any questions about the remaining artifacts, in case they shed some light on the matter. And determine which pieces to steal for the museum, of course."

Christine snorted. "Not that it will do much good. Without provenance, half the knowledge is lost already. Blast Bixby and his ilk; if they didn't pay outrageous sums for antiquities, there would be no incentive for tomb robbers to loot and destroy everything they come across."

I departed; as I walked down the hall, Christine moved on to cursing other archaeologists, most of whom, in her opinion, were little better than the grave robbers. I hoped Griffin was prepared for a long lecture.

I went down the hall, far enough for Christine's voice to be muffled, until I came to the parlor. It was also stuffed with curio cabinets and antiquities, and I made a mental note to mention it to Christine later. Possibly much later.

The light was good, so I cracked one of the windows and took a seat.

Finding the description of the ceremonial bowl proved no easy task; Bixby had apparently recorded each item as he received it, without any sort of index or regard to classification. But I was accustomed to such tedious work, having poured over many ancient tomes equally disorganized. There was nothing to do but begin on the first page and hope not to nod off before finding the entry I needed.

The breeze didn't stir the curtains beside me, but the scent of the ocean suddenly grew strong. At least it was preferable to mildew.

Bixby had apparently done quite a bit of collecting over time, buying objects and selling them when he tired of them, or wanted something new. He'd had atrocious handwriting, and it took me some puzzling to read. I had only gotten four or five pages into the ledger when a footstep sounded in the hall outside the room.

"Finished already?" I asked, not looking up from my work.

There came no reply. I lifted my gaze to see who stood there, and discovered the doorway empty.

I would have sworn I'd heard the scuff of a shoe…but perhaps I'd been mistaken. Houses did have a way of creaking oddly, after all, even ones not more than a decade or two old.

Banishing my unease, I turned my attention back to the ledger.

The entry for the stolen artifact lay on the sixth page. *"Ceremonial bowl(?),"* it read. *"Approx. 24 inches diameter. Restored from fragments. Sumerian? Depiction of an unknown sea god, surrounded by shark-men worshippers."*

Well. That was entirely unhelpful.

If only there had been a sketch, or a photograph, or some way of knowing what it looked like. The description certainly didn't sound like something worth committing murder over, not when there were items like the gold cosmetics-pot-cum-inkwell, which a thief could more easily pocket and sell. Either it was more impressive than it sounded, or someone wanted it for a very specific purpose.

A shiver ran down my back. The Brotherhood was gone, broken, so it couldn't be anyone with an occult goal in mind.

Could it?

The smell of ocean grew even stronger, and for an instant I heard the deep roar of the waves and the sucking of the tide on the strand. Out of the corner of my eye, I glimpsed someone standing in the doorway, silhouetted against the light. An irrational certainty gripped me that if I looked, I'd see the figure from my dream…

Feeling as if I fought against some strange compulsion, I forced my neck to unbend, my lips to move. "Who—?"

I saw no one. Moreover, there was no sound of tide, no scent of sea, beyond the usual fishy smell which hung over Widdershins.

Griffin and Christine's voices came from the back of the house, drawing nearer. A moment later, they appeared in the doorway. "Any luck?" Griffin asked.

I must have fallen asleep in the chair and dreamed the figure, the smell, the sound. Between the case itself, our visit to Stormhaven, Griffin's nightmares and my own, no wonder I should have odd visions upon slipping into a doze.

"Very little," I said, showing him the entry. "It doesn't sound like the sort of thing for which anyone would commit murder, I have to say."

"Agreed," Christine said, peering over Griffin's shoulder. "Gold and jewels is the usual sort of thing, not bits of broken clay. Perhaps if it had depicted a particularly attractive woman, or two men…never mind," she finished hastily, her cheeks going pink.

I pretended not to notice, but Griffin had no shame whatsoever. "Two men what?"

"Hmph. Don't try that look of wide-eyed innocence on me, Griffin Flaherty. There is a market for such objects, and given the, er, *nature* of the art, I can imagine purveyors turning even more cutthroat than the usual, as any buyers would have to be especially discreet." She frowned at the ledger. "But unless these 'shark-men' were disporting themselves in a manner not mentioned here, I can't imagine such would be the case."

"Thank heavens," I muttered.

She snorted. "Honestly, Whyborne, I assure you I am quite accustomed to such sights from many a tomb, and am capable of viewing them with perfect detachment. You have no need to dither about my embarrassment."

"It isn't *your* embarrassment I'm concerned for."

Griffin gently cleared his throat; I rather suspected, having stirred up trouble, he now tried not to laugh at us. "Perhaps we should concern ourselves with the case we actually have, and not some hypothetical one?"

I closed the book. "Yes, of course. Were your investigations more fruitful?"

"I found nothing incriminating in Bixby's correspondence," Griffin said. "Or at least, nothing I saw from a cursory inspection. As for the scene itself, I got down on my knees and examined the carpet. It was sodden with blood. According to the police, his assailant stabbed Victor Bixby forty-seven times, and I have no trouble believing it."

"Oh. That is…well, a great many times for an unknown assassin to have stabbed him while his nephew tried to stop the assault," I pointed out.

Griffin's expression darkened. "Allan Tambling isn't mad."

"I didn't say—"

"Perhaps he was frozen with shock. Wouldn't you be? Or perhaps he stepped away for a moment and returned only at the end of the assault, just long enough to clutch his uncle's dying body to him before chasing off after the assassin."

For the first time, it occurred to me Griffin might have a bit too much fellow-feeling with Allan to view the case with his usual detachment. Or Allan as he imagined him to be: a man unjustly confined in an asylum at the mercy of

Dr. Zeiler.

"I suppose?" I said, glancing at Christine for help.

She shrugged. "Stranger things have happened, and Griffin is the expert in this," she said, rather unhelpfully, in my opinion.

"I did find something out of the ordinary," Griffin went on. He pulled a slip of paper from his pocket and held it out for us to inspect. "I discovered this under the desk, as if it had been tossed or kicked there during the struggle. What do you make of it?"

The slip of paper was badly creased, as if someone had wadded it up in his fist. Smoothing it out, I saw one side was perfectly blank. On the other, a heavy hand had drawn a symbol depicting a stylized eye.

"What the devil?" I murmured.

"Do you recognize it?"

"It seems familiar." I tried to think from where, but couldn't quite place it. "I've seen similar occult signs in the *Arcanorum* and the *Al Azif*, although this one seems slightly different."

"Ah." He looked away. "That sort of familiar."

"It may mean nothing," I said hastily. "I might be mistaken. There may be nothing unnatural occurring."

"Yes." Griffin didn't sound convinced. With a sigh, he took out his watch to check the time. "Well, I'm off to confront...not otherworldly horrors, exactly."

"What are you on about?" Christine asked with a frown.

Griffin cast her a rueful grin. "Don't you recall? My parents wish to visit the museum today. We'll see you there."

CHAPTER 7

I SPENT THE first part of the afternoon in the library, as it was off limits to general visitors and thus an excellent place to hide from Griffin's family. Unfortunately, I eventually had to return to my office in order to get any actual work done. If I didn't wish to go too far out of my way, my course obliged me to cut through some of the public areas of the museum. The Ladysmith's architect had died screaming in a madhouse shortly after the building's completion, and his deteriorating mental state showed in its layout. I wondered what he'd think of Griffin's current case.

My stack of books made it difficult to see where I was going, let alone open and close doors, but I managed well enough until I reached the new Isley Wing, where a portion of Nephren-Ka's funerary relics were on display for the public. The mummy himself, along with some of the more grandiose items, was on world tour and wouldn't return to our museum until some time next year. But the sheer wealth of items Christine had uncovered meant plenty remained to display to our visitors, and the exhibit frequently had any number of spectators, even during what would normally be off times.

I hurried through the exhibit, hoping not to be seen. Over my stack of books, I glimpsed a group of people standing near one of the monumental statues of the pharaoh himself, but they seemed more interested in the statue than in accosting a museum worker with their questions. As I approached the discreet staff door at the other end of the room, I heard James Kerr say, "Well, don't that beat all! It's just like something out of the Bible, ain't it, Ma?"

"It surely is. Is this the one who held the Israelites in slavery and brought down all those plagues?"

"No, Mother, Nephren-Ka lived quite a long time earlier," replied Griffin.

Of course I'd managed to enter the hall at the exact same time as the very people I wanted to avoid. Should I greet them? Flee while I still had the chance? Which course of action would Griffin prefer I take?

"Whyborne? Is that you?" Griffin called.

I bit back a sigh and turned to them. "Oh, hello," I said, as if I'd somehow missed their presence earlier.

"Dr. Whyborne!" Mrs. Kerr beamed at me. "Oh, I'm so glad you and my boy are friends, I can't even tell you! Griffin mentioned you work here, and I was hoping we'd see you again. What is it you do, now? I'm sure he said in his letters, but when you get to be my age, the memory starts to go, you know!"

Her enthusiasm for our association piled me with guilt heavier than the books I carried. "I, ah, translate," I said. It wasn't precisely accurate, but close enough to the truth.

"It really is writing?" Ruth inquired, directing her gaze to a nearby case with a fragment of papyrus in it.

"Oh, yes, it is."

"All them little squiggles and snakes and birds and such?" Mr. Kerr said, as if he thought I played a joke on him. "Why would somebody want to write with birds and crocodiles, and not just plain old letters?"

"Yes, Whyborne," Griffin said with a grin, "why would they do such a thing?"

I shot him a glare, which he impudently ignored. "Very well," I said, shoving the books into his arms. "If you'll kindly deposit these in my office, I shall do my best to answer questions. I trust you remember the way?"

"I believe so," he said, without giving the slightest hint he'd visited me there on many occasions. Usually in order to have lunch together, but sometimes he would lock the door behind him and…

Oh dear lord, I couldn't think of such things, not while standing in front of his parents and cousin. "Well," I said, hoping my smile didn't look too strained, "what did you wish to know?"

Fortunately, Griffin returned before too long, and with Christine in tow. What sort of favor had he promised to get her to voluntarily play tour guide?

"Mother, Father, Ruth," he said, "allow me to introduce my friend Dr. Christine Putnam."

"Oh!" Nella Kerr's hands fluttered wildly. "James! She's the lady archaeologist we read about in the papers!" Lunging forward, she grabbed Christine's hand and shook it heartily. "It is just such a pleasure to meet you. Oh, I can't believe this! Me, shaking hands with the lady archaeologist!"

For the first time since I'd met her, Christine looked as if she wished to flee screaming. Given she'd faced down charging hippos, undead Guardians, and monstrous creatures from outer space, I didn't know if I should be amused or alarmed.

"Yes," she said, putting on a grim smile, like a woman en route to her execution. "Griffin said you wished to know about the exhibit."

Without giving them an opportunity to ask questions, she began lecturing on the deplorable state of archaeology in general, with specific examples of idiot tourists and fools searching for evidence of Moses. The Kerrs listened with somewhat stunned expressions on their faces, and I wondered if I should take the opportunity to slip away.

As I glanced to the safety of the staff door, I noticed Ruth lingering near the papyrus scroll she had asked about earlier, rather than remaining with her uncle and aunt. I had difficulty conversing with people I knew, let alone virtual strangers, but the instincts of my upbringing said I must at least offer to keep her company. Exposure to Christine had not yet been enough to overcome all the dictates of manners, so I approached Ruth resignedly.

"Have you any questions, Miss Kerr?" I asked.

She started a bit, as if she hadn't been aware of my approach. A pink blush spread across her cheeks, and she hastily looked down. "Oh, no. I'm sure you got better things to do than answer my silly questions."

"The only silly question is an unasked one," I said, a sentiment I was certain Christine would disagree with most vehemently. The museum didn't pay me to answer the questions of tourists, especially ones without the wherewithal to become donors, but a few minutes would make no difference. It had nothing at all to do with my feelings of guilt over deceiving Griffin's family about the truth of our relationship.

Well, hopefully I was deceiving them, at least, since I was doing a rather poor job of lying to myself at the moment.

"Then…how do you know what it says?" Miss Kerr asked. "I don't speak nothing but English, and not even that like my teacher wanted, when I did go to school. Ma always said there weren't no point in schooling a girl; not like fancy books were going to teach me how to raise children or kill a chicken the right way."

Shadows darkened her blue eyes. Of regret? Perhaps she had as little enthusiasm for her aunt's matchmaking as Griffin did.

"My mother taught me how to read," I said. "Not just English, but Latin and Greek as well. So, with all respect to your mother, I cannot agree with such a sentiment." A thought occurred to me. "Can you read? Ah, English? I don't mean to offer insult—"

She blushed and ducked her head. "I can read pretty well, sir. Better than I can speak it, I reckon."

"Egyptian hieroglyphs may not be the best starting point for the new student," I said, hoping I came across as diplomatic rather than patronizing. "There are some Latin inscriptions in the Roman exhibit through here; those use the letters you are familiar with, at least."

I set about explaining some of the very basics, choosing one of the simpler inscriptions. Ruth proved to be a quick learner, and even followed my explanation of how different endings implied a masculine or feminine or neutral person or thing. Her eyes lit up when we worked through the first phrase together and again when she immediately recognized a word from the first exhibit in the second. Had someone—her mother?—attempted to impress an idea of her own stupidity on her, to prevent her from becoming too clever?

"If you are truly interested, there is a Latin primer I can recommend," I said, when Mr. Kerr's voice echoed through the gallery.

"Ruth! Are you bothering Dr. Whyborne, girl?"

I turned, startled. As for Ruth, she turned painfully red and stared at the ground. "I—I'm sorry," she mumbled, although whether the apology was aimed at her uncle or me I didn't know.

"Not at all," I assured him.

Mr. Kerr looked less than reassured, however. What was wrong with the man? Miss Kerr and I had been quite properly introduced; it wasn't as if I were some stranger who had pressed his unwanted attentions on her.

"Very kind," he said, as his wife and Griffin caught us up. Christine had vanished, probably cackling to herself, having thoroughly discomfited the Kerrs in some fashion or other. "But I know how the girl can go on once she gets an idea in her head."

"The girl," as if she had no name of her own to recognize. I tried to think, but before I could say anything, Mrs. Kerr shot her husband a hard look.

"Don't be foolish, Pa," she said. "Really, Dr. Whyborne, I don't know where he gets these ideas! You won't find another girl as sober and hardworking as our Ruth in Kansas *or* Massachusetts, I'd wager."

Surely, I had missed some important context. Poor Miss Kerr looked utterly humiliated, and Griffin seemed torn between amusement and some darker feeling I couldn't quite identify.

I had no idea what I could say to make Ruth's lot better—in fact, given how I tended to botch even everyday human interactions, I'd likely only make things worse. "It was a pleasure to meet you, Miss Kerr," I said, bowing to her. "I will send the Latin primer to you via Griffin, if I may."

Griffin seemed to have mastered his emotions. At any rate, he rather smirked when he said, "Really, Whyborne, don't you recall you and Dr. Putnam accepted our invitation to dinner on Friday?"

"Oh." I folded my hands behind my back to suppress the desire to throttle him. "Of course. How could I have possibly forgotten?"

"You never mentioned this cousin of yours to me," I said much later.

Griffin had taken his parents and Ruth out to dinner again, leaving me to dine alone, unless one counted Saul, who was excellent company in some ways but not much of a conversationalist. Griffin returned shortly after nightfall and changed into some of his more disreputable togs for a trip down to the docks.

Now we made our way through Widdershins, toward the saloon where Allan Tambling had lunched and drank away his last afternoon as a free man. A heavy fog rolled in off the sea, and the gaslights shone dimly through it. Other strolling figures appeared and disappeared with suddenness, none paying any mind to us. The Daboll trumpet sounded in the distance, warning ships of the fogbound coast.

Griffin sighed. "I didn't think there was any reason to," he said. "I met her once, many years ago, before I even left for Chicago. She was just a child then. Of course, I was also, or might as well have been." His mouth twisted slightly. "A month or two after I moved here, I received a letter from her. It was clear to me either Ma—Mother," he correctly hastily, "or perhaps Father, had encouraged her to write."

"You don't have to correct your language or disguise your accent in front of me," I said with some exasperation. Our backgrounds could not have been more disparate, but surely I'd made it clear I didn't care about our differences in class.

"It's no disguise. I've spoken this way for so long it's become my nature. Besides, Mother would be the first to scold me for slipping into old habits."

I didn't wish to argue, so I didn't dispute his words. Instead, I asked, "And their intent in bringing Miss Kerr…?"

"How should I know?" Griffin asked testily.

"Perhaps they've sprung her on you in hopes you'll be so smitten by meeting face-to-face you'll propose," I suggested.

"Then they'll be very disappointed, won't they?" Griffin said. "At any rate, she seems quite nice."

"Yes." At the moment, I'd rather she'd been cruel or dreadfully stupid, or at least have given me some reason to dislike her. But the little I'd seen of her had seemed perfectly charming, like a countrified version of Miss Parkhurst.

"They're only staying for a few days. Can you not endure it for that long?"

On the one hand, I didn't want to endure it at all. On the other, Griffin had been kidnapped by my father's cohorts and almost sacrificed in an unholy ritual. I might know little of the Kerrs, but I felt relativity certain they wouldn't be feeding my blood to undead abominations any time soon. "So long as it's only for a few days, then yes."

"Of course it will be."

"Then, yes, I'll endure it." I felt a bit of a wretch; it wasn't as if Griffin asked much of me, after all. "What do you believe we'll learn at the tavern?" I asked, hoping for a change of topic.

Griffin pursed his lips. "Whether or not Allan met anyone there. Or if someone had the opportunity to slip something into his drink, which might have caused his later blackout. At this point, I'm trying to keep an open mind."

I had another question, one I half-feared to ask. "Griffin…er, have you… well, that is, have you considered Allan may very well have killed his uncle?"

Griffin's bearing stiffened sharply, although only someone familiar with him would have noticed. "Why would he have screamed in the street and summoned attention if he were a cold-blooded murderer? And where is the ceremonial bowl, if not taken by some thief?"

"The latter is a puzzle," I admitted. "But in truth, there are any number of things he might have done with it."

"God." Griffin came to a halt, glaring away down the street rather than looking at me. "You sound like…"

He didn't finish, but I easily imagined what he meant to say. Surely, those who had condemned him to a madhouse had spoken similar words, never believing his tale of eldritch abominations could possibly be real.

Damn it. I wished I had waited to speak my mind, until we were behind locked doors and drawn curtains, where I might safely take him into my arms. I pitched my voice low and hoped he understood. "I'm sorry, old fellow. I merely raise the possibility, because you know as well as I do not every man within Stormhaven's walls has been unjustly condemned. Some suffer from delusion, and…and we may not be able to help them. I only meant to ask if you had considered the possibility, not cast doubt on your judgment."

"Of course I have." He sounded as if the words had to be dragged across sandpaper to reach his tongue. "But I like to believe I am a fair assessor of character. Allan Tambling strikes me no more of a murderer than you do."

I didn't think there was anything to gain from an argument. I touched his elbow lightly. "Of course. You are more experienced in these matters, so I shall defer to your expertise."

He glanced at me, and I caught a flicker of doubt in his eyes before he smiled. "Thank you."

"You will question the bartender?" I asked.

"That is one of my goals."

"And I'm with you, because…?"

Griffin laughed. "Because I value your opinion. Don't worry, my dear—I have no plans to abandon you to the locals."

Given our past history, I doubted his word, but I followed him anyway. I would have followed him anywhere: to a saloon, or bathhouse, or hell itself. Did he understand that? He felt such shame at his fits and his past, but I could not possibly imagine loving him more.

Except I did. Every day. Which didn't really disprove my point.

CHAPTER 8

THE BARNDOOR SKATE Saloon was just close enough to the docks to be somewhat disreputable, but not so near as to prevent a gentleman such as Allan Tambling from paying a visit despite the slovenly air. A woman wearing a great deal of makeup called to us from her post near the door. "Hey, gents, buy a lady a drink? I'll make it worth yer while. One at a time or both at once, whatever ye prefer."

I removed my hat and gave her a little bow. "No thank you, ma'am, but I wish you well in your night's endeavors." She was still crinkling up her brow and trying to determine my meaning when we passed through the door and into the saloon.

Griffin chuckled. "My, my. I remember a time when you would have all but died from embarrassment from such a salutation."

"Then clearly my association with you has done nothing to refine me," I replied.

To my surprise, his smile faltered slightly. "I never intended to drag you down to my level."

What strange mood rode him tonight? "I rather like your level," I said. "And if I've become a bit more worldly, surely it is to the good?"

Instead of answering, he said only, "Keep close, unless there seems reason for us to split up."

The saloon itself seemed fairly typical of the few I'd seen: tables crowded with mostly male clientele and the occasional woman, a long tin-topped bar to one side, and frightful growls and yells from a corner in the back indicating a rat pit. The cartilaginous skeleton of the saloon's namesake hung on the wall behind the bar. No one paid us any particular attention; apparently, various sorts of strangers wandered in and out of this neighborhood on a regular basis.

Griffin led the way to the crowded bar. The bartender, a round man with an excellent mustache, gave us a smile as he wiped down a glass. "What can I get you gents?"

"A beer for each of us," Griffin said with a smile of his own. When the barkeep deposited the foaming glasses in front of us, Griffin reached into his vest and pulled out a small picture in a frame. "If you don't mind my asking, do you recognize the man on the right?"

I leaned in, as curious as the barkeep. The picture showed Ernest and Allan standing together with a woman I didn't recognize. Griffin must have taken the photo from their uncle's house. Had he gotten Ernest's permission, or simply helped himself?

The bartender squinted at the photo. "Ain't that the one I read about in the papers? The one who went crazy and murdered his uncle?"

"So the police believe," Griffin said noncommittally. "We're trying to retrace his steps. Apparently, he ate lunch here on Saturday. Do you remember him?"

"He was here? The madman? In my bar?" The barkeep's eyes lit up. "I guess we're all lucky to have escaped with our lives, eh? I wonder where he sat—maybe I can charge a little extra to drink in the same chair as the lunatic murderer!"

"You don't remember him?" Griffin prompted.

"No, sir, but Saturday is right busy for us. Fellows come in as soon as they get paid and start drinking, straight on to midnight. My help had to go home sick, and I was in such a rush, I wouldn't have known it if my own mam came in for a drink."

I had the feeling he wouldn't let such a minor detail interfere with an attempt to make money from having an accused lunatic in his bar. By closing time tonight, there would no doubt not only be the "murderer's chair" scheme in place, but he'd probably be selling some concoction as the "murderer's drink." The most expensive he had on hand, I assumed.

"But you've seen him in here before?" Griffin prodded.

"Not that I recall, no."

I had a feeling our visit would prove a waste of time. Griffin seemed to come to similar conclusions. "I see," he said. Pulling out his card, he handed it to the barkeep. "If you remember anything, don't hesitate to contact me."

I expected him to try questioning some of the regular customers, but instead he seemed content to sit and finish his beer. Trusting he had some plan in mind, I did the same. When we were done, however, Griffin simply left a tip, slid off his chair, and led the way outside.

The prostitute, thankfully, had left, no doubt having found more favorable prospects. "That's it?" I asked Griffin, once we had passed beyond the amiable gaslight in front of the saloon. How long would it be until that damnable electric light penetrated even a place such as this?

"Not what you expected?"

"No, I rather thought you'd badger or charm everyone in the saloon until you came upon someone who'd seen something."

"I might yet," Griffin admitted. "If we make no headway otherwise, I'll return on Saturday, during the hours Allan was here. But I hope to have him freed by then."

The fog had thickened while we spoke to the bartender; the street lamps cast only faint golden halos in the gloom. Objects seemed to appear suddenly from the murk, only to slink back into it once we'd passed. A cab rattled past, the bright clink of harness and clop of hooves muffled by the heavy mist. Our path had taken us nearer the docks than I liked, and I realized with a start I heard the lap of the ocean.

"Griffin, this isn't the way home."

"I know," he said in a low voice. "We're being followed. Don't look!" he added, when I would have cast a glance over my shoulder. "I hope to lose them on the wharves, so we can see who has such an interest in our doings."

My heart beat rapidly. Could our pursuer be connected to Griffin's case? Perhaps even the mysterious person who had knocked at the door before—presumably—murdering Victor Bixby before Allan's eyes? Or a simple footpad, or even a policeman?

Griffin led the way past the warehouses lining the waterfront. Mounds of crates and barrels awaiting receipt or transfer turned the area into a maze. Nets and lines formed added obstacles. The air stank of fish.

"Not much farther," Griffin murmured. "Just past this pile of crates up ahead, we'll duck off to the right and—"

Two men stepped out from behind the very stack of crates, blocking our path.

"Drat," Griffin said in an almost conversational tone.

Both men were roughly dressed and had the look of sailors about them. One lacked an ear, while the other sported exotic tattoos on his face. No doubt they knew this part of town far better than Griffin, and had slipped ahead of us, while their fellow came up from behind.

Griffin took his revolver from his coat and held it at his side. "Good evening, gentlemen," he said. "Out for a stroll?"

Footsteps approached behind us, and I turned to see the third man emerge from the fog. I took him for the leader, as he said, "You know what to do, boys. The dweller in the deep will feed on their corpses tonight."

With chilling howls, all three drew wicked knives and charged us.

Griffin fired, but the shot merely grazed the head of one of the men. He would have fired again, but was forced to leap to the side to avoid the slash of a heavy knife.

Then I could pay no more attention to his struggle, because the third man rushed at me, knife raised. Weaponless, I dodged around the other side of a stack of sacks, hoping to keep my skin intact for at least a few more seconds. A docker's hook lay atop the sacks. I snatched it up.

My assailant lunged at me. I yelped and jumped back, trying to swing the hook at his head at the same time. The tip of his knife parted my shirt and left a long rent in my vest. My wild jab with the hook kept him from gutting me.

"Going to make things hard on yourself?" he asked. "Why? Just close your eyes and the ocean will sing you to sleep."

I ran onto the pier, in the vague hope I might find some way of defending myself, or at least fending off his assault. The boards thudded beneath his boots as he chased me. Damn it, nothing but nets in need of mending, brushes with half the bristles missing, and an abandoned bucket of pitch.

My shoes slipped on boards gone slick from fog and foam. I fetched up against a piling and fell, the rough wooden pier stinging my palms, the hook flying out of my reach. The rogue laughed, a horrible sound, and I rolled onto my back to see him running at me with his knife extended.

I grabbed the bucket of pitch and threw it at him with all my strength, shouting the secret name of fire.

The pitch burst into flame, sticky gobs of it striking my attacker. He let out a truly horrific shriek, his knife falling to the ground as he frantically tried to beat out the flames. The gooey tar stuck to his skin, spreading with every movement of his hands, and within seconds he lay writhing in agony on the pier.

The one-eared man ran toward us, whether to help his friend or to kill me, I didn't know. Silently hoping this would work, I wrapped my arms around the piling I leaned against and concentrated on the waves below.

For an instant, nothing happened, and the running footsteps drew ever closer. Then, with an odd, rushing gurgle, a great surge of water poured over the pier, sweeping everything before it. I caught a final glimpse of the blazing man, the flames dying as he vanished over the side, followed by his cohort. The wave pushed at me as well, and for an instant I had the strangest impulse to let go of the piling. To ride the swell back into the ocean and dive deep…

The surge receded, although the sound of the waves grew, the bay becoming as chaotic as if I'd reached down with a giant hand and splashed it. Distant cries and curses echoed from the docked ships, now pitching up and down in their moorings, their sides scraping against the piers or else snapping ropes as they sought to pull free.

"Whyborne!"

Griffin ran to me, hand outstretched, his shoes splashing in the puddles left from the wave. "My dear, are you injured?"

"No." I accepted his hand up. His face blanched at the sight of my shirt, and he peeled back the edges of the slice, peering at the skin beneath as if he hadn't believed me. As for him, he had a scrape on the knuckles of his right hand, and blood on his coat. "What of you?"

"The blood isn't mine," he reassured me. Smoothing my ruined shirt back into place, he tugged on my sodden coat. "Thank goodness for the freak wave."

"Er, yes." I tried to look innocent, but my voice must have given me away.

His hands stilled. "It *was* a freak wave, was it not?"

"Well...not precisely."

"By which you mean not at all?" he asked in exasperation. "Damn it, Whyborne, you promised you would only experiment with the *Arcanorum's* spells under my supervision!"

"Perhaps," I allowed. "But it saved my life just now. How can you object to that?"

His face darkened. "I don't. But for God's sake, you'd just set a man on fire! Couldn't you have done the same, or blown the other man off the pier, or something? How many spells do you truly need?"

"The water spell comes easily to me," I said through gritted teeth. I certainly wasn't going to admit to him it wasn't really supposed to. "I've done no harm, except to a man who meant to kill me. If you'd rather have come upon me gutted here on the pier, then say so."

He paled, no doubt envisioning the scenario. "No. No, of course not. But you lied to me."

"I kept certain things private," I clarified. "Just as you kept private the fact you've been corresponding with Cousin Ruth."

He flinched, and I knew I'd won. "My correspondence with Ruth was purely innocent, from my perspective at least. You know that."

"Do I?"

Griffin ran his hand over his face. "Very well. Let's not argue. As you said, the spell kept you alive, and for that I am very grateful. We should leave, in case there are more of them about."

I had the grace not to show my triumph in my expression. "Who were the men who attacked us?" I asked, following him from the pier. "And what did they mean by 'the dweller in the deep'?"

"I don't know." The body of the tattooed man lay sprawled at the foot of the crates, a gaping hole in his chest where Griffin had shot him. Tattoos showed not only on his face, but on his forearms, emerging from beneath rolled-up sleeves. Griffin knelt by him and carefully lifted one wrist. "Ah. I thought I glimpsed that."

"What?"

He twisted the limp arm around, exposing the lines of ink to my sight. There, on the dead man's forearm was the same eye-like symbol Griffin had found in Bixby's study.

"They weren't random attackers," I said. "There's some connection to Bixby's murder."

"I'm afraid so." Griffin let the dead man's arm fall back to the dock and stood up, wiping his hands on his handkerchief. "Which, in turn, means there is something going on far larger than a simple theft for the antiquities market, or even the bloody death of Allan's uncle. I fear our investigation has turned over a rock, and all the unpleasant things hidden beneath are beginning to wriggle into the light."

"What are you thinking?" I asked.

"An unsolved murder, an occult symbol, a stolen relic…and now we are targets once again. Could this be the work of the Brotherhood?"

"It does rather seem like their sort of mischief," I agreed with a heavy sigh. "Very well. I suppose this means I have to visit my father."

The next afternoon, I knocked on the door to Whyborne House.

Griffin had offered to accompany me, but I overruled him. If the Brotherhood were involved, I felt fairly certain Father wouldn't kill me out of hand. I was less certain he would extend such protection to any one else, let alone my male lover.

The butler, Fenton, answered the door. "Master Percival," he said, his voice liquid with contempt. "I wasn't informed you were expected by either Mr. or Mrs. Whyborne."

"I'm not," I said shortly. As a child—and later, to be honest—I'd been terrified of Fenton. Now I mostly found him tedious. "I've come to see my father."

"He and Master Stanford are sequestered in the study. It is not a conversation open to interruption."

Stanford, in Widdershins? Not a good sign. Normally my older brother kept to New York, where he lived with his wife and children, while handling Father's various business interests in the city. But if the Brotherhood were involved in this mess, his presence made all too much sense.

Barging in would do me no good. "Very well," I said. "Inform Father I'm here the instant they adjourn. In the meantime, I shall visit Mother."

Fenton glared at me, but could make no reasonable objection, and so stepped aside.

The interior of the mansion had changed little since my childhood: dark paneled wood with the portraits of dead ancestors, relics from the Revolutionary War, priceless paintings, and antique vases. The house's gloomy, ponderous air pressed down on me, seeping into my lungs with every dusty breath, as if I walked the halls of a mausoleum. I couldn't imagine living here again; had I stayed any longer than I did, I should have gone mad.

How did this compare to the farmhouse where Griffin had come to manhood? I had no doubt it had been simpler, the furnishings plain, no gilded candelabra or clocks encrusted with emeralds. But warmer? That I'd never questioned, and now even less having met his parents.

Still, I'd always had at least one ally in this house. Mother lived in a room on the uppermost floor. Spacious windows let in plenty of light, the long curtains stirring in the slight breeze. Large bookcases lined the walls, their shelves groaning under the weight of paper and ink. A portrait of the Lady of Shalott hung above the fireplace; the lady had been modeled on my mother, painted shortly after my parents wed.

Mother lay on her divan, wrapped in a dressing gown and reading a book. As soon as I entered, she set it aside and rose, an expression of welcome on her face which undid some of the tense knot in my chest. "Percival! What an unexpected pleasure. Have you brought Griffin with you?"

Her hope to see Griffin brought a genuine smile to my lips, and I wished I could answer in the affirmative. We had never discussed it openly, but I felt certain she labored under no illusions as to the nature of my relationship with him. "I'm afraid not. His…well, his parents are visiting." It wasn't the real reason he hadn't accompanied me, but it sounded better than *I'm afraid Father might be plotting the end of the world. Again.*

She gestured for me to sit by her. "I see. And how is their visit going?"

I settled on the divan, taking the opportunity to study her face. Although she'd had two children with no more effort than any healthy woman, she'd been stricken suddenly near the end of her third pregnancy, and had delivered my twin sister and myself early. My sister hadn't lived long enough to even be named, and my life had been in question for some time after. Mother had never recovered from her illness, and I dreaded the day when she would inevitably succumb.

At the moment, however, she looked as well as she ever did: too pale by half, her skin nearly translucent, the lines around her eyes deeply graven by pain. But those eyes were still sharp and fierce as a hawk's, unchanged from my earliest memory.

"They are under the impression Griffin lives alone," I admitted. "I've met them, and they seem very kind, but they've brought a girl. Griffin's cousin, but only by adoption. Griffin scoffs, but I think they wish him to marry her."

A sigh escaped Mother, and she put a hand to my arm, squeezing sympathetically. "I always feared a difficult path lay before you."

What did she mean? I'd always believed her the one person in all the world who would care more for my happiness than the gender of the person I chose to be happy with. Had I misjudged? Did she mourn the wedding I'd never have, the grandchildren who would never be born?

I feared her answer, but I had to know. "Are you disappointed in me?"

Her eyes widened in surprise—then she hugged me fiercely, with all the strength in her fragile body. "Of course not! My only regret is the age we live in makes your road a hard one, never that you walk it. Ancient Greece would have been more amenable to you, I think. But I am very, very proud of you, Percival. You must never doubt it."

I hugged her back, although not too tightly, lest I hurt her. "I won't."

"Good." She sat back and brushed a stray strand of hair off my forehead. "I love Guinevere and Stanford, of course, but they have so much of their father in them. I've always felt as if you were more my child."

Perhaps she would have viewed us differently if she hadn't lost her health. I couldn't know. I'd never known her as the young socialite from Boston, just as a woman whose intense love of books gave her the only freedom she could have.

Given she'd learned to speak Latin, Greek, and several other languages as a girl, I wondered which life she truly preferred: that of the laughing, vivacious society woman Father had once recalled to me, or of the scholar? Had she ever felt she had a true choice, just as Ruth had clearly been denied a choice?

"But surely you didn't come here just to see me," Mother went on. "I always welcome your company, of course, but I suspect you had some other motive for returning here."

"Unfortunately. Do you know why Stanford is here?" I asked. If the Brotherhood had become active once again, Father certainly wouldn't have mentioned it to her, but she might have gleaned something from either his manner or my brother's.

"Your father refuses to say, and Stanford doesn't wish to speak of it." Her mouth flexed into a disapproving frown. "I suspect money lies at the heart of it, though. Certainly, they have been quarreling ever since Stanford arrived."

They had? That was new. I tried to remember them ever arguing about anything in my entire life, and failed. They had always been a united front against the world: Father and his adored eldest son, the perfect replica of himself.

"Oh." I rose to my feet. "Fenton says they aren't to be disturbed, but if they're speaking of money, they might go on all night."

"Undoubtedly." She took my hand and gave it a squeeze. "Go on, then. Send me a letter and let me know how Griffin fares, won't you?"

"Of course."

I made my way back downstairs. Fenton stood at the door to the study, as if guarding Father against the rest of the household, including me. Raised voices came from inside, although too muffled by the door to make out what they said.

I strode to the door. Fenton scowled. "Master Percival, I've already told you, Mr. Whyborne and Master Stanford are not to be disturbed! Now—"

The door behind him swung abruptly open, and Stanford collided with Fenton.

"Watch out, you stupid oaf!" Stanford snarled, giving the butler a hard shove which would have sent him sprawling, had I not managed to catch him. As soon as he regained his balance, Fenton snatched his arm from me, as if I'd done him some terrible insult by touching him.

"Stanford!" Father bellowed from inside the study. "Walk away if you must, but don't think to change my mind. Not another penny, do you hear?"

Stanford stormed off down the hall, headed for the entrance. "Send my things to the rail station, immediately!" he barked at a poor maid who had the bad luck to step out of a side room at that moment. A few seconds later, the front door slammed, the sound echoing dramatically through the house.

Fenton shot me a glare, as if I'd angered Stanford, then went to the study door. "Master Percival here to see you, sir. He wouldn't take no for an answer."

I thought Father might have growled. "Send him in."

Feeling rather like a Roman slave being shoved into the lion pit, I stepped past Fenton and into the study.

CHAPTER 9

FATHER SAT BEHIND his desk like a king holding court. The air reeked of cigars. I rather thought the blasted things smelled like burning socks.

Although I'd come here with every intention of demanding answers about the Brotherhood, I found myself asking, "What did you and Stanford argue about? Did I actually hear you threaten to cut him off?" Unlike me, my brother received a generous monthly allowance, in addition to his salary as Father's man of business in New York.

Father ground his teeth together, staring not at me but at the door through which Stanford had exited. "Your brother has fallen in with a bad crowd."

Hardly shocking news to me, but Father believed Stanford could do nothing wrong. "Mother said you were arguing over money. I assume the New York reporters want higher bribes than the ones in Widdershins to keep his indiscretions out of the papers?"

Father's glower confirmed it. "I don't understand," he muttered, more to himself than to me. "Stanford always had such strength of character, such inner fortitude! How can he be so easily swayed now?"

A bitter laugh burst out before I could even think to control it. "Stanford? A man of character? Surely you jest."

Father's glare was for me, now. "You were always jealous—"

"Me? Jealous of Stanford?" Heat flared in my chest, as if the coals of some banked fire had suddenly been raked over and exposed to the air. "I hated him for being the spoiled princeling of the house, allowed to run wild and do what he wished, without consequence. You never lifted a hand when he dangled me over the upstairs bannister, or threw rocks at me—"

"I did it for your own good!" Father's voice rose into a roar, and his face flushed. "To toughen you up! Cure you of your womanish ways!"

"Clearly, it failed," I snapped back. As his expression and manner grew more heated, mine went cold, the first flush of anger giving way to long-held rage. "And as for Stanford, you speak of his inner fortitude, as if agreeing with your every opinion was proof of his strength of character. Mindlessly parroting back what someone wants to hear, for no other reason than they wish to hear it, isn't strength, Father. Quite the opposite."

"If this is some attempt to get back into my good graces after the disaster you caused at Threshold—"

"My only regret about Threshold is not being able to save more people, especially Mrs. Hicks."

"Who?"

"No one you would ever notice. Or Stanford, I suppose." I shook my head. "Stanford was your mirror when he lived here with you. Now that he's among others, he merely reflects them instead."

His eyes narrowed at my defiance. "How dare you come here, malign your brother's character, and question my judgment? I should have you thrown out this instant."

"Is the Brotherhood up to its old tricks?"

The sudden change in topic brought forth a scowl. "No. You saw to that. If you had come to me, as you should have, we would have taken care of Blackbyrne, brought Leander back, and still had a powerful order. You're fortunate I forgave your blunder."

He almost destroyed the world, but I was the one who blundered? Of course I was; admitting anything else would suggest he was capable of error. "Are you certain they're gone?"

"Of course," he snapped. "Why? What's going on?"

So if not the Brotherhood, someone else must be responsible. "Are there other organizations like the Brotherhood? Other cults you're aware of?"

He stared at me, and a calculating look came into his eyes. Would he throw me out? Perhaps…but he hadn't amassed a fortune by ignoring anything which could pose a potential threat. Surely, he knew I wouldn't have come here without reason and asked himself whether that reason could signal some danger to him as well.

"Perhaps." Father sat back in his chair and lit another cigar. "Tell me what you know."

I'd brought the symbol of the eye with me, and as I explained the basic facts of the case, I placed it on the desk in front of him. Recognition flickered in his gaze, but he didn't interrupt. Was he actually listening to what I said, for once?

When I finished, he nodded slowly to himself. "Zeiler, hmm? There's a name I haven't heard for a while. He was a useful tool."

I straightened, shocked to hear it. "Zeiler is—was—in the Brotherhood?"

"Of course not," Father snapped, waving his cigar so the foul smoke drifted about his head. "The man was the son of a whaling captain. We had certain standards of breeding to uphold." As if the Whybornes hadn't fled to the colonies to escape the hangman's noose. But as that had occurred two centuries ago, no one recalled it but us, allowing our money to veil our unsavory past. "No doubt he aspired to be one of us. Upstarts like him delude themselves into thinking their degrees or quick-earned cash make them our equals." He snorted contemptuously. "At any rate, we'd use him for certain tasks his position at the asylum qualified him to do."

"Such as?"

"An incident in Chicago, for example. Some fool Pinkerton made a bunch of noise, and it was always possible someone might begin to credit it as truth. Dr. Zeiler went to Chicago, certified him insane, and that was the end of it."

I sat perfectly still. If I moved, I might throw up. Or attack Father with my bare hands.

Father noticed, of course. He scowled, opened his mouth as if to ask me what was wrong…then apparently connected the facts at his disposal. "Don't tell me Mr. Flaherty was the Pinkerton in question."

My throat went tight with fury, but I forced the words out. "Yes. He was confined to the madhouse for months, without any justice, and now I discover you were behind it?"

"I had nothing to do with it," Father said irritably. "I only heard about what happened later. Really, Percival, I can't believe you've been running about with a convicted lunatic! If you must carry on as you do, couldn't you find all the low men you wished on the docks? Your brother might have been indiscreet, but at least he knows enough not form an attachment with any of his women."

My hand curled into a fist. Spell words sizzled on my tongue. The *Arcanorum*'s weight tugged my coat pocket down, gravity itself reminding me of the revenge I could take, for both Griffin and myself.

No. I'd come here for a different purpose. I took a deep breath and swallowed the words, which turned to acid and chewed holes in my stomach. "I have no intention of discussing my life with you. Tell me what I need to know, or refuse and allow me to leave."

"Don't be so damned touchy," he groused. "I can't speak to Zeiler's involvement in the attack on you, or on Bixby. It's possible when he realized the Brotherhood wouldn't be the avenue to power and riches he'd envisioned, he found new allies. Or old ones."

"What do you mean?"

"This symbol you found." He tapped the ash from his cigar into a green-glazed ashtray. "It belongs to a group calling itself the Eyes of Nodens."

"What can you tell me about them?"

"Little enough. A few important men became involved with them from time to time, but the mainstay of their membership consists of sailors, sea captains, and others who rely on the ocean for survival. Such as Zeiler's father." He shifted uncomfortably in his seat. "I also know they are very, very dangerous. Stay away from them."

"Considering the Brotherhood almost destroyed the world, I find calling someone else dangerous rather hypocritical."

His brows snapped down over his eyes. "The Brotherhood had clear, logical objectives."

"Those being whatever would get you the most power and wealth."

"Of course." As if it were something the world owed him. "Don't complain, Percival—you grew up in comfort thanks to our doings, don't forget. Had we known what Blackbyrne truly intended, we would have put him down ourselves. We have no desire to overthrow the established order of things—we *are* the established order of things. Or were." He scowled again. "The Eyes, though…they're fanatics. Convinced they act as the eyes and ears of their gods on land, so they can know the doings of man."

"Their gods?" My heart sped slightly. "Is one of them called the dweller in the deep?"

"Perhaps. I didn't pay close attention to their raving. Fortunately for the rest of us, these creatures they worship are trapped in the sea."

"So what could they want? Why kill Bixby and steal the ceremonial bowl? What are they up to that they don't want us investigating?"

"How should I know?" He sat back and regarded me. "Stay away from them, Percival. Go home and have your Mr. Flaherty tell his employer whatever lies will convince the man of his brother's guilt."

"I can't do that."

"Stubborn as always." He gestured toward the door. "Enough. If you won't take my advice, then leave now."

"With pleasure," I said. But I felt his gaze on me all the way to the door, like the stare of a viper fixed on my back.

I went straight home, walking in a daze. The conversation with Father weighed on me: Stanford's troubles, our old disagreement about the proper course of my life.

Zeiler.

The door opened as I came up the walk; Griffin must have kept an eye out for me. "Whyborne?" he called. "Are you all right?"

My face must have betrayed me. I continued up the walk and into the house, keeping my eyes turned toward the ground. What right did I have to look at him, when my own family had done him such a terrible injustice? Oh, Father might claim he had nothing to do with it, and perhaps he even believed it true. But our money had funded the Brotherhood's activities. Our family line had helped keep it alive through the centuries since Widdershins's founding. And if Father had known, he wouldn't have stopped it. Quite the opposite.

"My dear?" Griffin shut the door behind us, and put a hand to my shoulder. "I take it things didn't go well? Is the Brotherhood…?"

"No." At least I could give him that much. "Father swears they haven't regrouped and aren't behind this, and I believe him."

"Then what's troubling you?"

He knew me too well. He'd always been able to see past every façade I strove to place between the world and myself. I'd resented his ability at first, then come to treasure it, but now…

"I have something to tell you," I said quietly. "And I'm afraid you'll hate me for it."

"No." His response came immediately: so sure, so certain. So unlike my constant second-guesses.

"You can't know until you've heard it."

His hand closed on my shoulder. "There's nothing you could say to make me hate you, my dear. You spoke to your father?"

"Yes."

"And he said something which upset you?"

I let out a bitter laugh. "This is my father we're talking about."

"Yes, well, that was something of a given, I suppose." His grip tightened on my shoulder, strong fingers pressing my gently against the arch of muscle and bone. "You didn't set him on fire, did you?"

"No," I said, "but I wish to God I had. He deserves it, and worse—they all do."

His sigh gusted against my cheek. "Talk to me."

"Zeiler." I hated the man. The urge rose in me to go to Stormhaven tonight, to force visions into his mind until he raved and screamed. Until everyone thought him mad, and he was sentenced to the same torment to which he'd condemned Griffin. "The Brotherhood employed him. That's why he went to Illinois. They sent him to silence you."

Griffin froze, his fingers still on my shoulder. But for how long, until he pulled away in disgust? "Father claims he wasn't involved," I said, bitterness burning my tongue. "But I know him—if he had been, he would have sent Zeiler to attest to your madness without a second thought. So it might as well be his fault, and I wish he'd died in the war and I'd never been born if it would have saved you this, and—"

"Hush." He turned me to face him. The color had drained from his face, but at least he wasn't shaking. "I…I suppose I shouldn't be surprised, given the Brotherhood was more than happy to sacrifice me last winter."

"This is different." I felt utterly helpless. "I'll cut off contact with all of them, immediately. Father, Stanford, everyone in my wretched family. I swear."

"No." He touched my face lightly. "Your mother is a kind woman, and doesn't deserve such treatment. She welcomed me with open arms, which is something I never expected. As for Niles, did he give you any useful information?"

I nodded miserably.

"Then it behooves us to make use of him, as he would have done with me." Griffin's voice went flat and cold. Rage showed in his eyes.

"I wish I had done everything differently." For the first time, I understood just how selfish all my choices had been. "If I had gone to Widdershins University, if I had followed Father and Stanford into business and the Brotherhood, I could have done something. Kept it from happening. It's all my fault…"

"Ival, no!" He pulled me roughly against him but I couldn't bear to return his embrace. "You're speaking nonsense. If you'd been the sort of man to give in to whatever Niles wished, how could you have also been the sort to stand up to him and the Brotherhood?"

"If I'd only thought—"

"As far as I know, thinking about something doesn't grant one omniscience." He gripped me tightly. "This changes nothing between us. I love you. I adore your mother. Your father can burn in hell for all I care, but the sentiment is hardly new to either of us."

It pulled a ragged laugh from me. "No, it isn't."

"Don't take too much on yourself. Just breathe." He stroked my back gently.

I hesitantly slipped my arms around him. "I've spent my whole life trying to get away from all of this, only to find it waiting for me at every turn."

"I know." He tilted his head back and kissed me gently. "I know, my dear. It's all right."

I kissed him back, even though it still felt selfish, as if I had no right, knowing what I did. When the kiss was done, he studied me carefully.

"So," he said, "what did Niles say?"

I told him everything. When I was done, he stared into nothing for a long time, his brow furrowed in thought.

"We don't know for certain Dr. Zeiler is actually involved," I pointed out, when he failed to say anything. "In this case, at least. Just because he was a tool of the Brotherhood doesn't mean he has anything to do with the Eyes of Nodens. The symbol was found in Bixby's study, after all—perhaps he had some connection to them, not his killer."

"I suppose," he agreed reluctantly. "We could ask Allan if he recognizes it. I should visit him again, anyway, so he knows he's not forgotten."

My stomach clenched at the thought of facing Zeiler, knowing now what I did. How much worse must it be for Griffin? "I'll accompany you."

"Your work—"

"Can wait." I brushed a lock of hair from his forehead. "We're in this together, Griffin."

He sighed and leaned against me. "I'm glad. I…I don't know how I would do this without you. You're my strength."

I didn't know how to respond to his words. I wasn't strong, or brave, or anything really.

But he made me want to be.

"No! His face—no!"

Griffin's cry pulled me awake from restless sleep. He sat upright, so tense the cords of his neck stood out. His shivers shook the bed with their intensity. A low moan started in his chest.

As he was in no position to object, I lit the night candle with a word. He flinched at the light, but his eyes stared unseeing into nothing, not even blinking.

"Griffin." I reached for him. "Griffin, it's all right. It's—"

He jerked violently from me. "No! Let go of me! You can't do this, you have no right; I won't let you!"

My voice trembled, but I kept my tone low and reassuring. "Shh. Darling, it's me."

He shuddered, but didn't pull away when I rested my fingers on his forearm. "Don't hurt me," he whispered. "Don't make me go back."

God, I hated these fits. I'd never before so vehemently wanted the death of a fellow human being as I desired Zeiler's at that moment.

"Of course I won't make you go back." I wrapped my arms around him. He trembled, his skin covered with goose bumps, even though it was a warm August night. "You're home. You're safe. No one will hurt you, or send you away."

"Home?"

"Yes, Griffin."

"Whyborne?"

I hadn't expected him to recognize me this quickly. Usually when his fits took him, he knew nothing around him for some time. "Yes." I pressed a kiss to his hair. "It's me. Your Ival."

He relaxed against me, letting me draw him down and twine my legs around him as well. Gradually, his trembling ceased, and his frantic pulse calmed.

We remained still for so long, I began to slip back into a doze, until he stirred against me. "I'm sorry," he whispered. His breath tickled the skin of my throat.

"You have nothing for which to apologize."

"I thought I was doing better. I hadn't had a fit in weeks, until this damned case…"

"I know." I tightened my hold on him. "I understand."

"You shouldn't have to. You shouldn't have to put up with this."

"Hush." I kissed him again. "I'm here because I wish to be. Because I love you as you are, right now, today."

He sighed. "I wish I could have met you before. If you'd known me as I was then…"

Would I have loved him? He had still been with Elliot at the time…and his partner Glenn...and heaven only knew how many others. Probably I would only have been another conquest, bedded and forgotten.

Or perhaps not. I liked to think some special bond existed between us, something which would have still found us here, twined together in this bed, or at least one much like it.

"You're speaking nonsense," I told him. "Here—rest your head on my shoulder and let me hold you. That helps, does it not?"

Another sigh, nearly soundless. "Yes," he admitted. "I...thank you."

"You don't need to thank me."

"You're wrong." He settled in against me, the weight of his head on my shoulder familiar and comforting to us both. "But I shan't argue."

"Very sensible of you," I said. Or meant to; it turned into a yawn, and thence into the heaviness of sleep. But when I woke a few hours later, I found Griffin staring at the ceiling, a haunted look on his face.

CHAPTER 10

FOG SHROUDED THE spires of Stormhaven when we alighted from our hired coach. Water dripped from the leaves of the stunted trees, the sound mingling with the roar of the ocean echoing from below the cliffs.

Dr. Peck met us in the foyer. I noticed Griffin very carefully did not glance at Dr. Zeiler's nearby door. Dark circles showed under his eyes, giving him a haggard look, especially combined with the bloodless pallor his face assumed once we reached Stormhaven.

I didn't look at Dr. Zeiler's office, either. Because if I did, I might not be responsible for my actions.

Perhaps there was no malice in Zeiler; perhaps he believed his treatment of Griffin simply followed the dictates of modern medicine. Perhaps he'd even thought he might help Griffin, by curing his predilections.

I didn't give a damn. The words of a dozen curses sizzled on the back of my tongue. I'd read far too much in the *Arcanorum,* spells which Griffin remained unaware of, spells I'd never intended to actually use. I could set a host of whippoorwills shrieking about Zeiler in the summer, and crows in the winter, to hound him from sleep and shatter his nerves. I could drive him as mad as the wretches around him, and God, a part of me longed to do so.

But Griffin feared for me. He wouldn't consider such a revenge an even trade, would berate me for using the *Arcanorum* in such a fashion, even for his sake. So I wouldn't. No matter the temptation.

"Good morning, Mr. Flaherty, Dr. Whyborne," Peck said, shaking our hands in turn. If he noticed the strain showing on Griffin's face, he didn't remark upon it. "Your message said you've come to speak with Allan Tambling again?"

Griffin nodded. "I have a question about something we found at the scene of his uncle's murder, which might shed light on who killed the man."

Dr. Peck's smile became somewhat pained. "You persist in your theory Allan isn't the one responsible? I'm certain you know your business, Mr. Flaherty, but trust we know ours just as well. Allan murdered his uncle, for reasons we do not yet understand. Violent delusions seem likely. Whatever the cause, once he killed Bixby, he found himself burdened with unbearable guilt. The only way to escape the horror of his own actions was for his mind to draw a curtain across his memories so he might believe himself innocent. A victim, even. It's a tragic delusion, but not as uncommon as one might think."

Griffin's expression had grown rather fixed. "Indulge me."

"As you wish."

Peck led us back to the wards as he had before. After we passed through the steel door, he asked the attendant on duty to bring Allan to the sitting room to meet us.

The air still reeked of urine and other foul things, and one of the patients seemed to be in the grip of a violent cough. Others sang to themselves, babbled, or stared at their hands with eyes gone gray with despair. I glanced at Griffin's profile and saw his brow furrowed and his mouth tight with suppressed emotion.

I hated this.

Some of the other patients occupied the sitting room, rocking or staring at nothing. Another attendant herded them away; they shuffled off, one of them protesting loudly.

A short time later, the attendant returned with Allan. The poor man had clearly lost weight even in the few days of his confinement, and his welcoming smile trembled. "Do you have news?" he asked hopefully.

Griffin looked stricken, although he quickly hid the expression and assumed an encouraging air. "I think we do indeed have some clues," he said, putting a comforting hand to the other man's shoulder. "Hold tight, Allan. You aren't forgotten in this place. We will have you out of here soon, I swear it."

Tears gathered in the corners of Allan's eyes, and he blinked rapidly. "Thank you. You have no idea what your words mean to me."

Griffin swallowed thickly. Reaching into his pocket, he withdrew the folded piece of paper. "I found this in your uncle's study." He passed it to Allan, who began to unfold it. "Do you recognize the symbol? Does it perhaps correspond to some tattoo your uncle had, or—"

With a frenzied shriek, Allan hurled himself on Griffin.

It happened so quickly, none of us had a chance to react. Griffin's chair crashed backward, carrying both of them to the floor, with Allan on top. The madman's hands locked around Griffin's throat.

The attendant and I both flung ourselves on Allan, seeking to pry him off. The attendant managed to get an arm around the lunatic's throat, but instead of responding to the chokehold, Allan continued to strangle Griffin. Griffin's cane had fallen to the floor, so I snatched it up and struck Allan a hard blow across both forearms, seeking to break his grip.

Either my efforts or those of the attendant worked, because his hold slackened. The attendant hauled Allan off Griffin, and I fell to my knees at his side. Griffin's face had purpled, and he gagged and coughed. Seeing my concern, he waved me off. "I'm fine," he managed to grate out.

I rather doubted it, but chose not to argue, instead helping him to his feet. Screams spread through the ward, accompanied by wild shouts, as Allan's howls excited the other wretches confined here. Attendants rushed in, no doubt summoned by the nurse on duty, and began to herd the patients back to their rooms, with blows if necessary to get them to cooperate.

"Take him to the fourth floor!" Dr. Peck ordered the attendant holding Allan. Turning to Griffin, he asked, "Dear heavens, are you injured? Come to the infirmary—"

"No." Griffin picked up the paper where it had fallen. "You devils! You've done something to him, haven't you?"

Peck took a step back, shock spreading across his face. "What on earth do you mean?"

"You've done something to Allan—mesmerized him, or put him under some sort of spell, or—"

"Control yourself, sir," Peck said, scowling. "You are distraught, I understand. It must be quite a blow to discover your client is a lunatic after all, but—"

"He isn't!" Griffin shouted, looking rather deranged himself.

I rather feared he'd end up condemned a second time. "Griffin," I said urgently. "Please!" I didn't want to believe it of Allan either, but the man had leapt on Griffin like a wild beast.

Griffin turned to me, eyes wide. "Don't you see? Allan was perfectly fine until he saw *this*." He waved the paper in my face. "The very symbol from the crime scene! Allan has been used—someone did this to him, before the murder."

"Um…" The theory sounded mad, but given his current state, I didn't know what Griffin would do if I expressed such an opinion.

His brows rose sharply, a look of revelation on his face. "Of course. They knew each other socially. Zeiler is behind it! He must be!"

As badly as I wished Zeiler destroyed, we had no evidence connecting Zeiler with the Eyes. As I flailed for a diplomatic way of saying so, Griffin bolted from the room, weaving in between attendants and patients. Peck and I exchanged a startled look then raced after him. At least Griffin couldn't get far —the steel door was always kept locked.

Unless, of course, someone was in the process of going through it. As we struggled to follow Griffin, the door swung open. He shoved aside the nurse coming in, knocking a tea tray from her hands, and darted into the central section of the building.

Blast it. I managed to reach the door before Peck, relying on my longer legs, and dodged the alarmed nurse. Yelling echoed from Zeiler's office, and my heart sank.

Griffin had flung open the door and seized the superintendent by his lapels, dragging him from his desk chair. I wanted to join him, to throw myself on Zeiler and beat him senseless for what he'd done to Griffin. But the rational part of me said this wasn't the way; brute force would do nothing but bring the matter to the attention of the police, whose sympathies would never lie with us.

"What did you do to Allan? Tell me, damn you!" Griffin roared at Zeiler.

"Get your hands off me! Help!" the doctor shouted.

I grabbed Griffin's shoulders and hauled him back, even as several attendants and Dr. Peck burst into the room. Griffin seemed to recognize a lost cause, and let go of Zeiler so abruptly I nearly fell backward.

"Calm yourself!" I exclaimed, clinging to Griffin's suit coat in case he decided to lunge at Zeiler again. "This will gain us nothing, and certainly not help Allan's case!"

The superintendent's face had gone purple with fury. "I don't know what you mean by this, but, Dr. Whyborne, you will take your friend and leave immediately. Just because you're Niles Whyborne's son doesn't mean your associates can assault me with impunity my own office. I will not have it!"

I wanted to strike him. Instead, I only replied, "Come along, Griffin. We're done here for now."

Griffin yanked free of my grasp, straightening his coat. "This isn't over."

"I think you'll find it is," Zeiler replied. The attendants closed in, and for a horrible moment I thought Griffin meant to fight them. Then he turned sharply on his heel and shoved past me and out the door.

I hastened after him. The attendants followed us out to the waiting carriage, whose driver cast a curious look at us. Griffin ignored him, climbing inside the conveyance and leaving it to me to say, "Home, please. As quickly as you might."

Griffin fumed in the carriage, his arms folded over his chest, a murderous look on his face. I waited until we cleared the gates before saying, "What was that about?"

"Zeiler did something to Allan. Mesmerized him, perhaps." Griffin pulled the wadded-up paper from his pocket and glared at it. "You saw for yourself, Whyborne—he was perfectly calm and ordinary until I showed him the symbol. I wager he has no idea why they've taken him to the violent ward. No memory of the attack, any more than he remembers…"

"Murdering his uncle?" I asked. "I thought…I mean, this new assault does weaken our theory Allan didn't kill the man."

"One of the men who assaulted us on the docks had this very mark etched into his skin. There is something happening here—something organized. It must be linked to the ceremonial bowl, somehow. A sea god, the ledger said. And the men who attacked us were sailors. Zeiler isn't, but Niles said he was the son of a sea captain. He has to be involved."

I didn't know how to respond. The evidence was tenuous at best, but Griffin could hardly be expected to think rationally when it came to the superintendent, and for good reason. Truthfully, though, we had nothing to link Zeiler with the symbol.

"We don't even know what the cult wanted with the ceremonial bowl," I said at length. "Or if Bixby might have been a member himself, rather than an innocent victim. Which has no bearing on Allan's innocence," I added hastily at Griffin's dark look. "Perhaps if we can learn more about the cult and what their motives might be, we can find a way to help him."

Griffin sighed and slumped back against the seat. "You're right."

"I'll take tomorrow to look into certain volumes at the museum."

"Thank you." Griffin stared out the window, his expression grim. "I have some ideas of my own to pursue."

I hoped they didn't involve an altercation with the asylum guards. But as Griffin didn't seem in the mood to discuss things, I merely touched the back of his hand lightly. We rode the rest of the way home in silence.

The temple loomed above me in the crushing black of the depths.

I no longer felt any surprise or confusion at seeing it. Rather, a sense of familiarity settled into my bones, as if I returned to a place I'd lived as a child, but had long forgotten existed.

A thousand fish swarmed before the temple, drifting along just inches off its surface, as if they too heard the song calling me within. Their bellies glowed with the ghastly light of corpse candles, and as they moved about, they more clearly illuminated the section of stonework nearest to them. Here was a carved limb, almost human but subtly, horribly not. There a face leered from a bas-relief, its mouth filled with shark's teeth.

A mixture of revulsion and curiosity shuddered through me. I didn't want to see the temple façade any more than I wanted to see the faces on the great statues flanking the door.

Did I?

One of the idly swimming fish crossed just above the lintel of the colossal entrance, casting its nacreous glow across what appeared to be a symbol carved there. Its shape…I knew it, I was almost certain.

Then another fish joined its brother, and, even as the dream began to fragment and fade, I beheld the stylized eye of the cult.

I spent the next morning in the museum library, amidst a stack of books and notes. Mr. Quinn, the head librarian, had been lurking about the entrance when I arrived. He unlocked or located the various rare texts I needed, caressing them with his white, spidery hands before passing them to me. Some of the staff swore the labyrinthine library demonstrated the final descent into lunacy on the part of the Ladysmith's architect, while others claimed it would drive those who stayed too long in its walls mad as well.

Which was an even more disturbing thought than usual. "Do you know anything about Stormhaven?" I asked Mr. Quinn. "The lunatic asylum, that is, not the cove."

Mr. Quinn stared at me with his strange, pale eyes. He didn't seem to blink as often as ordinary people. "My father died there," he said, but the note in his voice was more a sort of dreamy relish than the grief such a pronouncement would usually contain. "Syphilis."

"I…oh." Who would think to share such an untoward diagnosis with a colleague he barely knew? "I'm, er, sorry."

"Yes," he agreed. Not knowing what else to do, I nodded stupidly and fled into the depths of the stacks.

I found a small room where I could put my back to what I hoped was a solid wall, although after the discovery of hidden tunnels last December, the prospect was less than certain. The most promising book I'd chosen was von Junzt's *Unaussprechlichen Kulten*, so I turned my attention to the heavy volume with its forbidding iron hinges.

Some time later, the echo of footsteps interrupted my reading. The bizarre architecture of the library meant sound had a way of echoing oddly, making it impossible to tell how near or far the walker might be. I grabbed the heaviest tome out of my stack and held it tightly, just in case my visitor proved to be Mr. Quinn, come to strangle me under the influence of a symbol on a piece of paper.

When Griffin appeared at last from behind the stacks, I almost sagged with relief. My arms ached from holding the heavy book up, and I dropped it to the table with a loud thud.

"Hello," he said, a bit uncertainly as he eyed the book.

"Sorry. After…well. My imagination has run away with me," I admitted.

"So I see. How is your research coming?"

"Quite well." I wished I dared risk kissing him, but who knew if one of the librarians might be near. "And your morning?"

"A profitable few hours spent at City Hall."

"City Hall?"

"Tell me of your progress first; then I shall tell you of mine."

"As you wish." I cast a wary glance about for Mr. Quinn, but saw nothing to suggest he might be eavesdropping. "I've been looking through the *Unaussprechlichen Kulten* for any information on the Eyes of Nodens."

"And did you find anything?"

"Fragmentary hints and veiled suggestions, for the most part. Von Junzt believed the cult existed from ancient times, its name changing from place to place depending on the local dialect and deities. The one thing all iterations have in common is the worshippers believe themselves to act as the conduit through which their god—or gods, perhaps—can sense what passes on land. The god watches through their eyes, hears through their ears…and, when necessary, acts through their hands. It communicates with them through dreams. Supposedly, it also sings to the mad."

"Hmm." Griffin's brow furrowed. "Didn't I read something in the paper just a few days ago? Yes, I remember—the night of the murder! There was a disturbance at the asylum, with the patients screaming in their sleep."

What of the strange dreams I'd had? The things glimpsed out of the corner of my eye, the salty tang of the ocean…

No. My dreams had nothing to do with whatever monstrous thing sang to its followers from the depths of the sea. I was neither a cultist nor a madman. Any odd night terrors were merely the product of interrupted sleep, mingled with the stress of the case.

"What of your morning?" I said, hoping to turn the conversation to something else.

"Ernest spoke of seeing Zeiler socially. It stood to reason the good doctor might have somewhere in town to stay," Griffin replied. "And, possibly, to have the sort of clandestine meetings he couldn't conduct in his apartments at Stormhaven. I went through the deeds at City Hall and discovered he bought a house in Widdershins only six months ago."

"And you mean to break in and search it for anything incriminating."

"Of course." Griffin clapped me on the arm, before rising from his chair. "Let us find Christine and discover if she is willing to undertake a bit of law-breaking this weekend."

CHAPTER 11

AS IT PROVED, Christine was indeed willing to join us on Saturday night. First, however, we had to get through the dinner with Griffin's family.

Our destination was Le Calmar, the fanciest restaurant in Widdershins, so when Griffin and I dressed for the evening, we both paid careful attention to our wardrobe. Griffin, of course, looked handsome in anything, but I had to work at it.

My hair, in particular, posed problems; it had the awful tendency to stick in every direction, as if I'd forgotten to comb it. A judicious application of macassar oil could tame it for a while, and Griffin kindly offered to assist me.

Accordingly, I sat in the chair in front of him, as if he were a barber, and he laid a towel across my shoulders to protect my suit from the oil. Before beginning, he ran his fingers through my unruly locks, and I sighed in pleasure at his touch.

"You look very handsome," he murmured. "I can't wait to have you back here tonight, alone with me. It will make putting up with poor Ruth's lovelorn sighs worth it."

"Is she very taken with you, then?" I asked, as he pulled back and began to comb my hair into place.

"Me?" He chuckled. "Didn't you notice? I rather fear you'll break her heart. Father worries you're a cad poised to take advantage of an innocent farm girl, while Mother sees Ruth's future made."

"Dear lord!" That explained the strange way in which his parents had reacted at the museum. "Miss Kerr strikes me as an intelligent young woman, and we had a serious discussion of Latin. There is far more to her than simply who she might marry. Besides, I thought...well. They hoped you would become her suitor."

"So no tossing me aside for a respectable wedding?" he teased.

"You know better. Besides, Father would be horrified if I married some penniless country girl. *Whom* one weds is even more important than *if*."

"Poor Ruth. She does seem very nice. And, as you said, intelligent."

"Yes." I hesitated. "Have you…have you ever been with a woman?"

His hands stilled. "Do you truly want an answer?"

"I take it that means 'yes.'"

He resumed combing. "After I left Kansas, I was…desperate, shall we say, to prove myself normal. To convince myself the indiscretion with Benjamin merely resulted from never having had the opportunity with a woman. So I hired a prostitute at the first station we came to."

"Oh." This tale had turned sordid more quickly than I'd expected. Although given what little I knew of his adventures in Chicago, particularly in the bathhouses, it was probably rather tame in comparison. "And you, er, enjoyed the act?"

Griffin applied more oil to a particularly stubborn lock. "What is a food you don't particularly care for, but everyone else seems to love?" he asked nonsensically.

"Apples," I said.

"Apples? Really?" He laughed. "I am very fond of apples, myself. So if you and I shared an apple pie, I would very much enjoy the entire experience, beyond the simple fact of food giving nourishment to my body. As for you, of course it would sustain your health if choked down, but you would be left wishing it had been…"

"Raspberry."

"…raspberry instead."

"I see." And I thought I did. "And after…?"

"Informants I needed to charm. Nothing detrimental to the lady in question, I assure you. I am not quite such a scoundrel as to take advantage in such a fashion, and I parted with them all on excellent terms and, I believe, to their satisfaction. Why do you want to know?"

"Oh…no reason." Did he find Ruth attractive even if, as he said, he might prefer something else?

"Hmm." He didn't sound as if he believed me, but he let the matter drop. Whisking away the towel, he said, "There. You look extraordinary. I shall have to do battle with both the women and the waiters at Le Calmar for you."

I blushed. Why did he feel the need to say such things? I was quite aware I possessed no great beauty; quite the opposite, in fact. Only he had ever noticed me. "Thank you for your assistance."

"You're welcome." He stepped in front of me and leaned down, pressing his forehead against mine. "And tonight, once we are home again, I shall make a wreck of your hair. When you look across the table during dinner and meet my eyes, know I'll be imagining stripping off your clothes and flinging you onto our bed, to touch and suck you until you beg for release."

I made a small sound of protest. "We're going to dinner with your *parents!*"

"Then your night will at least be interesting." He withdrew. "I had best go to their hotel and collect them. And Ruth."

"I'll bring the book for her."

"And you call me a trouble maker." But he said it fondly. "I will see you and Christine in an hour."

"Goodbye," I said, and tilted my head back for a kiss. But he'd turned away without noticing, and I merely sat and listened to the door close behind him.

Christine's boarding house was close enough to the restaurant to walk, and the weather mild enough to allow it. She met me on the curb, looking rather impatient. She wore a fashionable dress, which meant sleeves large enough to contain a small child, and an enormous, feathered hat. "Let us get this farce over with, shall we?" she asked upon seeing me.

I offered her my arm, and she sighed loudly before taking it for appearances' sake. "Look upon it as a chance to show Miss Kerr what a woman may accomplish," I suggested.

"A good point. It would be a better one, if the Kerrs did not believe you and I were courting."

"The assumption is entirely their fault, not ours."

"You are a dreadful liar. Or you don't fully appreciate Griffin's devious nature."

I remained silent out of loyalty. Christine rolled her eyes but let the matter drop, instead choosing to turn the conversation to the director's absurd decision to allocate more funds to the American History Wing and, therefore, Bradley. By the time we were through abusing the director, the trustees, and of course Bradley, we arrived at the restaurant.

Our timing was, for once, excellent. As we approached, a carriage pulled up at the corner and disgorged Griffin, his parents, and Miss Kerr. They greeted us enthusiastically, Griffin shaking my hand as if we hadn't parted less than an hour ago. I was extremely impressed by Christine's fortitude when she refrained from making some sarcastic remark.

Mr. Kerr took his wife's arm, which left Griffin paired with Ruth. There was no reason to be jealous, I reminded myself as we followed them inside. And I wasn't, not of Ruth, anyway. She seemed quite a lovely person, and I had no quarrel with her. But Griffin seemed so relaxed, so *normal*, as her escort.

The two of us had eaten dinner together in public, many times. But never…like this.

"Oh, do stop scowling, Whyborne," Christine ordered.

"Forgive me." I reordered my expression hastily.

Fortunately, the waiter seated us immediately. It had been some time since I'd set foot in Le Calmar; had it been for Stanford's eighteenth birthday? Things had changed, of course, but for the most part it matched my memory: a large room filled with tables, each bearing a pristine white tablecloth and extravagant centerpiece. Waiters in white suit coats glided between the tables, pushing carts laden with covered dishes. A mixture of cologne, sweat, and cooked beef mingled with the perfume wafting from the roses and lilies in the centerpieces. The enormous windows looked out on River Street, and Mrs. Kerr let out a cry of delight when the electric street lights came on outside.

Christine ended up seated between Griffin and me, with Mrs. Kerr to my right, Mr. Kerr on her other side, and Ruth across from me. "Look at all the forks, Ma!" Mr. Kerr exclaimed.

"One uses them from the outside in," Griffin advised. "Shall we have champagne with our meal?"

"Please," Christine said, a bit too quickly.

Griffin ordered champagne, and I began to wonder just how much he intended to spend tonight. Our combined incomes kept us comfortably situated, and we didn't go out much so we had a little money set aside, but this lavish meal would certainly put a strain on our coffers. Like the Pinkertons who had trained him, Griffin charged a per-day fee and expenses for his cases, which meant he wouldn't receive a handsome reward should he somehow manage to clear Allan of the murder charges. Which, perhaps, was just as well, as such an outcome seemed increasingly unlikely.

The first course, chicken and leek soup, arrived and our glasses were filled. "A toast," Griffin said, raising his glass. "To friends and family."

Christine downed her champagne in a single gulp and motioned the hovering waiter for more. Fortunately, the Kerrs didn't seem to notice.

It seemed a good opportunity to offer Ruth the Latin primer; I pulled it from my coat and passed it across the table. "The book I promised, Miss Kerr. I hope you find it interesting." That sounded neutral enough, didn't it? Friendly but certainly not flirtatious. I couldn't even do flirtatious with Griffin.

"Oh!" She seemed surprised I remembered, and her cheeks went bright pink. "I, er, th-thank you, sir."

"So, Dr. Whyborne," Mrs. Kerr asked as we set into the first course, "what church do you attend?"

I choked on my soup. Christine helpfully pounded me on the back. "Er, um, First Esoteric," I said, when I recovered. I'd been christened there, anyway.

"Oh." Mrs. Kerr frowned a little. "Is that like Episcopalian?"

"It's a small denomination," Griffin said helpfully. "A few churches here, in Arkham, and Kingsport."

"So we won't see you at services on Sunday?" she asked, sounding disappointed.

"No."

"I belong to First Esoteric as well," Christine said quickly, which was an utter lie since I didn't think the church allowed non-Widdershins natives to even attend services, let alone join.

"Oh, you and Dr. Whyborne know each other from church?" Mr. Kerr said, as if he'd been wondering. Didn't the man realize we worked together?

"Yes," Christine said. "Parson, um…?"

"High Priest Thornhill," I whispered out of the corner of my mouth.

"Yes. His sermons are quite invigorating."

"The tiaras are most impressive," I added.

Everyone else stared at us as if we'd grown extra heads. Didn't most preachers wear tiaras? Since my greatest religious feeling had come as a small child building altars to Pan and Bacchus, I didn't really know for certain.

"Yes," Christine said, stabbing the soup with her spoon. "The tiaras are excellent."

"So, what do you think of Widdershins thus far?" Griffin asked his parents hurriedly. The waiters took away our soup and brought the next course, filet of beef and celery salad.

Apparently, they liked our town a great deal, which took us through the rest of the course and into the next, canvasback duck served with French peas. The champagne continued to flow, albeit mostly into Christine.

Some of it must have been going in Griffin as well, because halfway through the course, I glanced up to find him looking at me with a sly expression on his face. Seeing I'd noticed, he scooped up some of the peas and sucked them down one at a time in a suggestive manner.

I transferred my gaze to my plate, ears afire. Yet I couldn't help but look again, to find him licking some of the sauce from his knife.

The man was determined to be the death of me.

"Tell us about your work, Dr. Whyborne," Mr. Kerr said.

I jumped guiltily. What the devil had Griffin been thinking? My cheeks ached with heat, and other places ached as well, and dear lord, we were at dinner with his family and Christine. "Wh-what?" I stammered like an idiot.

Thankfully, Mr. Kerr didn't seem to notice. "Did you do the excavating over in Egypt?"

Beside me, Christine stiffened. "Er, no," I said. "I don't leave Widdershins much, if I can help it. Christine is the archaeologist, not I."

"Right, right, but who does the actual, you know, work?"

I closed my eyes. At least the threat of imminent death cured me of my untoward arousal.

"I have a large force of trained local men," Christine said frostily. "They do the heavy lifting, but I assure you I am very familiar with the workings of a shovel."

"Yes, but who directs them?"

I opened my eyes to see Christine's smile grow increasingly brittle. "I do, of course," she said, biting off every word.

"But you don't actually live out in the desert with them."

"And why the devil shouldn't I?"

All the Kerrs flinched at her language. I drained my glass of champagne and signaled to the waiter for more, wishing I could discreetly ask him to leave the bottle.

"What Christine means," Griffin said, "is she directs the excavations in their entirety, from deciding on a location to dig, to supervising the packing and loading of any artifacts removed. Of course it means she must endure some hardships, but nothing more than any other scientist in such a distant locale."

The Kerrs stared at her as if she were on display at the freak show. "The museum is cruel enough to ask a woman to do such work?" Mr. Kerr asked in horror.

"Indeed." Christine stuck her fork into the duck on her plate, then gave a sudden, somewhat alarming, grin. "The greatest hardship is the food, of course. Let me tell you about it."

In truth, I knew Christine rather enjoyed most Arabic cooking, but as with any foreign people, they had a great many dishes which sounded alarming to an American palate. I'd heard it all before, from the boiled sheep's head—eyeballs still in place—to spit-roasted whole camel, to what happened when flies—or rather, their maggoty offspring—found the perishable foodstuffs. I simply ignored her while I ate. From the greenish hue on their faces, neither the Kerrs nor Griffin found themselves able to follow my example.

The waiters brought the dessert course of pistachio ice cream and fruit, just as Christine ran out of steam. "Quite the story," Mrs. Kerr said with a pale smile. "How relieved you'll be to give it up."

Christine's spoon clinked loudly against the side of her ice cream bowl. "Give it up?" she asked, brows drawing down. "Why should I do that?"

Mr. Kerr chuckled. "Well, I don't expect Dr. Whyborne will put up with such nonsense."

If the man hated me, couldn't he simply challenge me to a duel? I started to make a stupid reply, but glanced up and saw Ruth watching me with a curious expression on her face, as if my answer actually meant something to her.

"My affection for Christine is predicated only on who she is, not on society's view of who she should be," I said, which was nothing but the truth. "As I trust hers is for me."

"Damned right," Christine muttered.

I didn't mean to say more, but Ruth still watched, and the words spilled out anyway. "We all have our talents in this world, and we shouldn't be…be ashamed of them." God, I sounded like a fool. "Whether it lies in archaeology, or languages, or harvesting the bounty of the land, or making a safe home for an orphan child. So. Er, yes."

"Well said," Griffin declared, raising his glass of champagne. Ruth clinked hers rather enthusiastically, and Mr. and Mrs. Kerr did as well, if with slightly less enthusiasm.

Lingering would only invite further awkwardness, so I gave the table a slight bow. "If you would excuse us, Dr. Putnam and I need to be on our way."

Griffin caught my eye and shot me a devilish grin. "Of course. I look forward to our next meeting."

CHAPTER 12

"BLAST GRIFFIN," CHRISTINE exclaimed. "I can't believe he's so selfish as to put you through this ordeal!"

We had left the restaurant behind us and were well on our way to her boarding house. Christine strode determinedly along the sidewalk, scowling furiously at the fog which had crept in while we dined, turning the night murky and damp. Hansom cabs emerged from the gloom and faded back into it, the clop of horses' hooves lingering long after I'd lost sight of them in the fog. A cloaked figure hurried past, hat drawn low over his face, and I politely looked away.

One of the electric lights made a strange sound and went out. I recalled reading in the papers about how often they failed, to the bafflement of the manufacturer, who swore the bulbs lasted five times longer in every other city in which they were installed. Yet another sign the blasted things were wrong for Widdershins, as far as I was concerned.

"You're being unfair," I told Christine.

"What isn't fair is how he uses you." Christine ground her teeth together. "Or Ruth Kerr. His parents believe there is a chance of a match, and instead of doing the honorable thing and putting an end to the matter, he allows them to continue in their assumptions. And Ruth! Right now, the poor woman is probably imagining a wedding which will allow her to move to Widdershins and escape whatever farming hell she's trapped in."

I stared down at the sidewalk, counting the cracks as we passed. "It's different for him than for us. Or for me, anyway," I added, since she'd spoken little of her own falling-out with her mother. Given Christine's temper, it must have been spectacular. "My father never approved of me and never will. I had nothing to lose by walking out of Whyborne House and living my own life."

Christine snorted. "Nothing to lose, except for a share of one of the largest fortunes in America."

A chuckle escaped me. "I suppose. But it never brought me happiness in the first seventeen years of my life. Why expect it to bring any in the next seventeen, or in the years after? It's different for Griffin. His family loves him and he them. You and I cannot imagine a normal life, but he can."

"Is he certain of his parents' reaction?" she asked hesitantly. "He mentioned a small indiscretion…"

"I don't know the details, but in essence, the community ran him out of town." I hated saying the words, but Christine deserved the truth. "His parents agreed it would be best if he left in haste. But later on they saved him from the asylum, so I can't condemn them too harshly. As for Griffin, he feels he owes them his life twice over."

"Oh." She knew little of Griffin's confinement, other than it had been unwarranted, but she surely guessed it had not been pleasant. "You don't believe there is anything to this absurd charade with Miss Kerr, do you? That he might actually go through with it and marry her?"

We had come to her boarding house and paused on the sidewalk. "No, of course not." I didn't, did I? "They will all leave in a few days, and our lives will go back to normal. His parents will be reassured as to his happiness here in Widdershins, and will overcome any disappointment the match with Miss Kerr didn't work out."

"Hmm. I hope you're correct. And for Griffin's sake, I hope he doesn't have to choose between the life he wants and the life society wants for him." She turned to the boarding house. "Good night, Whyborne. See you in church."

I turned my steps back in the direction of home. The streets had grown quiet. I quickened my pace. Another of the electric streetlights went out, just after I passed by. I glanced behind me. Even though no one had been there a moment before, someone now stood in the pool of darkness beneath the extinguished streetlight.

I came to a halt, heart pounding. Was I being stalked, perhaps by armed cultists, or was it some innocent passer-by?

An innocent passer-by who held perfectly still, nothing but a half-glimpsed silhouette in the blackness?

"Hello?" I called; thank goodness my voice didn't shake. "Who's there?"

The smell of seaweed and slime, of cold mud dredged from the bottom of the ocean floor, flooded from the figure. The hairs on my arms stood up, and I took an involuntary step back.

Even as I did so, a sudden, overwhelming conviction swept over me. The person in the shadows was my mother. I had to go to her. I had to go to her *right now*.

I swayed, but the rational part of my mind reasserted itself. It couldn't really be Mother. She was far too ill to leave the house. And why would she be alone here, without even a maid to assist her?

The shadowy figure whispered something to me, and I recognized Mother's voice, even though I couldn't make out the words.

"I-I can't hear you," I said. "Who are you?"

Another light went out. Then another. Darkness pooled around me, like black water, filling up the street. Something felt dreadfully wrong.

I ran.

Something hunted me, just as it had in my dream. My heart pounded—did I hear footfalls behind me, over the rasp of my breath? Shadows flickered on the brick walls of the buildings, as if ghosts raced me. The night air turned as cold and heavy against my skin as the sea.

A horrible compulsion to look back over my shoulder seized me. Like the curse on Lot's wife, except I doubted my fate would be half so benign should I succumb. I focused my gaze on the sidewalks and cobblestones, stretching my legs as far as they'd go, my lungs bursting with the need for air. Pain jagged down my side; I wasn't used to such exercise.

I paid no heed to where my feet took me, desperate only to put as much distance between myself and whatever followed. Did it follow?

At last I stumbled to a halt, my legs trembling and my throat raw. Tight bands encircled my chest, and I couldn't seem to catch my breath.

Where was I? The high walls of warehouses loomed against the night sky, and I realized with a little frisson of dread that I'd run straight toward the docks.

Toward the ocean, and whatever lay beneath it.

"No," I whispered aloud. It was just a coincidence. Nothing more.

"Talking to himself, is he?" asked a voice behind me.

I spun, too winded to gasp in shock. Two men stood behind me, dressed in passable, if cheap, suits: one brown and one gray. Both carried unsheathed knives in their hands.

"L-leave me alone," I ordered, drawing myself up. Why hadn't I paid more attention to where I fled, instead of letting blind panic take over?

The man in the gray suit smiled greasily, as if taking pleasure in my predicament. "Oh, no, we can't do that, Dr. Whyborne. You've led us on quite the little chase, you have. Not sure how you spotted us, but that don't matter now."

"You were following me?" But it didn't sound as if they'd been the ones under the blown-out streetlight. I felt certain in my bones whatever I'd glimpsed, it hadn't been human at all. "Who sent you? What is this about?"

They ignored my questions, instead exchanging a glance. "Don't know why himself said to get the drop on this one," said the man in the brown suit. "Doesn't look like he'd stand up to a stiff breeze, let alone put up a fight."

Swallowing back my fear, I forced my spine straight. "Walk away. Whoever sent you, just...just leave, and I'll do the same."

"Would you listen to that!" brown suit exclaimed with a laugh. "You've made a bad mistake, friend."

What I wouldn't give for Christine's pistol or Griffin's steady presence at the moment! But I'd faced down worse than these two, surely. I had resources. I just had to figure out what those resources might be. If we were only nearer the water, and I could sweep them away with a wave as I'd done their fellows.

"Better not take any chances, though," Gray suit said, and drew out a gun.

Thank God.

"You should have stayed with knives," I said, and spoke the secret name of fire.

The revolver exploded in his hand as the powder in the bullets ignited all at once. Something hot whizzed dangerously close to my face: no doubt the bullet he'd had chambered. While he screamed in surprise and agony, his partner stared at him in uncomprehending shock. I took the opportunity to kick the man as hard as I could in the knee.

He went down, clutching at the wounded joint. I didn't wait to find out what happened next. Instead, I ran as fast as my aching legs would carry me, away from the water and its whispered song.

"And you've no idea who sent those fellows after you?" Christine asked the next evening.

The three of us strolled along Slaughterhouse Road, pretending casualness on our way to breaking into Dr. Zeiler's house.

"It had to be Zeiler," Griffin said. He'd been utterly aghast to arrive home later that night and discover I'd been set upon. For once, he hadn't even commented on my use of sorcery.

"Or the dweller itself," I suggested, remembering the lights going out one at a time, the sense something terrible hunted me through the streets of Widdershins. I hadn't mentioned my delusion to Griffin and Christine, though, because surely that was all it had been. A bout of paranoia—or perhaps, even more likely, I'd somehow sensed the two perfectly ordinary men watching me, and my weary mind had confused them with the dreams which had haunted me. "Supposedly it speaks to its followers in some fashion."

"And ordered them to attack you?" Christine asked skeptically. "Whatever for?"

"Because it knows I'm helping Griffin, obviously."

She snorted. "That can't be the reason. Am I not also involved with this? Although why, I have no idea, after last night."

"Because you would be furious if we left you out," Griffin replied. "Really, Christine, do try to ask something harder."

"Very well. Why haven't I buried your body in the back garden yet?"

"Because you would never hurt Whyborne."

Christine huffed angrily. "Then you had best hope he doesn't tire of you, because I have a large number of shovels and am quite adept at using them, no matter what certain men may think."

Her voice had grown dangerously loud. "Please, concentrate on what we're doing, Christine," I said. "Fighting off murderous cultists is all well and good, but getting caught by the police might cost us our jobs at the museum."

"You have a point," she allowed.

All of us wore dark clothing, with Christine in her bloomers. Griffin carried his carpetbag, containing police lanterns, lock picks, and other articles, which might be of use.

We passed a drunken man staggering in the middle of the road; he had only one arm and one eye. Not old enough to have fought in the war between the states, and the injuries looked too well healed to have been incurred in the current strife with Spain. No doubt he had acquired them through injury or accident. He stared at the cobblestones as he wove back and forth, cursing and mumbling to himself.

From the similarity of the houses and the proximity to the factory, I guessed the cannery owners had originally constructed the neighborhood to house workers. "This is a rather…odd part of town for Zeiler to own a house in," I remarked. "One would expect him to have taken quarters somewhere a bit more in keeping with his status."

"Indeed, one would," Griffin said grimly. His green eyes watched our surroundings with the intentness of an eagle on a fish, and I could all but feel the tension radiating from him.

"I suppose it's possible his salary isn't such as to allow a house in a better part of the town, considering he's expected to live in the asylum," I suggested.

Christine snorted. "And you believe that?"

"I said it was only a possibility."

"Quiet," Griffin ordered. "We're here."

We fell silent. The house was larger than most of its neighbors and two stories rather than one; perhaps a foreman had initially lived here. Paint peeled from the boards, and a general air of decay hung about it, something as much sensed as seen. No lights showed from within, at least on the side facing the street.

Griffin paused, glanced causally up and down the street then turned into the narrow carriageway between the house and its fellows. My shoes crunched on the crushed shell lane, and Christine cast me a disapproving look.

Once we were away from the street, Griffin passed out the lanterns. "Keep yours dark for now," he whispered. He lit his, adjusting the shield until only a narrow beam of light emerged, which hopefully wouldn't be easily spotted by any passers-by.

The back of the house looked onto the Cranch River. A dilapidated dock protruded out into the dark water, and the air reeked of fish and sewage. The bulk of the cannery blocked out the stars across the river, not far downstream. Another house sat directly on the other side of the water, dark and dingy.

A flight of wooden steps led up to the back door of Zeiler's house. Griffin climbed them; they creaked softly under his weight. Taking his lock picks from the carpetbag, he knelt in front of the door.

I strained my ears for any sound while Griffin worked, but heard nothing save for the soft scratch of pick on lock, the barking of some distant dog, and the far-off whistle of a train. The lock gave way with a soft click. Griffin stood up, tucking his lock picks into his coat pocket. The carpetbag he concealed beneath a bush beside the steps. With a quick glance back to make certain we were ready, he eased open the door.

It creaked, a horrid sound which made me wince. Griffin opened it only far enough to shimmy through. Christine slipped in after him, and I tried to follow their example, but managed to jostle the door. Its rusted hinges let out a loud shriek.

"Sorry," I whispered, my face burning. Christine scowled and motioned me to silence.

The door opened onto the most deplorable kitchen I'd ever seen. The atmosphere was thick with rancid food and mold, and the dishes stacked in the sink looked to have been there for quite some time. Roaches scuttled away from the light of Griffin's lantern. My skin crawled at the sight. "The house might be in his name, but I can't imagine Zeiler consenting to spend much time in such a squalid place," I said in a low voice.

"Agreed," Griffin murmured back. "So the question is: who is it really for?"

The kitchen let onto a dusty hall, which showed tracks of mud and filth. Griffin motioned for us to remain behind, kneeling to examine the tracks. "The sort of boots one might expect laboring men to wear," he said, half to himself. "But see here—there are at least one pair of smoother soles. Those must belong to Zeiler."

An empty room, no doubt meant to be a parlor, occupied the front of the house; dusty curtains blocked out all light from the street. As we stepped inside, something caught my eye. I crouched, careful to keep the knees of my trousers off the dirty floor, and touched it. "Wax. Someone burned a candle in here."

"Many of them, it would seem," Griffin agreed.

The wax blobs seemed to indicate a circle. In between, ghostly lines of smeared chalk still showed. A dark stain covered the bare boards of the center of the room. "Is that…blood?"

CHAPTER 13

GRIFFIN DIDN'T SHARE my reticence about the floor; he got down on all fours and cautiously sniffed at the stain. "Yes."

I swallowed against the sudden dryness of my throat. "Do you think it's human?"

"I don't know."

Christine shuddered. "I don't keep up with the papers—have there been any unsolved disappearances lately?"

Griffin climbed to his feet. "This is Widdershins. People go missing all the time."

"Surely, that's true in any city," I objected.

"Perhaps." Griffin dusted off his knees. "Let's see what lies upstairs."

The steps creaked under our feet. Another large room filled the front of the house, directly above the parlor. This one appeared to have been converted into some sort of flophouse. At any rate, a number of crude pallets lay about the room, covered with disheveled bedding. A few personal items such as a corncob pipe or a chipped mug lay about, but it didn't appear as if anyone currently lived here.

"Do you think this is a gathering place? For the cultists, I mean?" I asked.

"Ready to admit Zeiler is involved with the Eyes, then?" Griffin returned.

I winced at his tone. "I only wanted proof."

"He's clearly involved in something," Christine said. She poked at the bedding with her boot, uncovering a rather gnawed-looking bone. "The devil?"

Griffin picked the bone up with a frown. "It looks like a dog's been at it. A bone from the butcher's, no doubt."

"Only if the butchers around here serve human flesh," Christine replied.

Taking it from him, she examined it critically. "It's the end of an adult human femur. Probably a man's given the size, but it's impossible to say for certain."

My heart beat faster, fear flickering along my nerves. I already knew these men were willing to kill, but this seemed worse, somehow. "Perhaps the same poor fellow whose blood is downstairs," I managed to say. My voice trembled only slightly.

"Perhaps." Christine carefully put the bone back on the bedding, then wiped her hands on her handkerchief "Let's finish up and leave here quickly."

"Agreed," Griffin said grimly.

Two more rooms lay at the back of the house. The first was a bedroom with an actual four-poster, and sheets which looked far cleaner than those in the front room. Perhaps Zeiler slept here? The only other furniture consisted of a washstand and a wardrobe, which proved to be empty.

The final room had probably started its existence as a bedroom, but now served as a sort of study. A desk took up much of the space. On the center of the desk stood a large pottery bowl.

Christine and I both gasped at the sight, and Griffin wisely got out of our path. The bowl was surprisingly large, but relatively shallow. Cracks showed where it had been expertly repaired, and I felt a flash of anger at whoever had put such work into restoring it for no other reason than to sell it at a higher price, rather than to further our scientific understanding. The fired clay had a reddish hue, with designs painted in black. My knowledge of pottery was sorely lacking, and I hadn't the slightest notion what tradition it might have belonged to.

The painting in the center of the bowl depicted what Victor Bixby had referred to in his ledger as an unknown sea god. Certainly the creature was a monstrous thing: part cetacean, part human, and part octopod. I didn't recognize its appearance offhand from any myth cycle familiar to me.

The creature didn't swim alone, but rather was accompanied by a group of humanoid creatures, long and lithe, with flowing hair, sharp teeth, and what appeared to be fins of some kind on their legs and arms. Some ancient legend of mermen or naiads, perhaps? They seemed strangely familiar…

Characters marched around the edge of the bowl, and it took only a moment's examination to identify them. "Look," I said, pointing without actually touching the bowl. "The text uses the Cypriot syllabary. I believe the language is…hmm…an archaic form of Greek." The lighting was terrible, and I struggled to make out the words. "There's something about singing…and the god answering? I think it's an invocation of sorts."

"Later," Griffin said. "We'll take it with us—the fact it's been found in Zeiler's house proves he is mixed up with Bixby's murder. The police will no longer be able to deny something strange is going on. With any luck, we can get Allan released immediately."

"I certainly hope so." I picked up the bowl and held it carefully. It was surprisingly heavy, and I cradled it against my chest to keep from dropping it.

We had just started back down the hall, when Griffin froze. "Did you hear that?"

Christine and I mimicked him, holding our breath. From the street outside came the murmur of voices, accompanied by the click of a key unlocking the front door.

Sweat slicked my palms against the bowl, and my heart sped. We were trapped—as soon as we started down the stairs, anyone standing in the hall would see us. And if they came up here, we'd surely be found. Even if we tried hiding in one of the back rooms, there was no egress save right past their sleeping space—assuming Zeiler himself hadn't returned for another look at the bowl.

Steps trod along the hall downstairs. Time was running out to make a decision.

Griffin seemed to come to the same conclusion. His mouth firmed and his eyes darkened as he drew his revolver. "Run for the back door," he ordered, before charging down the stairs.

Christine followed, her pistol drawn as well. Swearing under my breath, I bolted after them, the bowl a heavy weight in my arms. A rather surprised-looking sailor stared up at us from the lower landing. Without pausing, Griffin grasped the stair rail to brace himself and aimed a kick directly at the man's chest.

The man fell back heavily and Griffin leapt the rest of the way down the stairs after him, kicking him again when he tried to rise. A shout rang out from the front of the house—accompanied by a frenzy of barking.

My heart clenched in terror, recalling the enormous tooth marks in the bone upstairs. On the landing, Griffin turned and fired a shot, but the barking didn't cease. "Go!" he shouted at us. "Go!"

Shockingly, Christine obeyed him, running for the kitchen and back entrance. I followed her, glancing over my shoulder to see two more sailors and a huge dog crowding into the hallway. "Griffin, come on!"

"I am! Run, damn you!"

An instant later, his boots thudded on the wooden floor behind me—and the hellish barking of the dog grew closer as well.

We burst out the back door. I missed a step, jarring my spine but somehow keeping my feet. Christine, in a fit of apparent madness, ran straight for the rickety dock jutting out into the river.

I slowed, only to have Griffin grab my coat and haul me along with him, following Christine. "What are you doing?" I shouted.

"The river! It's deep enough; the dog will surely not follow us!"

"Dogs can swim! I can't!"

The dock vibrated under our feet, and the river spread out before us like a spill of ink. Terror burst in my chest; I tried to stop, feet skidding on the slimy planks, but Griffin's grip was implacable. "Griffin, no please—"

He flung himself off the end, dragging me with him. We had an instant of weightlessness as we fell—then the rank water slammed into me with physical force, knocking the air from my lungs before it closed over my head.

I thrashed wildly, no longer sure which direction was up. My lungs ached—I had to hold my breath, only I had none left to hold. Fear pounded through me with every heartbeat. I was drowning, just as I'd almost drowned the horrible night on the lake with Leander. The water roared in my ears, but I thought I heard the sound of distant singing as well.

A hand closed around the back of my coat, hauling me up. My head broke the surface and I gasped wildly, choking as a bit of water lapped into my mouth. "Be still, Whyborne!" Griffin exclaimed.

"Griffin—no—I can't—"

"Trust me and stop flailing, before you drown us both!"

The fear of doing him some harm cut through my panic. I forced my trembling limbs to be still and closed my eyes. "There we go," he said encouragingly, slipping one arm around my chest, beneath my arms. "Just relax and I'll get us to shore."

Far easier for him to say than me to do, but somehow I managed. He swam with powerful strokes, and within a few minutes, he said, "Here we are."

I dared open my eyes. To my unutterable relief, we'd reached a bridge abutment. Christine had already dragged herself up on shore beside it and stood uttering curses, which would have felled any of the sailors we'd just fled. I flailed about with my feet and found the bottom, and together Griffin and I stumbled out of the river. I collapsed instantly to my knees, swearing never again to leave dry land.

"Are you all right, my dear?" Griffin asked, thumping me on the back, as if worried I'd inhaled too much water. "Bathing in the ocean seems to be a popular pastime here; I assumed you could swim."

"No." I shivered. "I haven't been in the water since the night on the lake."

He didn't have to ask what night I meant. "Ah. Forgive me—I had no idea. Not to suggest it would have dissuaded me, since I couldn't leave you to get eaten by that monster."

"No. I…" Realization struck, and my heart sank. "Oh no! The bowl! I let go of it when I hit the water." Our one piece of evidence, and I'd managed to lose it at the bottom of the river. "I'm sorry. You should have let me drown."

"Don't be so absurdly dramatic, Whyborne," Christine said. "Even an expert swimmer wouldn't have made it to shore carrying that thing. Blast it all, why couldn't they have waited another ten minutes before returning to the house?"

"Indeed." Griffin stood up. "My equipment is lost as well. Even if they don't find the carpetbag, I wouldn't dare attempt to retrieve it now they've been put on alert."

I leaned against the bridge's footing. All of us were soaked to the bone with rank water and smeared with mud. Now that my heart had slowed its pace to something approaching normal, I became aware of the cool night wind on my skin, raising up goose bumps and making me shiver. "What now?" I asked.

Griffin shook his head. "For tonight, we go home, bathe thoroughly, and change our clothes."

"Out with it, Griffin," Christine said. "You have some scheme already in mind. I can tell."

He pressed his lips together in annoyance, but after a moment reluctantly nodded his head. "Even if we've no proof to show the police now, I think we can all agree we've seen enough to know Zeiler is indeed involved with the cult, and whatever they—and their god—might want, it's not likely to be our good. If we are to stop them, however, we must determine what, precisely, is their objective."

"And how to do you propose to do that?"

"There's one other place Zeiler might keep personal documents—a diary, notes in cipher, something."

I straightened in alarm. "Griffin, you can't mean…"

"I can. I do." Griffin stared off north across the river. "I mean to break into Stormhaven."

"This is a terrible idea," I said as I shut the door behind us.

We were both soaking wet and stank of river water, and I had little hope of salvaging my suit. Thank goodness I'd left the *Arcanorum* safely hidden in its drawer upstairs, instead of carrying it in my pocket.

Griffin made for the kitchen. "Help me with the tub." Although we had running water in the kitchen and water closet, the house was too old and too simple for a permanently installed bathtub.

"Are you even listening to me?" I demanded, hastening after him. "Griffin!"

He stopped and turned on his heel, his green eyes stormy and his brows drawn down. "You think breaking into Stormhaven is a terrible idea. I heard you."

"Shouldn't we discuss it?"

"I don't see what there is to discuss." His voice remained level, but I knew him well enough to hear the faint tremor of emotion beneath it. "I'm going to do it, no matter what you think. You're under no obligation to help or accompany me."

"Don't be absurd," I snapped, feeling the stirrings of anger in my own chest. "I'm insulted you'd even say such a thing."

He wavered slightly. "Forgive me. I didn't mean…"

"You did, but never mind." If he wished to speak harshly, I would do the same. "Allow me to be blunt: you have enough difficulties arriving in a carriage and walking inside with the blessings of the staff. Can you manage under more stressful conditions such as the ones you propose?"

He paled, as if I'd slapped him. "I'm not an invalid."

"I didn't say you were."

"Then stop trying to coddle me and help me instead!"

"I'm trying!" I flung out my arms in frustration. "Pretending there will be no difficulties involved won't help anything, except perhaps to get us caught by Dr. Zeiler. Do you want that to happen?"

He paled even further, but his expression grew more determined. "What do you suggest? Do you mean to let Zeiler and the Eyes carry out the whims of some terrible creature? To abandon Allan to his fate?"

"Of course not!"

"Because I won't. I refuse to let Zeiler carry out whatever horrors he has planned. I couldn't stop him from doing as he wished before, in Illinois. But I can now. I'll be damned to the lowest pit of hell if his plans, whatever they are, succeed because I'm too weak to stop him!"

"Griffin, please!"

"You don't understand," he went on, as if I hadn't said anything. "You *can't*. So either do as I ask or stay here."

His words carved little slivers off my heart. "I'm not your enemy. I already said I would go with you. I don't intend to abandon Allan to Zeiler, or the rest of the world to whatever Zeiler's god wants. I only ask these questions because I fear…I fear you are not thinking as clearly about this case as you might another."

Griffin laughed bitterly. "Really? Why ever would you think such a thing?"

I winced. "Don't be angry with me, my love. Please. Truly, I only wish to help."

"If you wish to help, start by trusting me."

"I do." I held out my hand. He reached back, twining his fingers with mine. "Tell me your plan."

"We need access to Zeiler's private quarters on the fourth floor. The only way to get it is to create a distraction, one large enough to throw the entire asylum into chaos."

"What sort of distraction?" Did I really want to know?

He rubbed at his eyes with his free hand. "Assuming Stormhaven works on a similar system to the one I'm…familiar…with, the patients are locked in their rooms overnight, and released in the morning. Those who aren't permanently restrained, at any rate. Beginning at nine o'clock at night, the attendants begin to herd them back to their rooms." His mouth thinned slightly. "The usual way of things is to force the patients to remove all their clothes in the open doorway and hand them over to the attendant in exchange for a nightshirt. Then they are l-locked away for the night."

I tightened my grip on his fingers. He squeezed back, but didn't look at me, concentrating instead on Saul, who had wandered in to investigate his food bowl. "All of this is supposed to be completed by nine-thirty," he went on. "As you can imagine, there is a great deal of movement and disorder already. If something were to happen to the power lines leading to the asylum at precisely the right moment—say if someone felled them with an ax—the entire place would be plunged into darkness. It would cause absolute pandemonium, at least for a short period of time."

"If you simply cut down the poles, won't it seem suspicious?" I asked. "If Zeiler thinks you are responsible, he'll go to the police. And as you've attacked him in front of witnesses once already…"

Griffin's green eyes flashed with suppressed anger, and he pulled his hands free from mine. "Do you have another suggestion?"

I tried to recall what I'd read about electrical lighting in the papers. "Don't the poles sometimes fall over during storms?"

"So you wish me to, what, just wait until a convenient storm comes along, and…" he trailed off as my implication sank in. "No."

"My wind spell—"

"Damn it, Whyborne—"

"*Griffin.*" I cut him off, and a bit to my surprise, he fell silent. "You want to find out what Zeiler, or whatever creature controls him, is up to, do you not? Surely, you must agree that slipping in and out of the asylum undetected is of vital importance. Or do you want to end up in a jail cell for destruction of Widdershins Electric property, while the Eyes have free run of the town?"

I knew I'd won the argument when he looked away. "No."

"I know you fear for me. But have you seen any evidence to suggest the spells and the *Arcanorum* are doing whatever it is you imagine they'll do to me?" When he didn't respond, I let out a heavy sigh. "How can you ask me to trust you, when you aren't willing to do the same for me?"

He winced. "I do trust you."

"Then let me help you." I took his hand again. "I love you."

His gaze softened, and he gave me a small smile. "I know. I don't deserve you."

"Don't be foolish." I bent to kiss him. "Now, let us prepare the tub and be out of these wet clothes. We shall take turns scrubbing each other's backs."

It got a chuckle out of him. "Why do I suspect it isn't my back you're most interested in scrubbing?"

"Because you have a wicked mind."

"It's why you love me."

"Well." I kissed him again. "One of the reasons, anyway."

Chapter 14

GRIFFIN WANTED THE opportunity to scout the area around Stormhaven and make certain of the particulars of the plan. He also did not wish to get caught, which meant arriving after dark but before the patients were shut away for the night. Thus, it would be at least another day before we could infiltrate the asylum. His family had asked to see the waterfront, so the next morning he convinced me to meet them after church.

Although much of the waterfront was given to the business of ships and the activities of sailors come ashore, a group of enterprising businessmen had converted a stretch along the southernmost edge into a respectable area where swimmers might bathe in the ocean. Other entertainments sprang up on the nearby pier, and it had become a popular area during the warm summer months. I'd never gone, as I disliked crowds and none of the entertainments sounded appealing to me, so it was with some trepidation I made my way to the area around one o'clock Sunday afternoon.

Soon I found myself meandering through a crowd of families, couples, and large groups of friends; I seemed the only one by myself. The attempts of a brass band to make up for a lack of talent with volume vied with hucksters yelling at me to win a prize by shooting clay pigeons. The aroma of roasted sausages didn't seem at all appetizing despite the claims of the proprietor he supplied President McKinley's table. I tried to ignore the shrill laughter of a gaggle of young girls as I passed by. Everywhere was sound and motion: singing, screaming, running, and my nerves stretched thinner and thinner with each passing moment.

Griffin had asked me to meet them near the carousel, which I found without much trouble, at least. Wooden horses galloped, tigers roared, and swans sailed around and around in a stately dance. Whoever had carved and painted the carousel animals had a master's touch; they almost looked real, like actual creatures frozen in the midst of life. I found the effect eerie, unnerving even, although it didn't seem the riders shared my sentiment.

"Whyborne! Over here!"

I peered about until I spotted Griffin and his family near the sausage vendor. Griffin had apparently made use of his parents' hotel room to change, for instead of his Sunday best, he now wore an outing shirt with blue stripes and a straw hat. I had to admit they looked rather fine on him.

"Glad you could make it, Dr. Whyborne," Mr. Kerr said when I approached.

"Is Dr. Putnam not with you?" his wife asked.

"Uh, no. She had another engagement," I said apologetically. In truth, I hadn't the courage to ask her to accompany me. After the dinner, she likely would have responded with murder, either Griffin's or mine. Possibly both.

"What shall we do first?" Griffin asked, rubbing his hands together delightedly. I realized with a bit of a shock that he actually enjoyed this sort of thing. "A turn about on the carousel?"

"Oh, may we?" Ruth asked wistfully.

"It sounds like fun." Griffin looked at the rest of us.

"Not for me," his mother said. "I'll stay here and watch, though."

Manners dictated I offer to keep her company. "I shall remain also."

Griffin seemed disappointed, but neither his father nor Ruth noticed, and in a moment, the three of them departed to stand in line for their turn on the carousel. I folded my hands behind my back and hoped Mrs. Kerr didn't wish for conversation.

The hope proved short lived. "Dr. Whyborne," she said, almost as soon as the others were gone, "I hope you don't think I'm a meddling old hen, but, well, sometimes it takes a woman to see things a woman's way, you know."

"Er, yes?" I asked, although I had no idea what she could possibly mean.

She took my response for encouragement, though. "How old is Miss Putnam?"

"Dr. Putnam," I corrected automatically. Thank goodness I'd left Christine out of this, or my body would be washing up with the tide. Why the devil did the woman want to know such a thing, anyway? "I'm not sure, actually. A year or two older than me, I believe."

I knew Christine had started her university career at a slightly later age than most men did, and I had begun early. Both of us had completed our coursework at our respective alma maters rather more quickly than the norm, however, perhaps due to the fact neither of us had ever socialized, vacationed, or even returned home during our years of study.

"You men don't have to think of such things, but she's far past the age most girls marry," Mrs. Kerr said matter-of-factly. "If you have marriage with her in mind, you'd better not dawdle about too much longer, or else most of her child-bearing years will be done and over."

Oh dear lord! I stared fixedly at the carousel, barely seeing the swirl of color and riders. "Y-yes," I managed.

"And if you don't, you have to let the poor woman know, so she can find a man who'll do right by her before it's too late."

"I, er—"

"Dr. Whyborne? Is that you?"

I turned hurriedly to the speaker, grateful for any rescue. Maggie Parkhurst and a group of young women had come up behind me. Rather than her usual sober suit, she wore a summer-weight dress and a straw hat with a ribbon. Her hair seemed different as well, although I wasn't certain how, precisely.

"Miss Parkhurst! Hello!" I probably sounded like a fool, but I was ready to enter into any conversation, as long as it didn't involve marriage. "Lovely weather, isn't it?"

Never mind. I most certainly sounded like a fool.

"Oh, yes, very lovely. Do you come here often? That is, I mean, I've never seen you here before," she said, her cheeks turning pink. The ladies behind her all stared at me in fascination, and I began to wonder what on earth she might have said about me.

Griffin returned with his father and Ruth. His hair was mussed from the ride, and his eyes sparkled. "Miss Parkhurst! A pleasure as always."

He made introductions, and I soon gathered the other ladies boarded in the same house as Miss Parkhurst, or were friends with women who did. Within minutes, they chatted delightedly with Ruth.

"Oh! The kinetoscope!" one of them exclaimed; she seemed rather excitable. "You *must* see it, Ruth, you really must!"

"Yes, come with us," Miss Parkhurst encouraged.

Ruth glanced hopefully at her uncle. "Oh, may I?"

"I suppose," was as far as he got, before they all hastened away, Ruth in their midst.

If Ruth could escape, I decided I could as well. "Excuse me," I said, "I need a bit of air."

The crowd seemed to press in on me from every side, but for once my height served to my advantage. I spotted a place on the end of the pier that was very nearly deserted. I hastened to it, and stood staring out over the rolling waves, feeling as though some constriction had eased from around my lungs.

What was wrong with me? Even a cursory glance at the revelers behind me showed other people had no trouble with boisterous crowds, and some even relished them. And although I might not have minded viewing the kinetoscope, the promise of winning cheap prizes by shooting clay pigeons or tossing a ring onto a milk jug held no appeal for me. I'd rather be curled up in a chair at home, reading a book or petting Saul.

Griffin clearly enjoyed it, however. Had he wanted to come here before, but never mentioned it because he knew I would hate it? I'd never meant to hold him back from anything, no matter how trivial, and it hurt to think I had.

With a sigh, I turned my attention back to the waves. Under ordinary circumstances the view would have been peaceful, but even that was impossible here. Crudely built bathing houses lined the strand. Children buried each other in the sand while their parents lounged about on blankets, eating sausages and ice cream. Meanwhile, men and women in revealing bathing costumes sported in the waves, laughing and splashing one another in a shocking display of informality.

A group of young men, perhaps students from Widdershins University, charged down the narrow beach and into the water. They were all well-formed, their striped mohair bathing suits showing off their figures to excellent advantage. One in particular caught my eye; he cut through the waves like a seal, hair golden in the sun when he surfaced, graceful and laughing.

"Ice cream?" Griffin asked.

I started, a bit guiltily. He stood beside me, proffering a small cup of vanilla ice cream and giving me knowing look.

"Yes, thank you." I took it from him, trying to pretend as if my face wasn't on fire.

Griffin leaned casually against the railing beside me, sampling his own ice cream. "Nice view," he said, glancing out at the ocean.

"I wasn't...that is, I hadn't noticed."

"Mmm hmm."

"Where are your parents?" I asked, seizing on the first change of topic which came to mind.

"Listening to the brass band, I believe." He gave a little shrug. "I wanted to spend time with you. Like this. Without getting chased by dogs, or attacked by cultists."

"The day is still young."

"Point taken." He glanced at me. "I must say, I didn't expect you to wear a full suit to the shore."

I brushed self-consciously at my coat. "It's what I always wear."

"I know. I didn't mean it as a criticism." He turned his gaze back to the ocean. "Although I wouldn't mind seeing you in one of those bathing costumes."

"Good heavens! I'd look a complete fool." Griffin would no doubt cut a fine figure so attired, but I was all angles and bone.

"I disagree," he said. "Will you have your picture taken with me?"

"What?" I asked, surprised by the non sequitur.

Griffin inclined his head to where a man with a camera had set up shop at the far end of the pier. "He's taking portraits, and the price is reasonable. I thought we might have a memento."

"What about your family?"

He shrugged. "Once we're back with them, I'll suggest we have a group portrait done, if they wish. But I'd like something with just the two of us."

"Oh." I'd had my picture taken a few times: family portraits for the most part. It hadn't occurred to me Griffin would want such a thing. "Yes. Let's."

His happy smile made my heart ache. "Wonderful."

The photographer was more than willing to take our picture: I in my suit, my hands folded in front of me, and Griffin looking far more carefree in his striped shirt and straw hat, leaning casually against the pier railing so one arm was behind me. Even though I wouldn't have chosen such an outing, the knowledge Griffin wanted to share it with me left a smile on my face, and I hoped the camera had captured it.

"There," Griffin said when we'd finished. "Not so bad, was it?"

"No, of course not." I cast him a fond glance, then recalled his family might come searching for him at any moment. I directed my gaze back to the water.

At first I thought this section of the ocean clear of bathers, before glimpsing a pale shape moving beneath the waves. I waited for the swimmer to surface for air, but he failed to do so, instead continuing his underwater course north, toward the mouth of the Cranch.

I must be mistaken. Perhaps the shape was a stray dolphin or some other sort of sea life. No human could remain submerged for so long.

For the briefest of instants, its back broke the water, revealing sleek skin, fins and an unmistakable human-like form.

"Did you see that?" I exclaimed, grasping Griffin's arm and pointing.

Griffin shaded his eyes against the sun sparkling from the sea. "See what?"

"The creature..." But when I looked again, the shape was gone.

Griffin returned around four o'clock. "I mean to go up to Stormhaven tonight," he said, glancing at the clock. "But I have a few hours to pass beforehand. Oh, that reminds me, I'll need to borrow your binoculars."

"Of course," I said. I sat in our study, pouring over the *Arcanorum* for any clue which might help us.

He dropped onto the couch beside me. The sun had conjured up more freckles on his nose and cheekbones, and the blue stripes on his shirt lightened his eyes. "Did you enjoy the pier?"

"I suppose."

"Perhaps it would be better with just the two of us," he said. "Although I dare say you enjoyed one part of it."

I set the book aside, wondering what he was about. "The ice cream?"

Griffin leaned in. The scent of his cologne, mingled with the salty tang of sweat, rose from his skin. "The bathers. One in particular, I think."

I swallowed against a sudden constriction in my throat. Heat rose up my neck, and I said, "I-I didn't mean to linger."

"I'm not upset." Griffin's fingers brushed my shoulder, and his breath toyed with the small hairs around my ear. "He was very handsome. Perhaps we shall return some time so we can watch together."

To my mortification, my body roused at the idea. "Th-that would be indecent."

"I'm an indecent fellow," he murmured in my ear, even as his hand stole down to cup me through my trousers. "And you like it."

I turned my face to accept his kiss. He pressed me back against the couch, moving to straddle my lap, his erection hard and straining against mine through the cloth of our trousers.

"Come to bed with me," I whispered when the kiss ended. I wanted him, wanted the feel of his skin under my hands, the taste of his desire on my tongue.

"Yes." He slid off my lap. I rose to my feet and took his hand, drawing him after me to the bedroom. The evening breeze stirred the curtains, which did little to block the stream of late sunlight into the room. I kissed him thoroughly, savoring the taste of his mouth. He nipped my lower lip lightly with his teeth when I drew back.

I removed his clothing one piece at a time, baring his skin to the light, kissing every inch. He fell back on the bed with a languid sigh, stretching his arms above his head and letting me do with him as I wished. I pulled his drawers off last, nibbling at his thighs, his knees. He smelled of sandalwood and musky desire, of everything good in the world, and I rubbed my face against his leg like a cat.

He laughed. "Get undressed and come up here."

I did so, half-wishing for the kindness of candlelight rather than the revealing glow of the evening sun. My gawky limbs hardly seemed likely to enflame anyone's passion. But his eyes followed my every move, the pupils wide with lust, his hand idly stroking his erection.

His hunger fed mine; I ached for his touch, for the velvety slide of his member against mine. I stretched out beside him, and he rolled against me, his lips wandering from my mouth to my throat. I gasped and arched as he kissed and licked his way farther down—then bit me on a sensitive spot on my stomach, making me curl up with a short exclamation.

He looked up at me with a wicked grin dancing on his mouth. "Ticklish?" he asked, although he damned well knew I was. And bit me there again.

"S-Stop!" I ordered through laughter. He didn't, so I thought it quite justified to retaliate with a pillow to the back of his head.

"No fair!" he exclaimed, trying to grab it from me.

Then we were wrestling, laughing like a pair of boys, no thought in the world except each other and this moment. I managed to pummel him a bit more with the pillow, until he pinned me under him. Catching my jaw with his hand, he turned my face to his. "I love to hear you laugh."

I answered with a kiss which began sweet and turned more passionate. His body felt incredible against mine, skin on skin, the heat and flex of his muscles beneath my hands. I rolled to face him, and his hand settled on my cock, stroking in long, delicious movements, which drew a moan from me. I wrapped my own hand around his erection, at the same time tossing a leg across his, pulling us tighter together.

"Look at me," he panted. "I want to see your face."

I did as he asked, even though it left me feeling far more exposed than any bareness of my skin. His green gaze locked with mine, threads of rust and blue texturing his irises. A flush of passion darkened his cheeks, and his lips parted. His hip twitched beneath my leg, thrusting his length against my eager hand, and his breathing came quick and rough.

"I love this," I whispered. "All of it. Your touch, the way you make me feel, so alive…"

"Ival…" He closed his eyes, body shuddering, his cock twitching in my hand as he spent himself.

I closed my eyes as well, curling into him, biting his shoulder as I thrust against his grasp. With a low growl, he rolled me suddenly over onto my back, mouth hot at my throat, biting and sucking hard enough to leave a mark.

His passion was my undoing; I felt the familiar tightening in my sack, the rush of ecstasy, cresting and cresting like a wave until it broke, spilling over his grip and drawing a long, low cry of completion from the very depths of my being.

We lay still and silent for a few minutes, our breath evening out. Then Griffin sat up and stretched, before going to the washbasin. A few moments later, he passed a fresh cloth to me, to wipe away the evidence of our passion.

Once we were done, he came back to bed, and we lay side by side in the warm afternoon, without even a coverlet over us. Before I'd met him, I'd been fully naked only when I bathed; now it seemed natural to lie here with him. Some of the reading I'd done suggested many lovers only partially divested themselves of clothing, but I had no intention of depriving myself of the sight of his exquisite body.

We were silent for a while, but he must have been thinking deeply, because eventually he said, "Sometimes I wonder what would have happened if I'd never gone into that basement."

I hadn't expected this turn of conversation. Although on reflection, perhaps I should have. Perhaps today's carefree excursion more closely echoed the life he'd once lived.

"Well," I said, "I suppose you would have remained in Chicago, with the Pinkertons. Last December, Blackbyrne would have successfully resurrected Leander and summoned the horror he meant to wear Leander's skin. I would be either dead or some sort of thrall, and Threshold would be a smoking crater. Well, it *is* a smoking crater, but the entire town would be dead and monsters roaming the hills unchecked."

Griffin gave me an odd look, and I wondered if he hadn't wanted so literal an answer. "Do you know why I chose Widdershins as the place to start my new life?" he asked abruptly.

"I assume because it's quiet?" In truth, it hadn't occurred to me to ask.

Why wouldn't someone wish to live here?

He slipped his hand into mine, linking our fingers together. "I remember it quite clearly. I'd begun to recover from my confinement—gained weight, stopped jumping at my own shadow, learned what it was to be a human again instead of a caged animal." I squeezed his hand, and he squeezed back, but continued speaking without interruption. "I'd begun to think ahead to my future. Over breakfast one morning, Pa asked about my plans for the future. I couldn't stay there indefinitely, of course, not after having been run out of town once already. I told him I wanted to open my own detective agency. Ma asked where, and I realized I didn't have an answer.

"Father read the paper over breakfast, and it lay on the table between us. I glanced down and saw the headline. THE FINAL JOURNEY OF THE BLACK PHARAOH: NEPHREN-KA AND HIS TREASURE STEAM THEIR WAY TO AMERICA. And below: *Archaeological Find of the Century to Make Landfall in Widdershins Next Week.* I just blurted out: Widdershins."

I turned my head to look at him incredulously. "You must be joking. You're here because of *Christine?*"

He grinned ruefully. "I'm afraid so. Once it came out of my mouth, I thought, why not? Widdershins must be as good a place as any. I made arrangements and ended up here almost a year ago. Of course, I knew within a week I'd made a terrible mistake."

His confession took me aback. "You…you did?"

"I've never seen a town so determined to keep its secrets." His fingers tightened on mine. "A terrible environment for a private detective who hopes to thrive. Still, I had some funds set aside, and I've always enjoyed a challenge."

"By which you mean you're as stubborn as a concussed mule."

He laughed. "Perhaps I am." The laughter died away, and his gaze grew thoughtful. "Do you…do you believe things happen for a reason?"

"No."

"No?"

I shrugged. "If things happened for a reason, as you say, all it would have taken to keep Blackbyrne from almost destroying the world would have been to prevent Leander from drowning. A mild cold to keep us off the lake would have done it."

"No greater scheme? No plan we cannot comprehend?"

"A greater scheme, which required an innocent young man to die, before nearly resulting in the destruction of the world?" I shook my head. "No. Forgive me, but I can't."

He smiled, a bit wistfully. "Do you truly believe in nothing?"

I held up our entwined hands. "I believe in this. With all my heart."

His smile lost its sadness, and he drew my hand to his lips. "As do I, my dear. As do I."

CHAPTER 15

GRIFFIN'S SCOUTING TRIP that night confirmed the asylum's routine, so the next day, we rode a pair of rented horses up the coast road toward Stormhaven.

"Couldn't we have hired a carriage?" I asked, jouncing along on the horrible beast. Knowing it had an inexperienced rider on its back, it insisted on stopping every three feet to munch on the dry grass alongside the road, ignoring my every attempt to get it to move again. "Or walked?"

"A carriage is more difficult to conceal than a pair of horses," he pointed out. "And if things should go awry and we have to flee, it will be quicker and easier on horseback than on foot. I thought about renting bicycles, but it didn't seem practical."

I tried to imagine cycling up the steep coast road. I'd die from exhaustion before we were a mile out of town.

"Perhaps you're right," I granted as my hellish mount stopped yet again, this time to release a copious stream of urine into the road. "Let us hope no one smells horse on us."

Griffin planned for us to pass ourselves off as attendants once we entered the asylum. Accordingly, we both dressed in simple suits similar to those worn by the asylum staff. As the female nurses wore uniforms, which Griffin couldn't easily acquire with only a day's warning, we'd elected not to inform Christine of our plans.

"No one will notice," Griffin said. "They will be far more occupied by other considerations."

"What of my height?" At over six feet, I towered a good five inches above the average man, including Griffin, which made me unfortunately noticeable no matter how much I stooped.

"It is a concern," he admitted. "But in the darkness and confusion, chances are no one will remark on it."

His plan seemed to be leaving a great deal to chance and hope. But I had no better scheme, so I remained silent and concentrated on convincing my mount to obey. Was there a spell in the *Arcanorum* to encourage recalcitrant beasts, or perhaps mesmerize them? If so, perhaps I should learn it against some terrible future which would require another excursion on horseback.

We kept our ride leisurely, not wishing to attract any attention from passers-by. Not that there were many such; the coast road was little used now these days, when the casual traveler could board a train to any but the smallest villages. The evening was fine, with a soft breeze across the bay making the electrical wires hum on their poles.

We paused for dinner just south of the headland where Stormhaven lurked. Griffin tied up our horses alongside the road and took sandwiches from the saddlebags. At his suggestion, we climbed down the rocky slope to the narrow strand of beach below and found a secluded spot to sit and eat. The setting sun cast the shadow of the cliffs over us. Gulls screamed by the thousands, swirling around their roosts, and the last plovers and sandpipers raced back and forth along the stony beach. Griffin rested his hand on my thigh as we ate and stole kisses between bites. What would it be like to be this free with one another in the ordinary course of life?

We returned to the horses just as night fell. Griffin took one of the lanterns from the saddlebags and lit it with a match. He had scouted the area the evening and night before, locating a place to conceal our horses and verifying the asylum operated on the expected schedule. It did, leaving us with another hour to hide the horses and make our way to the electrical lines.

After a quarter-hour ride, Griffin led the way to a copse of trees on the landward side of the road. These were less stunted than those closer to the edge of the cliffs, and thus offered more cover. Hopefully, no other travelers would pass by, tempting the horses to make some sound of either greeting or alarm.

Once the horses were hobbled, Griffin pulled a replacement carpetbag from the saddlebags and began to fill it with the equipment he'd brought: extra kerosene, rope, grappling hook, and chalk. After passing a second lantern to me, he shouldered the bag, and we headed out.

"We should choose poles close to Stormhaven," he said. Flitting bats had replaced the gulls overhead. Tendrils of mist crept in from the ocean, promising of fog to come. "That way we can act quickly, before the staff has the chance to restore order. And have the wind blow from the sea, so as to bring the fog in more quickly."

The rough wood of the electrical poles loomed into the beams of light cast by our lanterns. Griffin inspected the closest one. "You're certain you can send them over?"

"Of course." I measured the space between it and its fellows. "Er, you might wish to stand well clear. And out of the way of any flying debris."

He rummaged in the carpetbag and handed me the chalk. "Just remember not to touch the lines once they're down."

"I won't."

Looking rather unhappy about the situation, he removed himself to a safe distance. I went to the nearest pole and began to sketch a sigil on its splintery surface.

As I worked, I chanted, my focus sharpening. Although I did not truly understand the principles on which the *Arcanorum's* spells worked, I did know the ability of the caster to focus his or her will was paramount in implementing them. Practice had sharpened my focus, until I could block out almost any distraction.

Wind stirred the hair on the back of my neck, bringing with it the scent of the sea. The humming of the electrical lines overhead grew louder. Finished with the first pole, I moved on to its neighbor, again sketching the sigil and speaking the words. The wind intensified, the crashing of the waves against the cliff growing louder. Fog streamed around me, and grains of sand scoured my exposed skin. The stunted trees thrashed in the darkness, and the wooden pole groaned.

One more should do it.

I repeated the action on the third pole, and the wind roared up into a gale, the leaves stripped from the trees, sand and debris pelting me. The wires howled like tormented things, the poles bending in the wind, until suddenly there came a loud crack from the second one I had marked.

My heart sang along with the wires, exaltation filling me. I tasted the salt on the wind, and a giddy feeling slid along my nerves, whispering I had done this. *Me*. Like the moments when I lay with Griffin and realized anew I was the one who made him hard and aching and desperate for release, this filled me with a sense of power, sweet and heady.

Lifting my hands above my head, I concentrated on all three sigils at once, shouting the words into the world as I demanded the very universe bend its laws to my will.

The cracked pole gave way before the gale, overstressed wood shattering. The first pole went next, dragged down by the weight of its fellow. Broken lines snaked through the air, sparks dancing and popping.

I lowered my arms, even as the wind died away. A moment later, I heard Griffin's footsteps, and his lantern cut through the gloom. "Well done, my dear."

"I'm glad you approve," I said smugly.

He gave me a rueful grin. "Well…whatever else I may think of your researches, as you call them, you did cut a rather commanding figure a moment ago. I find myself regretting we must act in haste."

I flushed, but secretly his words pleased me. Taking out my handkerchief, I quickly wiped away the three sigils, so only smudges of chalk remained. No sense leaving behind any evidence to be puzzled over by whoever came to inspect the lines in the morning. As soon as I finished, Griffin led the way up the last slope of hill, until the outer wall of Stormhaven loomed up before us.

Griffin took out the rope and grappling hook. Eying the distance to the top of the wall, he swung the grapple a few times before tossing it. The sound of iron striking brick seemed hideously loud, but with any luck the fog helped to muffle it. Griffin tugged on the rope; apparently satisfied the grapple was secure, he climbed the wall.

I handed up the lanterns. He lowered the rope again, and I clung to it, doing my best to help as he hauled me up as well. The stones scraped against my clothing and I left some skin from my knuckles against them, but eventually I crouched on top of the wall.

The night beyond was utterly black; between the fog and the darkness, I would never have known the asylum existed save for the faint echoes of cries from within. "We must move quickly," Griffin said. "Come!"

We dropped from the wall. Griffin led the way, using the tiny sliver of light from his lantern to guide us to the side ward whose door he had decided to attempt. Given the conditions, I would have been lucky to find even the huge front door, but Griffin navigated quickly across the wide lawn, until the stone walls loomed in front of us through the streamers of fog.

The sounds were louder now: screams and cries, accompanied by wild laughter. Lanterns flashed past windows, the staff struggling to get the patients back under control. Would anyone be hurt in the chaos? I hadn't thought so far ahead, but now I worried our plan might end up with innocents getting injured, or worse.

As Griffin said, we needed to hurry.

We reached the door. This part of our plan depended on no one noticing us breaking in. From the sounds inside, I doubted anyone had attention to spare for the doors, but there was always the chance of ill luck.

Griffin took his lock picks from inside his coat, while I aimed the lantern beam at the door. Within a matter of seconds, the lock clicked and he hastily put away his tools. Opening the door, he stepped inside with all the confidence of someone who belonged there, and I tried to mimic him.

It was chaos, just as Griffin had promised. Even with the "less troublesome" patients here on the ground floor, several screamed in terror, and I heard the sounds of a struggle. An attendant with a lantern shoved a patient into a room, ignoring the man's protests this wasn't his bed, and slammed the door. "Back to your rooms, you damned bastards!" he yelled. "Or you'll be fucking sorry for it, I promise you!"

How he expected them were to find their rooms in the blackness, with no lanterns or candles of their own, I had no idea. Griffin kept his light directed at the floor; hands grabbed at him, and he swung it out of their reach.

"That you, MacCauly?" the attendant yelled.

Griffin stepped up to the man. For an instant, I had no idea what he meant to do, until the attendant let out a muffled grunt and crumpled to the ground. Bending over his prone form, Griffin snatched up the man's keys.

"Come on," he said. "He won't be out long."

The door out of the ward opened onto the one in which we'd visited Allan. We found more of the same: patients crowding the wide halls, shuffling about in confusion, yelling and weeping.

"Give me the light!" one of the inmates shouted, grabbing at Griffin's arm. Griffin shoved him back, and for a minute I thought the madman might start a fight. Instead, he spat a curse at us, railing and shrieking at our backs as we fled.

Griffin unlocked the door into the central section of the building, his hand shaking in the lantern light. As we started through, however, Zeiler's voice boomed out. "Send all the attendants and nurses to the first three floors! We must regain control of the patients!"

If Zeiler glimpsed us, it would all be over. Griffin froze in the doorway, and several patients, perhaps sensing the chance to flee, began to jostle me from behind. I grabbed Griffin and yanked him back, leaving the inmates to do as they wished.

"Is there another way to the fourth floor?" I asked him urgently.

He nodded. "Y-yes. The Kirkbride asylums are all built on the same plan. It should be this way."

We hurried back to the end of the ward, took a turn, and found ourselves at another locked door. Griffin's hands shook too badly to get the key in the lock, so I took it from him and opened the door. We darted through, and I secured it again behind us.

This stairwell was far narrower than the grand mahogany stair near the main doors, the risers and rail made from cast iron. Running feet and the shouts of nurses rang down from above, but none made for the first floor, for which I was grateful.

I shone the beam of my lantern at Griffin's face. His color was awful, his jaw clenched, and his lips tight against his teeth. Still, he winced at the light and shoved my arm down. "Are you trying to blind me?"

"I only wished to take a closer look," I said. "Come—from what Zeiler said, the fourth floor will be clear of attendants. We just have to get there."

A scream echoed from somewhere above, and Griffin flinched. "Yes."

"Can you make it?"

He straightened his shoulders with obvious effort. "Yes. I can." His hand found mine briefly and squeezed, and I marveled silently at his courage. I didn't know if I could have even come here, let alone kept any shred of equilibrium, if I had suffered such things. "Let's go."

An iron grate barred the stairs at each floor, no doubt to keep back the patients in case they were somehow able to escape from their wards. We let ourselves through each one with the keys. Other attendants and nurses rushed past, but none of them paid any attention to us, too focused on restoring order to do anything other than assume we were doing the same. At last we reached the top of the stairs, and I unlocked the door.

Griffin stepped out first and I followed, locking the door again behind me. When I turned back, it became immediately apparent why Zeiler hadn't been concerned with leaving anyone to handle the patients of this floor. Unlike the other wards, there were no shuffling lunatics, no hurrying attendants or hastily closed doors. The place reeked of filth of every kind, and the only sound was a faint moan, which might emanate from one of the floors below. The doors to the little rooms were shut fast, and I had the feeling these patients weren't allowed to roam free under any circumstances.

A sense of dreadful curiosity drew me to the nearest door. Unlike those of the other wards, which had a Judas grate to allow the night watchman to observe the patients when he chose, these were made entirely of bars, like a cell in a prison. The only furniture consisted of a single, filthy bed. A man lay on it, his face thickly bearded, his slack gaze fixed on the ceiling. Heavy iron cuffs chained him to the bed, and I knew he'd not be able to move more than a few inches.

A sense of revulsion swept over me. What had he done, to be restrained like this? Would poor Allan end up like this if we weren't able to secure his freedom? Was he here somewhere now?

If we found Allan, could we set him free? Take him with us? Surely, Griffin must have contacts able to conceal him for a time, at least until we got to the bottom of the matter.

"God," Griffin whispered. I turned and saw him staring through an open door. Not a cell; it looked like some sort of utilitarian room at first glance, lined with cabinets of various kinds. Only at second glance did I see the chairs meant to act as shackles to immobilize patients, the cage-like "cribs" so narrow anyone inside could not so much as turn over. A so-called treatment room.

An open cabinet stood along the wall, filled with jars and wire. This must be one of the electro-therapeutic devices Zeiler had mentioned before. The jars were chemical cells, and the wire meant to connect with…

An array of probes lay on the table in front of it, some of whose use was made obvious by their shape. Bile stung my throat, and I glanced at Griffin, whose empty-eyed gaze had locked on the probes.

If he slipped into a fit now, we'd be caught for sure. I had to get him out of here. "Griffin," I said, low and urgent. "Hang on. We're almost there. I know you can do this."

He swallowed convulsively, then nodded. "Yes. Just…lead the way."

I did so, trying not to think of him locked in one of those cribs or chairs, let alone receiving shocks from the instruments. I wanted to take him far from here, wrap my arms around him, and shield him from every possible harm. But I couldn't.

I led him further down the ward, wondering how many men might be confined here. Unlike the first floor ward, these walls weren't painted a cheerful yellow. Instead, strange, swirling lines and symbols covered the raw plaster. I stopped to look at them, certain I'd seen many of the sigils in the *Arcanorum* and other occult tomes. A symbol hung above every cell, with sigils and lines twisting out from it, both inside the cell and to tangle with its neighbors.

What the devil was Zeiler doing with these men?

Griffin tugged at my hand. There was no time to gawk, I reminded myself. As we hurried down the ward, I shone my lantern into each cell, hoping for a glimpse of Allan. The wretched patients were little more than huddled shapes, for the most part, with the occasional gleam of eyes. The low moaning grew louder, and I realized it came from a cell halfway down the ward. Through some trick of the ventilation, the scent of the sea strengthened as we approached, drowning out the foulness of human effluvia. The air grew heavy and damp, smelling of salt and rot, dead fish and cold, cold mud.

My footsteps turned sluggish, as if mired in sludge. I needed to keep walking…and yet for some reason I felt compelled to look into the cell. Everything seemed to move very slowly, as if I'd slipped into some strange dream.

My feet came to a halt altogether, and I shone the beam of my lantern on the moaning man. The occupant of the cell crouched with his back to me. Unlike the shabbily-clothed patients I'd seen thus far, he seemed to be naked, his vertebrae strung like stones beneath his skin. Tattoos of strange design covered his arms and part of his back. Had he been a sailor, perhaps? Even one of the cultists?

The moaning fell suddenly silent. When the madman spoke, his cracked voice lilted strangely, like a child half-singing the words of a taunt. "You hear its song."

My breath caught in my throat. "I d-don't know what you mean," I lied.

A low laugh started…then spread to the other cells, until we stood in the midst of a whole ward of laughing, cackling, giggling lunatics. "Don't you?" the sailor asked. "It sings to you as it sings to us. In our dreams."

"Whyborne," Griffin said urgently, but he seemed very far away. On the other side of the world, or at the bottom of a well.

I took a step closer to the cell, fascinated by the tattoos on the sailor's back. Was it a trick of the light, or had they begun to *move?*

The lunatic sprang to his feet, slamming into the bars, mere inches from my face. *"It sings to you!"* he screamed, spittle flying everywhere.

No, not spittle—sea foam. Somehow—I didn't know how—the ocean had risen into Stormhaven, an inch of water splashing beneath my feet, the scent of the murky depths filling my nose. It wasn't possible—it would take a cataclysm indeed for the ocean to rise so high, and surely the building would have been swept away. But where did the water come from?

What was happening to me?

"It's coming!" the madman howled, shaking the bars of his cage. "The dweller in the deep is coming! The god is coming, singing; don't you hear it, *don't you hear it?"*

A hand touched my arm.

Chapter 16

I screamed and spun, to only to find myself face-to-face with the girl—Amelie—who had given me the flower on our first visit. She screamed as well, and I stumbled back, tripping over my own feet and falling to the floor.

The perfectly dry floor.

"Whyborne! Are you all right?" Griffin exclaimed, dropping to his knees by me.

"What happened to the water?" I asked, hysteria kicking my voice into a higher register than usual.

Griffin stared at me in bewilderment. "Water?"

"The floor…it was flooded…" But obviously that wasn't so. "Never mind."

Griffin helped me to my feet, his brows drawn with concern. At least his worry for me seemed to have relieved his impending fit; perhaps only one of us would end tonight thrashing about on the floor. "Are you all right, my dear?" he asked anxiously.

"I'm fine." The atmosphere of the ward had surely played tricks on my mind.

Amelie drew closer, peering up into my face. "You're here," she said, and poked me in the chest. "Actually here."

"Er, yes. And so are you." I looked about uneasily. Surely, she shouldn't be on this floor at all, let alone in a male ward.

She nodded solemnly, her red-gold hair rustling about her shoulders. Her bare feet were stained with grass, as if she'd been running wild outside just moments ago. "Yes. Follow me."

She walked purposefully away from us, heading deeper into the ward.

Around us, the inmates groaned and screamed and snarled like…well, like mad things. Thankfully, none of them tried to speak to her.

"What should we do?" I asked Griffin uncertainly. Amelie seemed as if she had some destination in mind, but there was no knowing what it might be.

Griffin shrugged. "We follow her."

I supposed we had no choice; we could not, in good conscience, let her wander alone amidst a bunch of violent men, even ones who had been restrained. As we followed her, I continued my examination of the patients, but to my disappointment didn't spot Allan amongst them.

Amelie led the way to the end of the ward, where the heavy steel door stood open by just a crack. Was that how she'd managed to get in? Hadn't the nurse said something the first day about Amelie somehow getting through locked doors?

She boldly pushed the door open, and we followed her into the centermost portion of the asylum. A single glance confirmed we'd reached our destination. The superintendent's living space was much finer than the rest of Stormhaven, at least the parts I'd seen. To one side was a large, comfortable parlor, while to the other lay a dining room with a long table for entertaining. A cupboard filled with cut glass and china stood against one wall.

"Ooh, pretty!" Amelie exclaimed, and ran to peer at it closely.

Griffin sighed. "Zeiler won't keep anything incriminating lying about where anyone could find it. Let's search his chambers. See if you can convince the young lady to follow us."

She pried at the front of the cabinet, so I hurried over to her, visions of her happily breaking the glasses and summoning every attendant in Stormhaven dancing through my head. "Er, come along, now," I said.

She let me lead her away, but not without numerous glances of longing back over her shoulder.

A little hall opened off the back of the parlor. Griffin led the way, and Amelie danced after him, her skirts swishing about her knees, as if we strolled down a country lane. "I like your eyes," she said, smiling winsomely at me. "They're pretty."

Griffin chuckled. I blushed. "Er, thank you. You're, um, very kind."

"Will you kiss me?"

"Good heavens, no!" I exclaimed. Griffin muffled a snort of laughter, curse him. At least he had regained his equilibrium, even if it was at my expense.

Two doors opened off the short hall. The one on the left appeared to lead into Zeiler's bedroom, and the one on the right to a small study. Griffin chose the study, which contained only a chair and curtain top desk, at which Dr. Zeiler might write his private correspondence. The desk had been left open, the chair shoved back, no doubt when the sudden darkness interrupted the doctor's evening. His writing set was out, a pen lying abandoned on its side, atop what appeared to be a half-composed letter.

Griffin went to the desk and began to rifle through it with quick efficiency.

Amelie stood too close and stared fixedly at my face, as if something about me fascinated her. I, in turn, resolutely watched Griffin and prayed we'd be out of here soon.

From somewhere outside, a board creaked, as if beneath a footstep.

Beside me, Amelie froze, her gaze locked on the door, which we had foolishly left open. Griffin gestured frantically for me to shutter my lantern, which I did, plunging us into darkness. My mind immediately populated it with horrors: an insane murderer, creeping in on silent feet to chop us apart with an ax. Or perhaps, something worse, something which whispered words I couldn't quite make out in the voice of my mother…

"Is anyone there?" called a woman. One of the nurses, no doubt. "I heard you, so come on out if you're here, or things'll go worse for you!"

I felt Amelie shudder. Her hand touched my arm lightly in the dark. "Stay here," she breathed in my ear.

She slipped away before I could stop her, bare feet almost silent on the floorboards. Once she left the room, however, she began to sing nonsense in a loud voice.

"Amelie! I should've known!" the nurse exclaimed. There came a loud crack, as of an open hand on flesh, and Amelie fell silent. "Shop that infernal noise. Now no tears, or I'll give you something to cry about, I will. Come on, you stupid slut, it's back to your room with the others."

My hands curled into fists…but Amelie had deliberately sacrificed her comfort for our mission, and the only way to repay her was to soldier on. I listened for what seemed like forever in the dark, but was probably only a few minutes. Eventually, Griffin unshuttered his lantern, the beam blindingly bright.

"Here," he said, voice pitched low as he held something out to me. "I spotted it just before we heard the nurse. What do you make of it?"

I took the paper from him. "It's a copy of the inscription from the ceremonial bowl," I replied. "And a translation—fairly accurate, I think…oh. Oh dear."

"What is it?" Griffin asked.

"It's an invocation to summon the god." I looked up and met his eyes, saw my dread reflected there.

"Summon? As in…?"

"Yes. They mean to release the dweller of the deep from its ocean prison and set it free upon the land."

Griffin swallowed hard. "Why?"

I shook my head slowly. "It doesn't say…but I can guess. Power. Revenge. The favor of the god, whatever form that favor takes."

We stood in utter silence for a long moment, both of us contemplating the horrors a man like Zeiler might loose on the world. As if summoned by our thoughts, the superintendent's voice echoed faintly from somewhere outside the room.

"Damn it," Griffin hissed. Grabbing my hand, he pulled me after him into the hall, and then the sitting room.

"…it doesn't happen again," Zeiler said from the southern stairwell.

We dashed to the northern stairwell, plunging down the wide steps just as the beams of lanterns appeared at the southern landing. "Who's there?" Zeiler called.

Blast the man for spotting us. Griffin didn't hesitate, however, dragging me down the stair after him, even as Zeiler yelled for us to stop. Had he seen our faces, or recognized us?

The stair let us out on the first floor. More shouts echoed from above, along with pounding footsteps coming down the southern stair. Griffin rushed to the front door, flung it open, and hauled me after him out into the foggy night.

We dashed across the lawn. My heart thudded in my chest, and a stitch formed in my side, but I pressed on over the damp grass. More shouts came from within—did they think us escaped patients, or intruders? Either way, it would be a matter of minutes before every attendant in the place turned out to search for us.

Griffin ran unerringly to where we had left our things at the foot of the wall. He threw the grapple, cursed when it failed to catch, and tossed it again. The clang of metal against stone echoed through the foggy night. "Who's there?" someone shouted.

Griffin scrambled up the rope, perching on the top of the wall to haul me after. Lantern light cut through the fog when I was halfway up, and there came another shout of alarm. "You there! Stop!"

Something—fingers?—brushed the bottom of my shoe. I didn't look down, focusing instead on Griffin's face. With a last heave, he pulled me atop the wall. The knees of my trousers scraped the stone, but I didn't care.

We dropped from the wall, as the shouts grew louder behind us. Griffin ran and I followed him, tripping over rocks and the uneven ground and leaving Stormhaven behind us.

Later that night, I found myself at the bottom of the ocean.

The cyclopean architecture loomed overhead, clinging to the sides of a great trench, its spiky towers and nonsensical angles clear to my sight despite the utter darkness of the abyss. Muck sucked at my feet as I walked down a great thoroughfare, and all the detritus of the miles of ocean above my head floated down like strange snow. A hellish glow showed far off in the distance, as if the great crevasse opened in places onto the bowels of the very earth. Columns of boiling water streamed up from the vents, and monstrous life grew thickly nearby. Fish floated past, flashing green and blue lights, like fireflies trapped on the bottom of the sea.

Somewhere, my mother sang.

I ran to her, the weight of the water no obstacle. She needed me, I knew it, but I still couldn't make out the words she sang.

There: she waited in front of the great temple. She'd escaped somehow. And yet the realization, which should have brought joy, instead filled me with dread. I slowed, every instinct shrieking at me to turn, to run, even though this was my mother, who I should be rushing to save…

No, wait. It wasn't mother, but Griffin. He stood alone in front of the temple, head bowed, tattered clothing drifting in the current.

He needed me.

Despite my mounting horror, I forced my feet forward, one step, then another. As I approached, he raised his head and looked at me. His irises had turned to gold, the pupils the oblong slits of a cuttlefish eye.

When I arrived at the Ladysmith the next morning, I found a small package from my father waiting for me at the museum. Taking it to my desk, I tore open the brown wrapping paper. It contained a slender volume of thoroughly modern origin and a note.

Percival,

I assume you've, as usual, not taken my advice, and have continued to delve into the matter with the Eyes. As I mentioned when we spoke, my fellows and I were in the habit of keeping watch over other organizations with similar interests. Here is what we gathered on the Eyes; the information is twenty years old, but that shouldn't matter when it comes to a cult spanning millennia.

And no, I did not have it in my possession the night we spoke, nor did I know for certain I could obtain it. I didn't wish to encourage you by mentioning its existence, but you've always been damnably stubborn.

I would tell you to be careful, if I thought you'd listen. Instead I say, for your mother's sake, at least, don't be foolhardy. Although I haven't agreed with your decisions, your actions of the last year suggest I may have underestimated your courage.

Yrs truly,
Niles Foster Whyborne

I read through the note several times. What the devil was the man about? Although I was grateful for whatever assistance the volume might provide, Father never did anything without some advantage to himself. Did he think to woo me back into the fold with such a gift?

Let alone his baseless flattery. *"I may have underestimated your courage"*—did he think me Stanford, to lap up such extravagant praise? I was well aware I had no more courage than the next man, and far less than someone like Griffin.

No doubt he intended to lower my guard. Probably he meant to ask another favor of Griffin, and thought I would argue his case for him, despite his possible involvement in Griffin's confinement. If so, he would have to resign himself to eternal disappointment, as he had with all other matters concerning me.

Putting such useless speculation aside, I opened the volume he'd sent and examined it. Written in plain English, using only the simplest of ciphers—the Brotherhood had indeed been confident no one would ever breach their secrets. Generations of wealth and power had a way of instilling a sense of invulnerability, I supposed. Just look at Stanford.

I took the volume with me and returned to the library. If the Eyes truly meant to raise some blasphemous creature from the depths of the sea, and unleash it upon the land, we had to find some way of stopping it. Surely, between the *Arcanorum*, the Brotherhood's investigation, the *Al Azif* and the other resources of the Ladysmith's library, I could discover its weakness.

I hoped. The alternative was too awful to consider.

If something happened to Zeiler, would the creature simply find another vessel to do its work? How widespread was the cult? Was Zeiler its slave, driven to enact its will, just as poor Allan had been unable to control himself at the sight of the cult's symbol? And if not, what did he hope to gain from unleashing it? Then again, crushing the world beneath the heel of one's god had proved tempting to men throughout history; how much more so if your reward came in this life instead of the next?

Zeiler. Hate flashed through me, and I tasted seawater in my mouth. I could turn my sorcery against him. Find a spell in the *Arcanorum* to force him to do my bidding.

Griffin would never forgive me. My use of magic already worried him; if I took things much further, he'd be furious. And if the dweller simply used one of its other minions instead, it would all be for nothing. I had to find a way to stop it from rising.

I blinked and realized my mind had drifted. Lack of restful sleep was beginning to take its toll on my ability to concentrate. I focused again on the words in front of me.

The air pressed heavy against my skin, like water. Strange sounds echoed from elsewhere in the library. Footsteps. Rustling paper. Even someone singing.

Mr. Quinn wouldn't like that. This was a place for quiet research, not frivolity.

The song grew louder, though. Haunting and beautiful and unearthly, it both called to and repulsed me.

I had to go to the singer. I had to.

Seaweed and barnacles clung to the library's shelves, currents stirring the pages of books. Fish darted past my face, and the light had a strange, bluish quality. I walked out through the underwater library, into the great, sunken city with its mad geometry. How had I not realized the city and Widdershins were one and the same before? That this terrible place was my home?

Of course it was. And the singer was my mother, or perhaps Griffin, who was in terrible danger. I picked up my pace, hurrying through the titanic city, making for the temple where everyone I'd ever loved was being held prisoner—

"Whyborne? What are you doing?"

The words meant nothing. Nonsense sounds, spoken by an unrecognized voice. I had to hurry.

A hand closed around my wrist, jerking my arm aside. I spun on my assailant with a snarl. No one would keep me from the singer.

"Whyborne!"

I fought, wrestling against the hands grabbing me. Whoever this was, I had to get away, Mother needed me, Griffin needed me—

"Ival, stop!"

Griffin?

I blinked. I stood on the familiar sidewalk of River St., in front of the department store. Griffin gripped both my arms; several people had stopped to stare, but I was too aghast to feel embarrassment. How could I have not known Griffin? For that matter, how had I gotten here in the first place? "Griffin, I—I'm sorry!"

Worry creased his brow. He loosened his hold on me, although he didn't let go altogether. "Are you all right, my dear?"

"No," I said miserably. "I don't think I am."

Chapter 17

I sat behind my desk, cradling the cup of coffee Griffin had fetched for me, unable to bring myself to look at either of my friends. Griffin had brought me back to the museum, alerted Christine something odd had happened, then had her sit with me while he found coffee. No doubt he'd been worried I'd wander off in an unseeing daze again.

"I'd come to meet you for lunch and find out if you would accompany us to the park later on," Griffin said. He perched on the arm of my chair, one hand resting lightly on my back. "As I was climbing the steps to the museum entrance, you walked out. I spoke to you, but you didn't acknowledge me at all. It was as if you didn't even know I was there."

"I didn't," I said. "I thought I was in an undersea city."

Griffin let out a hiss of fear. "The dweller—it couldn't touch your mind, could it? You aren't one of its followers, or mad."

"No, but…I've been having dreams."

The silence which followed my admission made me cringe. "You've what?" Griffin asked at last.

I told them everything—the nightmares, the strange hallucinations, all of it. When I was done, I continued to stare fixedly at my coffee, awaiting judgment.

Christine was happy to provide it. "What the devil were you thinking?" she demanded. "Why would you keep something like this to yourself?"

I buried my face in my hands. "I told myself they were just nightmares. As Griffin said, I'm not one of its followers, or a lunatic—"

"Not that one could tell from your actions!" she snapped.

I lifted my head and shot her a glare. "They were just dreams! And visions. That's all."

"Well, it's a good deal more, now."

"You seemed to be making for the docks," Griffin said.

"The ocean. The dweller was calling me. I suppose it would have been rather disappointed when I drowned in the bay." I let my hands drop to my lap. "I'm sorry. I should have said something."

"Indeed you should," Christine agreed.

Griffin's hand tightened on my shoulder. "Is there any way to…I don't know, shield your mind from the dweller?"

"Perhaps. The cult seems to be more interested in opening their minds to the god, not blocking it out. I didn't get much reading done before the, er, incident, but the folio Father sent spoke of something called the *oculares* potion. Rather than rely on holy lunatics or years of meditation in order to communicate with the dweller, they were attempting to develop some sort of serum to act as a short cut. Even a sane novice could take it and receive the sendings of their god."

"Did they succeed?" Griffin asked.

"No idea. The information is twenty years out of date. But if Zeiler is trying to develop it…"

"The fourth floor." Griffin's skin took on a grayish cast. "He's experimenting on them."

"Possibly." I hoped, for Allan's sake, we were wrong. If only we'd been able to find him while we were at the asylum!

"So what next?" Christine asked. "If the growing intensity of Whyborne's visions are any indication, the summoning will surely occur sooner rather than later. How are we to stop them?"

Griffin rubbed tiredly at eyes ringed by dark circles. New lines bracketed his mouth; this case had taken its toll on him. "I'm not certain. Perhaps I will keep watch on Zeiler's house, assuming they haven't abandoned the location. Or speak with my contacts on the docks, among the sailors. But I cannot do much today." I heard the frustration in his voice. "My parents and Ruth wish an excursion to the park, and I thought—"

"No," Christine said.

Griffin cast her an irritated look. "Christine…"

"Don't you 'Christine' me, Griffin Flaherty! Whyborne may do as he pleases, but I refuse to take any more part in this absurd charade."

Griffin's mouth tightened. "I don't have a choice!"

"Yes, you do." Christine's brows lowered and her eyes flashed with anger.

"Don't you understand? We could be arrested if anyone found out the truth!"

"Are you seriously trying to convince me your own parents would turn you in?" She flung up her arms in disgust. "And if you're so worried about it, why involve poor Whyborne at all?"

"Because I wanted him to meet them."

"Which could have been accomplished at the museum. The rest of this—

dinner, a turn around the park—why? Do you like showing off your friendship with Niles Whyborne's son, or do you just enjoy tempting fate?"

"Christine," I started to object.

Griffin overrode me. "Damn it, Christine, do you think I like living this way?"

Oh.

It shouldn't have hurt. I'd certainly prefer things to be otherwise as well. To live in some other world, where everything was different, where we could embrace in the park like any other pair of lovers. But his words bruised me inside my chest, aching with each intake of breath.

What had Griffin said, when he spoke of his time recovering from his experiences in the asylum? That he should have felt disappointment his inclinations hadn't altered, despite the cures inflicted on him. Did some part of him secretly hate the things we did together? Hate me for evoking these feelings in him? Did he wish he had waited, remained merely friends, so he would have been free to try to make a normal life with Ruth?

Was he free? We had agreed not to touch anyone else, so long as we were together. But of course he could break things off any time he wished.

Christine glanced at me, and perhaps something of my thoughts showed on my face, because her mouth pressed into a thin line. "Make my excuses to your parents, Whyborne?"

"I'm not letting Whyborne out of my sight," Griffin said firmly. "Not after what just happened."

I started to object, to say I'd go home and wait there. I was weary to the bone of this pretense. If Griffin hated his life with me, he could find another more easily without my presence. But he had a point, as much as I was loath to admit it. If the dweller attacked my mind again, there was no telling where I might end up. Drowned off the end of the pier seemed most likely.

"You're right," I said. "I'll come."

Christine let out a little huff, but said nothing further. Then again, given the glare she leveled at Griffin, she didn't need to.

"The park seems rather empty," Miss Kerr commented later that evening.

The setting sun cast long shadows over the green lawns and shady oaks. At one end of the small park, a fountain gurgled happily; at the other sat a large monument marked with the date of the town's founding and a list of its original inhabitants. It neglected to mention a mad sorcerer had founded Widdershins, or that most of the families listed had carried on his nefarious traditions.

"At least there's a carriage for hire," Mr. Kerr said with a nod to the lone vehicle at the stand. Its driver appeared to have fallen asleep.

His wife patted my arm. "A shame your Dr. Putnam couldn't join us."

"Er, yes," I said, hoping she didn't intend to start lecturing me on marriage again.

Griffin gestured to the carriage. "Would you enjoy a turn about the park,

Miss Kerr?"

A blush crept over her cheeks. "That would be lovely."

"Will you keep my parents company for a few moments, Whyborne?" Griffin asked. I supposed he wanted to be certain someone would be keeping an eye on me. Then again, the park wasn't so large. Did he expect to be distracted in some way, during which I might wander off?

I didn't care for the direction my thoughts tended. "Of course," I said, struggling to keep my tone neutral rather than bitter.

It was just a role he played, I told myself, as he escorted Miss Kerr to the carriage. His parents and Ruth would leave in a few days. Hopefully the elder Kerrs would be satisfied when Griffin wrote to them that Ruth, wonderful as she might be, was not the wife for him.

But would he be satisfied? Or would he still wish for everything to be different?

"Want to have a seat and enjoy the evening?" Mr. Kerr asked while the carriage rattled off.

I followed them to a bench. Mrs. Kerr sat in the center, so I positioned myself as close to the end as possible without falling off.

I'd thought Griffin content with our quiet existence in our little house. How could I have been so wrong? And if I was wrong about that, what else might I have mistaken? Was it possible he meant only to soften the blow when he bid me farewell and wed Miss Kerr?

No. He would have said something. He wouldn't be so cruel.

Unless he hadn't yet decided. Unless he was caught between the twin prods of his inclinations and his desire for an ordinary life. A life he wouldn't have to hide from the family who had welcomed a frightened orphan into their midst and raised him into the man I'd fallen in love with.

Griffin loved me, I knew it. But love wasn't always enough, was it? He'd known many men in Chicago, his own partner included, who found pleasure in the shadows but lived in the light, their standing in society assured by a wife and children. Doubtless, he wanted that for himself. And why shouldn't he? He'd make an excellent husband and devoted father.

My selfish heart rebelled at the thought. I stared down at my hands, loathing squirming in my gut. How could I chain him in the shadows with me, when by his own admission he longed for something else?

Griffin's parents chatted beside me on the bench, but I was far too wrapped up in my own misery to pay them much attention, until his mother straightened sharply. "What's that fellow doing?"

The note of fear in her voice caused me to look up. The carriage had reached the far side of the little park and come to a halt. For a horrified instant, I imagined the stop was to give the couple privacy, so Griffin could…what? Kiss Ruth? Propose to her?

Then I realized the driver had fallen from the carriage and clutched his arm, blood bright on the crushed shell drive. A man in the dress and tattoos of a sailor had thrown open the door and climbed into the passenger compartment, a knife in his hand.

"Griffin!" The cry tore from my throat. I sprang to my feet and ran for the carriage, stretching my long legs to their farthest. Griffin grasped his assailant's arm and the two men struggled for control of the knife, which seemed to be inching closer and closer to Griffin's chest. "Hold on! I'm coming—"

A hand grabbed my wrist, spinning me around. I found myself staring into the face of a tattooed sailor, his pale skin burned from sun and wind, his lips drawn back in a triumphant grin. I tried to pull free from his iron grip, but he yanked me closer. "Yer coming with me." A knife glittered in his other hand. "It's up to you in how many pieces."

No! I kicked at him, but he evaded my blows. "Have it yer way," he said, bringing the knife down.

The sailor's head snapped back, as James Kerr's fist plowed into his jaw. The knife fell, and the sailor followed it to the ground, dropped by the powerful blow.

There was no time to secure him. Mr. Kerr and I both ran for the carriage, where Griffin still fought off his attacker. Sea water filled my lungs, and made it hard to move, but…

No, wait. That wasn't right.

Cyclopean architecture loomed on every side, overlain on the prosaic trees and fountain of the park. The temple towered directly before me, and Griffin called out…but was it the real Griffin, fighting for his life, or the dweller?

No. No, not now! Not when Griffin needed me! I dug my nails into my palm, striving to hold onto reality, or at least, the reality around me. But I saw the mephitic glow in the distance, the fronds of the great creatures which seemed both worm and flower, and heard a song in a voice not remotely human. The world stuttered around me: park, city, park, city, alternating on every step. Did I breathe water or air?

The horses neighed and fidgeted, upset by the fight, held in place only by a white-faced Ruth, who'd had the presence of mind to seize the reins. The sailor's tanned face twisted into a snarl, muscles bulging beneath his suit, as he struggled to press the knife into Griffin's chest. Its tip rested against the lapel of Griffin's coat. Griffin's lips drew back from his teeth; he blinked and his eyes were golden with oblong slits, then human again.

I seized the sailor's nearest leg and fell back, using my weight to drag him with me to the ground. He let out a furious cry, and I spared a moment to wonder exactly where the knife might be, and if he would stab me instead.

Griffin leapt down, aiming a vicious kick at our assailant and sending the knife flying. Disarmed, the man bolted. For an instant, I thought Griffin would chase him down, but instead he fell to his knees beside me. "Whyborne? Are you hurt?"

I tried to swallow, but my spit had grown thick and clogged my throat.

Miles of black water stretched above me, so I closed my eyes and tried to focus my thoughts. "The dweller. It's trying to take over my mind."

Griffin's hands closed tight on my shoulders. "Fight it, Whyborne. You must fight it."

"What's wrong with him?" asked a male voice from somewhere high above me. Fathoms above me, in a world of light and wind, while I drowned in a sea of crushing darkness.

If Griffin answered, I didn't hear. An arm around my shoulders urged me up off the muck of the sea floor. Somehow, I managed to rise to my feet. Opening my eyes, I saw again the park, although other shapes trembled in the corner of my vision, ready to rush back in again.

"I'm sorry," I said, although I didn't know if I actually formed the words, or if there was even anyone to hear them. Or if I wandered alone on the ocean floor, amidst the splendor of a kingdom so ancient not even legend remained to tell of it.

"Shh, shh, it's going to be all right, my dear."

"I'll try to shut it out." I blinked at the temple. "God, Griffin, *look* at it!"

"It's not real. Don't pay any attention to it. Focus on me, Ival."

Pain spiked through my head, as if something huge pressed against the inside of my skull. I gritted my teeth and distantly wondered if the Kerrs thought I'd gone utterly mad.

Somehow, we arrived back at our house, although as far as I knew I'd stumbled across a decaying black plain, barely avoiding great rifts which belched out sulfuric water. Starfish swarmed over the rotting corpse of a whale, like a heaving carpet of spiny limbs, and I gagged at the sight.

"Here we go," Griffin said, tumbling me into my bed. "Hold on, Whyborne. You can fight it; I know you can. You're the strongest person I've ever met." Griffin gripped my arms tightly, pinning me to the bed, as if I'd tried to rise. "I won't lose you, not to this. I won't! Do you hear me?"

A great current stirred in the underwater city, sucking me back toward the temple and the thing singing inside. To my horror, I saw the barnacles had fallen away from the statues outside, revealing the faces of shark-men, their mouths full of row upon row of teeth, their hair curling like the stinging arms of an anemone.

The song grew louder, and I could almost understand what it meant, what it said. Pressure spiked in my head, and I screamed in defiance.

No. No, I would not hear its damnable words. It sought to enslave me, to make me its hands and eyes and ears upon the land, as it had done with Zeiler and the sailors. I couldn't fight its pull, but there must be some defense.

Will was everything in magic. I had to focus my intent, even when my mind insisted I was in an abyssal city of nightmare.

I tried imaging a barrier, a wall, somewhere safe. It didn't work. What wall had ever sheltered me, after all? Where had I ever felt safe? Not in the house where I'd grown up, at the mercy of my father's whims and my brother's cruelty. The string of apartments I'd lived in had barely received any imprint of my personality; they were nothing more than somewhere to snatch a few hours of sleep and store my belongings. Not until Griffin had asked me to move into his house had I ever felt at home.

Safe. Wanted.

And I was home now; I knew that much at least. How *dare* the dweller take it from me? The only person who had such a right was Griffin. I would not allow some monstrous creature to force me out one second before I had to go.

I bent all of my will to imposing an image of my room onto the colossal city before me. I clearly pictured the location of the window, the wardrobe, the feel of the sheets against my bare skin. The way it smelled, of cedar and lavender, of sheets soaked with sweat and spend after we made love, of the breeze blowing through the curtains. Even of Saul's fur, which had a peculiar sweetness to it. I imagined his purr, vibrating his entire body as he curled against my leg.

Then I locked the door and shut the window.

Something lurked outside the room I'd built in my mind. Something huge, its shadow drifting across the drawn curtains. Water lapped against the walls, but couldn't get in.

I was safe.

I opened eyes which felt gummed shut, caught a glimpse of warm candlelight and sensed Saul's purr against my leg. Griffin sat in the chair by the bed, his hand locked in mine, his mouth curled in a worried frown.

My eyelids grew too heavy and fell closed again. Exhausted from the struggle, I slipped into a mercifully dreamless sleep.

CHAPTER 18

I OPENED MY eyes and found the soft glow of the night candle illuminating the confines of my bedroom. The chair where Griffin had sat, keeping watch over me, was empty now, and even Saul had abandoned his place on the bed.

I sat up, taking in a long, shaky breath. My mind seemed my own, for the moment, at least.

I still wore my trousers, but someone had taken my coat and vest, removed cuffs and collar, and opened my shirt to the waist. Griffin, presumably. I remembered him holding on to me, bringing me to my bed…

In front of his family. He'd brought me to the house he supposedly lived in alone, to a bed in the room allegedly unoccupied. Perhaps he'd found some way of distracting his parents, or sending them away before they realized…

As if to make a mockery of my fragile hopes, the sound of voices echoed from below, up the stair and through my half-open door. "Your ma and Ruth are at the hotel. Now quit evading my question, boy!" Mr. Kerr exclaimed.

Griffin's voice held a note of misery such as I'd seldom heard. "I'm sorry, sir," he said, a little of the rural accent of his youth slipping into his voice. "I didn't want to lie, but…I didn't want you and Ma to be disappointed with me."

"I love you, son, but if you want to stay part of our family, you've got to stop this. You've got to."

I couldn't listen. Not to this. Moving to the edge of the bed, I tugged on my shoes, buttoned my shirt, and found the rest of my clothing. I had too many things to take with me at one go—perhaps I could hire someone to remove them for me, for surely I'd never set another foot here. But I had a small valise, and I pulled it from the wardrobe and stuffed whatever came to hand into it: my shaving kit, some socks, the *Arcanorum*. The hideous Valentine card Griffin had given me.

I'd keep it in my desk, wherever I ended up. Perhaps I'd take it out each February to remind myself of the few months we'd snatched from fate, before the world forced our lives back onto their inevitable courses.

My throat tightened with unshed tears, but years of pretending not to care, not to feel, helped me smooth out my expression. Picking up the valise, I went to the stairs.

Griffin and his father were in the front parlor; there was no hope to evade them. Upon hearing my step, Griffin turned to the hall. His eyes widened at the sight of me.

"Whyborne—"

"I'm not under the dweller's influence," I said hastily. What had he told his family about the attack, about my bizarre fit?

His brows drew together. "Then what are you doing?"

I glanced past him at Mr. Kerr, but the man refused to even look at me. Perhaps he blamed me for seducing Griffin. If it would make things easier for Griffin, I'd take all the blame, and gladly.

"I thought it would be better if I…if I left," I said, struggling to keep misery from my voice.

Griffin's lips parted with shock. "Why?"

I nodded in the direction of his father. "What else should I do, when you've no other choice? I can't ask you to give up your family, give up a normal life, for…this." I gestured bleakly at myself. "For a life in the shadows."

"Listen to him." The floor creaked under Mr. Kerr's boots. "Ruth will make you a fine wife. A year from now, you'll be glad to have been saved from this, just like a drunkard's glad to be saved from the bottle."

Griffin looked between us, his green eyes dark with unhappiness. "Pa, please. I'm sorry you found out like this; I'm sorry I lied. But can't you at least try to understand? To accept this is how I feel?"

His father reached out and gently gripped both Griffin's shoulders. "I can't because I care about you. I want you to have a real home. A family of your own. Someone who'll love you, who'll take care of you. Somebody to be for you what your ma has been for me."

"But I already do," Griffin protested.

Grief twisted Mr. Kerr's features. "No, you don't. He don't love you. It's just pleasures of the flesh, and the worst kind at that. Whatever you think you have, it'll never last. Let it go. Be happy."

"I *am* happy." Griffin blinked rapidly, his eyes overly bright in the gas-lit hall. "I'm sorry I can't be the son you wanted, but can't you…can't you at least try to love me as I am?"

Kerr bit his lip, tears shining on his lashes. "I do love you. But if you continue on like this, I can't have nothing to do with you. Nor your ma, or Ruth. It ain't natural."

For a long moment, no one moved. Then Griffin let out a sigh and bowed his head. "Leave."

I couldn't breathe through the bands constricting my chest. "I...of course."

"Not you." Griffin took a step back from his father and toward me. "Him."

What? I couldn't have heard right. I balanced on a razor edge of pain, because this had to be another delusion.

But it wasn't. Kerr's eyes widened. "You don't mean that."

Griffin folded his arms over his chest, shoulders hunched, as if expecting a blow. "Please. Just go."

"You're really choosing him over your family?"

"Whyborne *is* my family."

Moving slowly, as if sure Griffin would change his mind, Kerr went to the door and opened it. Pausing on the threshold, he said, "Your ma and I will pray for you."

Then, wiping his face as if to dash away tears, he hurried out, leaving the door open behind him. As he reached the iron gate, Griffin looked up and after him, wetness shining on his lashes. "Bye, Pa," he said in a small, lost voice.

I stepped past him and gently shut the door. When I turned back, he flung himself into my arms, his whole body shaking against me.

"I just wanted them to love me," he whispered into my coat. "To not wish they'd picked some other boy from the orphan train."

In that moment, I hated Kerr for doing this to Griffin. How could anyone raise such a son, brave and clever and wonderful, and then just throw him away?

"I'm sorry, my darling," I said, holding him tight. "I never, ever meant to make you choose between us."

Griffin shook his head and pulled away, just far enough to look up at me through eyes brimming with tears. "You didn't. He did."

"But—"

"Don't you understand?" His arms tightened around me. "I l-love Ma and Pa, but...I can't lose you. I can't. Not to the dweller, or to society, or to anything else."

He kissed me, hard and desperate, his teeth bruising my lip. "Don't leave," he begged between kisses. His breath had gone ragged, and he trembled against me. "God, Ival, please."

"I won't."

"Show me." His hip pressed against my thigh. His fingers slipped from my hair, shaping my body, tugging at my coat. "Show me you feel the same."

"Yes."

I took his hand and pulled him after me. The night candle yet burned in the bedroom, and Griffin pulled away long enough to drag the chair from the bedside, before sliding out of his coat.

I went for the buttons on his vest, kissing him as I did so. We undressed each other, our breathing ragged and raw. I sat on the edge of the bed, and he moved to straddle my lap, the hot length of his member pressing against mine. Threading his fingers again through my hair, he tilted my head back to kiss me, his hips flexing to rub our bodies together.

"My dear." His voice rasped with emotion.

"Yes," I breathed back.

Griffin shoved me back onto the bed, stretching his body over mine, his hands tracing the contours of my chest and sides. I ran my fingers across his shoulders, gasping and arching under him. He nuzzled into my neck, biting lightly on my ear until I squirmed against him, before tracing my throat with his tongue.

"Say you won't leave me," he begged. "I'm broken and scarred and selfish, but I swear, you're the most important thing in the world to me."

"I'm not leaving you," I insisted. How could he think otherwise, considering our current activity? "I'm yours, for as long as you want me."

He stilled and pulled back, his face revealed to me in the soft glow of the night candle. "What if I want you forever?"

My breath caught. I'd never allowed myself to consider our relationship in the long term. Griffin wouldn't have invited me to move in had he not found my company agreeable, but I'd striven not to let my fancy stray beyond the next few months, perhaps the next holiday. Because, of course, he would tire of me, or the burden of our secrets would grow too great, or he would one day wake up and realize he could do better than a gawky, bookish creature such as myself.

His expression faltered; I'd hesitated too long. "I…forgive me, I shouldn't have…"

I rolled over and took him with me, so I was on top. My heart pounded and I couldn't quite catch my breath, but I framed his face with my hands and stared directly into his gaze.

"Yes," I said.

His smile bloomed, better and brighter to me than a thousand electric bulbs. He flipped us back over, bending down over me and whispering, "Say it again."

"Yes." I kissed the nearest patch of exposed skin within reach, on his arm. "Yes. I-I wish to be with you until the breath leaves my body, until the last stars burn out and the earth falls into the dying sun."

His lips pressed against mine with bruising intensity, his arms and legs flexing to rub his body against mine. The feel of skin on skin made me groan into his kiss. He caught my tongue in his mouth, sucking hard, his erection leaving a slick trail on my belly.

"I want you," he panted, when he finally pulled back. "Want in you."

My mouth went dry with lust and anticipation, so I only nodded frantic agreement. He grabbed one of the pillows and stuffed it beneath my hips, before retrieving what we needed from the nightstand. When he turned back to me, he paused, running his gaze over my exposed form. Heat suffused my cheeks at his scrutiny, but my cock bobbed against my stomach, responding to the hunger in his eyes.

"My Ival," he murmured.

Slick fingers pressed against me, and I breathed deep, opening to him, letting him do anything he wanted. I'd always trusted him with my body, and with a great deal of my heart. But I'd always held a little something back in reserve, a part which refused to think of a real future with him.

I could blame it on my knowledge of the uncertainty and fragility of life. We'd almost died on more than one occasion, and for all we knew, the dweller would emerge onto land and kill us all by the end of the week. But I'd be lying if I blamed my reticence on anything other than my own fear, my determination not to be surprised when he finally left me.

He shifted into position, and I clasped my legs against his flanks, feeling the broad head of his cock press against my passage. "Griffin?"

The candlelight turned the light sheen of sweat on his forehead into gold. He stopped, not moving, his eyes nearly black with desire. "Yes, my dear? Is something wrong? Shall I stop?"

"No." I swallowed hard against the constriction in my throat, the fear which tried to steal away my words. Why had intimacy of the body always come easier to me than that of words? Was it because I had built my life around language, and so believed something once spoken had a weight and a truth it hadn't before? "I just…You chose tonight. Chose me. And I just wanted to say I choose this, too. A life with you."

He pushed into me. I gasped, back arching, legs tightening, seeking to draw him deeper. I abandoned words and let my body speak for me, reveling in the feel of him opening and filling me. He bent over me, beautiful, the muscles of his shoulders taut, his curls stuck to his forehead by sweat. Bracing himself with one hand while he stared into my eyes, he wrapped the other around my aching member.

A sharp cry of ecstasy escaped me, and I writhed under him, wanting to thrust and be thrust into. I ran my palms over his arms, his shoulders, his chest, before catching the tight buds of his nipples in my fingers and pinching. Now it was his turn to hiss in pleasure.

"You are everything to me," he whispered. "The light to guide me through my days. The cove shielding me in the storm."

"Griffin…"

He shifted slightly, changing the angle between us, and the head of his cock dragged over just the right spot inside me. My whole body jerked, electrified, and I gasped, "There!"

He obliged, keeping the angle, his fist tugging on my cock even as he sent shockwaves of pleasure through me with every thrust. I couldn't possibly last, and I had just enough breath in my lungs to call his name as the tidal wave of my orgasm crashed down over me.

CHAPTER 19

GRIFFIN GROWLED WORDLESSLY when I clenched around him. A moment later, his head went back, spine arching, pushing hard against me. Then he collapsed forward, catching himself on his palms.

For a moment, there was no sound but our breathing: rough and ragged, returning only gradually to normal. With a sigh, he eased gently away from me, pausing only long enough to brush a kiss across my forehead before padding to the washbasin.

"Stay where you are," he said. He returned shortly with a wet cloth, cool against my overheated skin. I sighed happily.

The bed creaked under his weight. My limbs felt boneless and heavy, and I wanted badly to sink down into sleep. But instead I turned onto my side to face Griffin, catching his near hand in mine. "Will you be all right?" I asked.

A shadow passed over his face, but he nodded. "Yes."

"Given my relationship with Father, I can only imagine how you must feel," I said. "But I know it's hard for you."

"Yes." He shifted closer, tangling our legs together. "Maybe a part of me knew this was coming, ever since the first time I left Kansas, and the last few days have been my final, foolish attempt to stave off the inevitable. Or perhaps I truly did believe I could have it both ways."

"If I hadn't succumbed to the dweller's influence…"

"Hush." He kissed me tenderly. "You haven't done anything wrong, so stop apologizing. Just…hold me, please."

"Of course." I wrapped my arms around him, and he laid his head on my shoulder. Together we lay in warm silence, but it was a long time before either of us could sleep.

~ * ~

We both slept poorly; although Griffin didn't have a full fit, he woke me thrashing and whimpering several times, in the grip of nightmares. Sleep returned slower and slower with each awakening. In the end, we both rose and dressed with the dawn.

Which turned out to be just as well, given Christine chose to pound on our door before we'd even finished breakfast.

"Ah, good, you are still alive," she said when I opened the door.

"Er, yes," I said. "I take it Griffin sent word?"

"He said you'd been attacked by cultists, were unwounded, but under some sort of psychic assault from the creature. I would have come immediately, but unfortunately, I chose last night to attend the opera, and it was quite late by the time I returned to the boarding house and found his note waiting." She eyed me closely. "So what were the two of you doing when you were attacked, and why the devil didn't you ask me to go with you?"

"It was just a trip to the park!" I exclaimed, exasperated. "And Griffin did invite you, remember?"

Her eyes widened. "Oh. I had no idea. I'd assumed something happened to divert you from your planned evening."

"Unfortunately, no." I glanced behind me to make certain Griffin hadn't come out into the hall, then stepped onto the porch with Christine. "His parents were there," I said in a low voice. "They...found out."

"Oh." She pursed her lips. "I did warn him. Well, how bad is it?"

"Griffin told his father to leave." I normally wouldn't speak of our intimate life with Christine, but I needed to talk about it to someone. "The man threatened to cut off all contact if Griffin didn't give me up, and, well, there you have it."

"Good for Griffin," Christine agreed, as though I hadn't just said something extraordinary. "He seems to have learned his damned lesson, so we can all look forward to a great deal less drama in the future."

"I...well, I suppose." I lowered my voice even further. "But Griffin...he said...he wants our arrangement to be *permanent!*" The last word came out as more of a squeak than I'd intended. "Um, assuming we don't all die in the next few days, anyway."

"Well at least there's one thing he's sensible about."

I folded my arms over my chest. "I don't think you're taking this any of this very seriously."

"I think it's too early to deal with any of this before I've even had coffee, especially having been up half the night worrying about you."

"Oh." I winced. "I'm sorry. Please, come inside and have breakfast."

"Thank you."

I'd assumed she'd keep my confidence, but as soon as we entered the kitchen, where Griffin poured a cup of coffee for her, she said, "Congratulations on coming to your senses and asking Whyborne to put up with you on a permanent basis."

"Christine!" I exclaimed. Forget the griddle; Griffin could just fry our breakfast eggs on my face.

"What?" she asked, taking her coffee from Griffin.

"I meant it as a confidence!"

"Well, I assumed Griffin knew about it already, considering," she said with a shrug.

Griffin unsuccessfully tried to hide his smile behind his own coffee. "Indeed. Thank you, Christine. I am pleased Whyborne agreed to such an arrangement."

"You blasted well ought to be." She sat at the table and began to stir sugar into her cup.

Griffin winced. "Yes, well…you were right. I should never have taken things as far as I did. It was selfish of me."

"Indeed, it was." She sipped her coffee and made an appreciative sound. "Ah, much better than the swill the landlady makes. Now, tell me what happened yesterday."

I let Griffin relate the facts. When he finished, Christine absently tapped her spoon against her cup. "They seem rather keen on killing you and Whyborne. Zeiler, at least, perceives you as a threat, which I take to be a good sign."

"I don't think they were going to kill me," I said, remembering the threats of the sailor. "He told me to come with him, and didn't try to use the knife until I refused."

Griffin frowned. "That makes no sense."

"I agree. And they were certainly trying to kill me when I encountered them earlier."

"Perhaps they know their god is trying to take over Whyborne's mind?" Christine suggested.

"Which only begs the question: what does it want with Whyborne?" Griffin replied.

"Perhaps it knows I can use magic?" I suggested reluctantly, not happy to give Griffin more ammunition for his argument against my using the *Arcanorum*.

"Perhaps." He didn't sound entirely convinced, however. "I'll go to the docks today and discover if there is anything I can learn. Someone must have seen or heard something that might be of use. Or if I can find one of the cultists and get him alone, I might force him to tell me when they intend to summon the dweller, and why they're interested in you all of a sudden."

It didn't seem like much of a plan to me, but I had no better suggestion. Christine seemed to come to the same conclusion, pursing her lips unhappily. "As you wish. I'll go to the museum and attempt to do something useful, in the hope monsters from the deep don't overrun the world. Send word immediately if you need my assistance."

"Of course," Griffin said.

"And what about me?" I asked. "Do you want me to come to the docks with you?"

Griffin winced. "It may not be safe for you," he said carefully. "If you were to suddenly be overcome by the dweller's influence…"

I didn't like it…but I couldn't argue, either. "You're right," I said unhappily. "I'm a liability now."

"No." He reached out and put his hand over mine, squeezing gently. "Stay here and look through the *Arcanorum* and folio your father sent."

Christine drained her coffee and rose to her feet. "Well, then. I shall see you gentlemen later. Good luck, Griffin. You too, Whyborne. And hold steady: your mind is too fine to waste on some aquatic monster."

The tips of my ears grew warm at her compliment. "Thank you."

Once she left, I said, "I assume you wish me to stay home so you can bind me to my chair, to prevent me from wandering off in the dweller's grasp again?"

Griffin gave me a flirtatious smile. "Well, there is something to be said for the idea of tying you up and having you at my mercy."

I shifted in my seat, my trousers suddenly uncomfortably tight. "Be serious."

"I don't think we need to go quite so far as to bind you all day," he said, sobering. "Do you have any warning before the dweller takes over?"

"A bit." I remembered the taste of saltwater in the library, the flickering images from the park.

"I have a pair of handcuffs. I'll leave them with you, and take the key with me. If you find yourself falling under its influence, cuff yourself immediately to something heavy."

"Oh." It seemed as good a plan as any.

He leaned over and kissed me on the cheek, before rising to his feet. "And if you don't have to use them, we'll keep them out for later."

A few hours later, I sat in the study, pouring over both the notes from the Brotherhood and the *Arcanorum* in hopes of finding something, anything, which might thwart the dweller's followers. The handcuffs lay on the desk beside my books, a constant reminder the creature might reach out to me at any moment. Was its influence stronger at times, perhaps correlating with the tides? Or had my ability to eventually lock it out of my mind convinced it to find other, easier prey?

Despite what Griffin said, in truth, I was a liability. What if we should find some method of putting a halt to the Eyes' plans, and, at the moment I was most needed, the dweller should take over? What if it succeeded in doing more than it had so far, of truly turning me into its puppet?

What if Griffin was hurt because of me?

No. I couldn't allow it to happen. There had to be a way to stop the creature, and I would find it. I had to.

And if I didn't? If the visions grew worse, stronger? If it turned me into a slave, or broke my mind, leaving me a raving lunatic?

I tried to return my concentration to my reading, but it proved difficult. Saul wandered in and curled up in my lap, but even his purr failed to soothe my nerves. How long would I have to sit here helplessly and wonder?

A knock on the door startled me from my thoughts.

Odd. I wasn't expecting anyone. Perhaps Griffin had discovered something and sent me a message, asking me to come to him?

Dislodging Saul from my lap, I went to the door. On the other side stood the sailor who'd attacked me in the park yesterday, a bruise shadowing his jaw where James Kerr had struck him.

I tried to slam the door in his face, but he was too quick for me. "There'll be none of that, Dr. Whyborne," he said, leering at the sight of my fear. "We tried to do this the easy way, but ye wouldn't cooperate. Yer choice, but I'm thinking yer friend wishes ye'd picked the other option."

My heart thudded. My friend? Griffin? Did they have Griffin?

A carriage sat at the curb. At the sailor's signal, someone threw open the door so I could see inside. Another man, this one dressed like an attendant from the asylum, sat inside. Beside him, pale and terrified, was James Kerr.

"We saw him at the park with ye," the sailor said. "So the boss hopes his life is important to ye. Myself, I'm hoping it ain't, because then my friend gets to put a bullet in the geezer's head." He rubbed his jaw.

I stood frozen, staring at the man who had broken Griffin's heart only a few hours ago. Who had thrown away the only son he'd ever had, for no other reason than Griffin had fallen in love with me.

I hated him for the tears I'd wiped from Griffin's eyes. For not caring he'd raised a good, brave man.

But I couldn't let him die.

"Very well," I said. "Take me to your master."

CHAPTER 20

THE ATTENDANT DROVE back to Stormhaven, lashing the horse the entire way. I sat beside Kerr, our abductors across from us. A jolt knocked the older man into me, but when I reached to steady him, he pulled sharply away.

"I'm sorry," I said. "Don't worry. It will be fine." I rather suspected it wouldn't be fine at all, but felt I had to say something.

I received a glare in return. "What have you involved my boy in?"

"Keep it quiet." The sailor waved a knife leisurely in my direction. "That goes double for ye. Ye done for George with his own gun. Try to cast a spell on me, I'll cut yer bloody tongue out."

I obeyed, but my mind raced, searching for any way out. At least Nella and Ruth hadn't been taken. Had the cult chosen James because the police would more quickly investigate the disappearance of a respectable woman? Or had he simply been convenient?

Thank God they hadn't taken Griffin. I could only pray nothing happened to reveal his disguise.

What would he think, when he returned home to find me gone? That the dweller had taken me, mind and body? Surely, Mrs. Kerr would turn to him for help finding her husband, wouldn't she? Would Griffin realize our disappearances were related, or would he put it down to coincidence?

The carriage rounded a bend, jolting through potholes. The weather had turned breezy, and I caught glimpses of the sea far below, the waves lashed to whitecaps well out into the bay. The scent of salt water and dead things reached me even here...or was it yet another sending from the dweller?

No. I clenched my hands, driving my nails into my palms to center myself. I would not let it into my mind; I would not let it plant visions in my head. I wouldn't. Not now, not when any distraction could doom both Kerr and myself.

The gates of Stormhaven loomed up before us, opening to welcome the carriage, then shutting with a clang behind us. As the driver came to a halt near the steps, the door swung open, disgorging several attendants.

I tried to think of some way to fight back, but with Kerr hostage, no solutions came to mind. I had to trust an opportunity would present itself within the asylum, so I didn't resist when they hauled me roughly from the carriage. They hustled us both inside. Kerr tried to protest, yelling they couldn't do this, that his wife would have the police arrest them all. A blow silenced him.

"How brave, to strike an old man," I said with an outrage I hoped covered the fear pounding through my blood.

"We'll do a lot worse to you," the attendant sneered. "Take the geezer to the ward and lock him up where he can't cause trouble. It's the fourth floor for this one."

I cursed, digging in my heels, but they dragged me relentlessly to the stairs. Where were the other doctors? Dead? Enslaved? If I called for help, did anyone remain to answer my pleas—assuming they didn't put it down to the ravings of yet another lunatic?

Or would anyone even hear me over the screams already filling the air? Shrieks echoed all around, from every floor. Did the patients feel the coming of the dweller?

The cries grew louder as we reached the fourth floor. The attendants unlocked the door onto the ward and dragged me inside. The ward somehow seemed even worse in the daylight. The stench of waste and sweat filled the close, late-summer air, and I struggled not to gag. Chains rattled and beds creaked, and sobs and moans mingled with the shrieks of terror.

Zeiler awaited us, amidst the painted swirls and arcane symbols decorating the floor, ceiling, and walls. At the sight of me, his mouth twisted into a triumphant smile which turned my blood cold. "Dr. Whyborne," he said. "So kind of you to join us at last."

"What do you want with me?" I demanded. My voice shook, despite my best efforts to hold steady.

Zeiler stepped closer. "I want to show you something," he said. Drawing forth his pocket watch, he held it up, letting it spin and catch the light.

Had the touch of the dweller driven the man mad? What on earth did he mean by this? And yet…there was something oddly fascinating about the way it swung, how it glittered in the light.

"That's it. Relax," Zeiler murmured. "Listen to my voice."

There was an odd symbol cast on the watchcase. An eye?

Something pressed against me, but it wasn't a true physical force. Something pushing, nudging, carried on the sound of Zeiler's sonorous tone straight into my brain. "My voice is all that exists. Let go. I know you're troubled. Who among us is not? But I can take the pain away. The regret."

My shoulders slumped beneath the weight of those regrets. I had cost Griffin his family. If Kerr died here, he would lose even more. And now Griffin was off somewhere and I didn't know where, and if the cult had caught him…

"I know you've carried burdens, which would break any man," Zeiler went on. The watch twisted and turned, and found I no longer wished to look away. "Lay them down and let me take them for you. How wonderful it will be to allow someone else to make the hard choices."

A feeling of relief flooded me. I could stop fighting. Stop worrying. Rest. Let Zeiler make all the decisions…

No.

"Just let go and let me tell you what to do."

To the devil with that. I hadn't let my father tell me what to do. Why should I let this man, this monster who had imprisoned Griffin in an asylum, who had tried to kill us, do so in his stead?

"Let go."

"No!" I tore my gaze from the pocket watch, feeling it like a physical effort. Fear coursed through me, diluting anger, and I stumbled back into the attendant behind me.

Zeiler took a step back, his eyes going wide in surprise, before narrowing in anger. "I see. It would have saved us all a great deal of trouble had you cooperated, Dr. Whyborne. But that's been the case from the beginning."

I forced my shoulders straight, horribly aware of the attendant behind me and of the other two in front. Perhaps I could use the wind spell to knock them aside and make a run for it? But the doors were all locked, and the alarm would surely spread quickly. Not to mention they'd still have Kerr in their hands.

Still, I had to do something. If I could just stun them, maybe I could find a weapon and turn the tables by taking Zeiler hostage.

"What do you want from me?" I asked, buying time while I began to trace the sigil on my palm, I hoped discreetly. "You've gone to a lot of trouble to get me here."

"I didn't realize you were a sorcerer when we first met," Zeiler said. "But you made a mistake, when you encountered my men alone on the street. You left one alive to tell the tale of how you conjured fire from the air and made his comrade's gun explode in his hand. I'm sure your father is very proud of you."

The devil? "My father?"

Zeiler arched a brow. "Jones, please stop Dr. Whyborne from casting a spell."

The attendant behind me roughly seized my arms. I kicked back at him and tried to struggle, but his hands were like iron. One of the other men stepped up and slugged me in the jaw.

My head snapped back, and stars spangled my vision. My head swam from the blow, and I couldn't summon the concentration for even the simple fire spell.

"Let go!" I choked out, struggling pointlessly in their grasp.

"The Brotherhood looked down on me," Zeiler said, as if there had been no interruption to our conversation. "They thought my lineage wasn't good enough to join them. Oh, I didn't know it at first. I was a naïve fool.

"My father captained a whaling ship, but when he died, it destroyed our family. We almost starved—my youngest sister did starve! The Eyes of Nodens helped—they look after their own, but they are not by and large wealthy men themselves. But I persevered and clawed my way out of the gutter. I became a respected man, a doctor, and, at last, the superintendent of this very asylum."

His face darkened. "But none of my accomplishments mattered to the Brotherhood. They used me, and I let myself be used, waiting for my reward. But there was no reward save contempt. They—your father—looked down on me for my heritage, no different than the men who kicked my mother when she begged on the street, no different than the ones who let my sister starve."

"My father," I started to say, but the attendant cuffed me on my aching head.

"Will die screaming," Zeiler said with a malevolent grin. "The Eyes value me. They know I can help them to greatness. Behold." He gestured to the sigils and swirls. "The electro-therapeutic cabinet inspired me. All those individual cells, linked together to generate a powerful current. Could I not to the same with the minds of those already attuned to the touch of the dweller in the deep? Could I not link them together and turn Stormhaven itself into a giant psychic battery, capable of bringing the god onto land?"

Damn it. I knew this electrical craze would be the death of me. "And then what?" I asked, surprised my voice didn't shake with fear. "What possible good can come of this?"

Zeiler laughed. "With a god at my command? Your imagination must be very limited indeed, Dr. Whyborne. My word will be law, and men will bow before me. I will raise up the Eyes, reward them for their service, and cast down everyone who spat on us. Starting with your father." He took a step closer to me, his eyes burning with a mad light. "But my psychic battery isn't finished. Unlike a chemical battery, it requires a special type of mind to complete the circuit. Someone whose will has been shaped by the use of sorcery. Imagine my joy when I discovered not only could I finish my great work, but I'd use Niles Whyborne's own son to do it."

Oh God. I had to get away, before they used me to create horror. Had I thought myself a liability earlier? The truth was far worse. If I didn't escape, I'd be responsible for the deaths of everyone I'd ever loved.

I redoubled my struggles, striving to bite or kick. One of the attendants swore and struck me across the back of the head, adding a new burst of pain to my already aching skull.

"You believe it a good thing you resisted mesmerization better than that fool Allan?" Zeiler asked; it was hard to hear him through the ringing in my ears. "I assure you, we have other ways of breaking your will. Gentlemen, take him to one of the seclusion cells and calm him down. I'll prepare the injection."

Injection? Did he mean the *oculares* potion? Dear heavens, the dweller already entered my mind far too easily—what would an injection to do me?

I fought them with all my strength, but they routinely handled far more violent men than myself, and easily dragged me down the reeking hall, past the other inmates. Screams and howls rose from every room, the madmen struggling against their bindings or slamming into the doors, as if in a panic to get out before the monster in their dreams erupted into reality.

My jailers flung open a door to a windowless room with a sink. Tiles covered the walls, and a drain pierced the center of the floor. Chains hung from walls and ceiling and curled across the floor. The attendants finally released me with a shove, which sent me into the wall.

"Strip," one of them ordered.

I spun and faced them, my breathing growing faster. "Wh-what?"

"Take off your clothes."

"No!" I gathered my feet under me and tried to run past them, but found myself seized again. One of them locked his arm around my neck; I clawed and fought, but the pressure was relentless, and my consciousness faded before it. Just before blackness entirely clouded my vision, he let up; while I gasped and wheezed for breath, I felt hands on me, stripping first my jacket, then fumbling at the buttons of my vest.

"Be careful—he's got some nice stuff," said the man who had been strangling me. I struggled, and he tightened his arm again, as casually as if he did this every day. "Maybe we can get a good penny for it."

Perhaps they *did* do this every day; at any rate, in a frighteningly short time, they removed every stitch of clothing from my body. While I gasped for breath, they snapped manacles around my wrists and ankles. I swayed, but the chains attached to my arms kept me from falling. I found myself standing naked, arms out, my legs slightly spread.

Before I had time to feel anything besides utter humiliation spiked with terror, one of the attendants took a rubber hose from the sink and attached it to the spigot. A moment later, a jet of ice-cold water hit me full on. Every muscle went tense on instinct, my chest seized, and I choked on the spray. I twisted my head desperately to one side, trying to keep the stream away from my nose and mouth so I could breathe, and ended up with an earful of cold water.

I strove to concentrate on the water spell, to turn their weapon back on them. I felt the water's weight on my skin, tasted it in my mouth. It began to curl around me, taking form…

"There'll be none of that, Dr. Whyborne," Zeiler said. One of the attendants hit me again, breaking my concentration, and the water splashed harmlessly to the ground.

The drenching seemed to go on forever, until I shook so hard I could barely keep my weight from depending fully on the chains. My teeth chattered, and my thoughts turned sluggish. I couldn't get enough breath, and my toes burned in the cold runoff rushing to the drain.

Dear God, did they mean to kill me?

"Enough," Zeiler said.

The stream of water thankfully disappeared, but my shaking didn't stop, the air sucking warmth from my bare skin. I blinked water out of my eyes and tried to focus on the doctor. He approached me with a syringe, its needle glittering in the single light of the room. Both the attendants watched avidly, and humiliation and fear scalded me in turn, to be thus exposed to their rude gazes.

Zeiler seized my arm. I tried to protest, but my teeth chattered too hard. The needle stung as it punctured my skin; I caught a glimpse of swirling blood as he pulled back the plunger to make sure it was correctly seated.

The he pushed it in, and molten lead poured into my vein. I screamed and tried to pull away, but he gripped my arm and the chains held me fast. The potion moved inside me, like some sentient thing, squirming through my vein, up my arm, into my shoulder.

What would happen when it reached my heart?

"That should do it," Zeiler said. He turned and made for the door. "Come. We have things to do, and time grows short."

The last attendant out turned off the electric switch, so the only light remaining came through the door. Then it swung shut, and the lock grated home, leaving me alone in the dark.

The *oculares* potion crept through my shoulder and coursed downward, following the great vein and describing an arc across my chest. I tried to will it back, but of course it was impossible; I could only stand there in my chains, naked and freezing cold, and wait for the inevitable.

I'd fought off the dweller before, but with the damnable potion in me, the chances of doing so again seemed slim. Still, I tried to imagine the warm blanket of my home around me, the doors locked against the monsters outside, but the cold had sapped away too much of my strength.

Then the potion reached my heart, and was sent rushing out through the rest of my body.

I wasn't alone any more.

CHAPTER 21

I TOPPLED FORWARD, hands and knees striking the floor of the undersea temple. I had the impression of something immense, something nearly beyond comprehension, trying to fold itself to fit inside my skull. Pain spiked through my head, and I tasted blood.

Currents stirred my hair as something approached. A pair of familiar shoes came into view, then stopped, as if waiting for me to acknowledge them. Feeling as if a tremendous weight pushed down against me, I struggled to my feet. I was fully clothed, my ordinary suit heavy against my skin.

Griffin stood before me, but his eyes were gold, with the misshapen pupils of a cuttlefish. He—it—didn't look triumphant, as I'd expected. Quite the opposite, in fact.

The thing with Griffin's face spoke, and the *oculares* must have truly broken down the final barriers, because at last I understood what it had been trying to say to me all along. It was what Amelie had tried to tell me on my first visit to Stormhaven.

"Help me," it said. "Help me!"

Even though I knew it wasn't him, the plea in my lover's voice sent an ache through my heart. Where was the real Griffin? What had become of him?

What had become of me? The undersea temple seemed so very real.

No. I had to focus. "What are you?" I asked. "You aren't Griffin, so stop pretending."

It cocked its head to the side and blinked its strange eyes. "We take the forms we find in your mind." Its voice was still Griffin's…and yet I felt as if some vast, subsonic song preceded it just slightly, too low to hear save as a vibration in my very blood and bones.

That didn't sound promising. "We? There are more of you?"

"Yes." Griffin paced past me, and I lost sight of him.

And I hung naked from my chains, back in Stormhaven. But the rank scent of the sea filled the windowless room, and ocean water swirled around my feet. Blood slicked my upper lip, running from my nose and eyes. I licked it away. "Why are you doing this?"

A flicker, and I was neither in the temple nor the asylum, but swimming, my body vast, cutting through the ocean. Moving up and up, from heavy darkness into lighter regions, drawn helplessly by the tether of chanting voices, the weight of the water lessening, and it *hurt*...

"We do nothing," the dweller snarled, and I stood in the temple again, clothed but still tasting blood. "For millennia, we have watched the land, touching the minds of sensitive humans. They are our eyes and ears, the tools we use to explore places we cannot easily go."

"But you're coming to the surface now!" I argued. "You intend to dominate the land, or at least Zeiler seems to think so."

"You know nothing." It was suddenly far too close to me, misshapen eyes glaring into mine. The pressure in my head spiked—

—and I hung from my chains. "Help me!" Griffin screamed in my face.

The stone floor of the temple met my knee yet again, and I sucked in lungfuls of water. My thoughts scattered like a school of fish before a shark. "You need my help," I managed to gasp. "Why?"

The thing walked past me, hands clasped behind its back. "Humankind worshipped us as gods," it said with a sneer. "Tiamat. Nodens. Poseidon. But in this new age, men have cast aside their deities. They seek now to control."

Blood floated from my nose to swirl in the water in front of my face, staining whatever currents moved here in the depths. "Control?" What was it Zeiler had said? That he would have a god at his command? "Do you mean to say Zeiler is summoning you against your will?"

"We can survive on the surface, on your land, but it is painful to us. Long ago we retreated to the depths in which we spawned, content to watch." The thing masquerading as Griffin came to a halt in front of me, horrid eyes unblinking. "This Zeiler wishes to force me to the surface, to do his bidding. I have touched his dreams many times. His father belonged to us. From his ship, which hunted whales, the father showed us many things, showed us the growing strength of humankind. But we did not understand the threat they posed.

"Then this insect began to experiment, to link minds together. In desperation, I found your dreaming mind and called to you for help, but you would not hear me until now." The dweller looked away. "When it is too late."

"No." The creature before me was utterly alien, no matter what forms it plucked from my mind. Its thoughts crowded my own, heavy and strange. Its kind had made use of humans throughout history, turning us into servants of their curiosity, but right now, it needed help. "It isn't too late. Perhaps I can still do something to stop Zeiler."

It looked back at me, and I tried to focus on Griffin's familiar features instead of its eyes. Where was the real Griffin right now? Was he hurt? Captured? Dead?

"You would help me?" it asked in his voice, and yet not.

I swallowed, tasting blood and seawater. "You don't want to come to the surface, and I certainly don't want you here. So yes, I will do whatever I can to help you."

"Good." It smiled a ghastly smile. "With the *oculares* opening your mind, you can draw on my power. Do so."

"Er, all right?" I said, not at all sure what I had just agreed to.

The pressure in my head spiked. I screamed, spine arching, and blood trickled down the back of my throat.

I was in the asylum, alone, naked, and freezing. My arms hurt, and warm blood slicked the manacles, where I had struggled against them unknowing.

Power flooded into me: wild and unbridled as the waves pounding the rocks. I felt as though I might cast every spell in the *Arcanorum* at once without effort: call up a storm, or raise the dead, or burn Widdershins to the ground. I'd go to Whyborne House and make my father listen to me for once in his damned life; I'd track down Stanford and make him weep and beg. I'd make Griffin's parents sorry they had ever hurt him. Then I'd take Griffin home and fuck him hard, for hours.

A key grated in the lock, catching my attention. The door swung open, and the night watchman shuffled in, shining his light into my eyes. The smell of sweat and musk rose from his skin, and I knew his intent even before he shut the door again and began to unbutton his trousers.

"Well now," he said, pulling out his hardening member, "let's see what sort of fun we can have."

"Yes," I said with a smile like a shark's. "Let's."

The power of the dweller poured through me. It was easy, so very easy, with the dweller's thoughts weaving through my own. I reached out with my will as if with a physical hand, grasped the flame in the watchman's lantern, and urged it into an inferno.

Glass shattered from the heat, the kerosene igniting all at once. The watchman let out a cry of surprise and terror. It turned into a scream as the flames caught on his sagging trousers. He shrieked and flailed, beating at the fire, but it wouldn't go out until I willed it.

I didn't will it until his movements stopped altogether.

I hung from the chains, smelling roasted flesh and hair and clothes, the tide crashing on the rocks beneath Stormhaven beating in my blood. I was there, but I also swam through the water, up and up, drawn inexorably by the call like a harpooned whale.

A hum filled the room, the painted sigils on its walls and floor glowing. I felt the minds of the other captives around me, bent and broken, mesmerized by Zeiler into summoning the dweller.

I had to break the circuit. I twisted, tugging on the chains, power and magic slithering through my veins. None of it would help me here. If I tried to melt the chains, I'd roast myself within the small enclosure of the room.

The door swung open, and a young woman entered. I had to struggle through the alien thoughts coating the inside of my skull to remember her name. "Amelie," I said.

She stepped lightly past the smoking heap which was all that remained of the night watchman, pausing only to spit on his corpse. No doubt I wasn't the first helpless inmate he'd meant to victimize, just the first who could fight back. Turning from him, Amelie pulled a pin from her strawberry hair and set to working the locks on my chains. As she did so, she rested her hand lightly on my shoulder.

Something about the humanness of the touch shocked me back into myself. The dweller was still with me, but pushed to the back of my mind. I realized with a flush of horror I was completely naked in front of her. "Oh dear heavens! I-I'm so sorry. Please...well you can't really close your eyes, I suppose, but, er, oh."

My face felt unnaturally hot, and the situation only became worse when she paused what she was doing and cast a thoughtful gaze over me.

"You're pretty," she said.

Why didn't I know any spells which might actually be useful? Like conjuring a decent suit from nothingness?

The manacle fell away, and I hurriedly did what I could to cover myself with my hand. I swore Griffin would never find out about this. Or, good lord, Christine.

Assuming any of us survived.

I stumbled a bit when I was free, my legs aching from being forced into a single position for...how long had it been, anyway? How long had I been in the dream sent by the dweller, while it crawled through my brain?

How much longer did I have before the dweller reached the surface?

I closed my eyes, felt a strange shock go through me, like a vibration of some huge drum. For an instant, I was in the ocean, trailing streamers of kelp wrapped around my limbs as I swam toward the surface. Lithe shapes cut through the water around me, their mouths filled with serrated teeth, their hair the stinging tentacles of an anemone. But they were helpless to save me from my enslavers.

The sea tasted different here. It tasted of the land.

I/we were close.

I opened my eyes again, staggering and disoriented. I could feel the dweller as a pressure in my mind, feel the sluggish churn of the injection in my veins. "We have to hurry," I gasped.

Amelie led the way out of the room. I tried not to look down at the body of the dead man. A part of me was horrified at what I'd done, but I remembered his hands unbuttoning his trousers, the way Amelie had spit on him. Remembered, too, Griffin's nightmares.

Remorse washed away, like sand before the tide.

I paused at the doorway, studying the glowing lines of magic. Leaving the room would remove me from Zeiler's battery and break the circuit. Which likely meant he'd know of my escape instantly.

There was nothing for it. I stepped out, felt something like a pop in my ears, a tingle rushing across my skin. The ward now lay eerily silent, all the inmates motionless on their beds or their floors, staring into nothing. Had the psychic battery drained them somehow? Would it have done the same to me, had the vast power of the dweller not poured through me?

"I brought clothes," Amelie said, picking up a neatly-folded bundle from the floor outside. "I stole them from the clothing room on my ward."

"How did you know…never mind." I communicated telepathically with a monster from the deep. Asking how Amelie had known I'd be here, or what I'd need, seemed absurd in light of that. I took the bundle and shook it out, only to find she'd brought me a woman's dressing gown and a pair of embroidered slippers.

I stared at the dressing gown—paisley, with a great deal of lace at the collar and cuffs—in dismay. "Do you like it?" Amelie asked anxiously.

"Well, at least the slippers match the gown," I said. There was nothing for it; my only other choice was to go naked, which I certainly had no intention of doing. I pulled on the dressing gown; the sleeves ended just below my elbows, and the hem swished around my calves, but at least it had a belt to fasten about my waist. "Thank you. And thank you for your rescue."

"Do I get a kiss?"

"No," I said firmly, sliding my feet into the slippers. "I don't suppose you know where there's a men's closet on the way out?"

Now. The urge reverberated through me, pushing me forward, my head ringing like a bell. The surface was above me—I could see the moon—too close, too bright. It was almost too late.

But I'd broken Zeiler's spell. Why was the dweller still trapped?

I felt the dweller's thoughts fill me, carried on the hellish drug Zeiler had injected into my veins. It was here with me, and I was there with it, and for a moment I didn't know what was happening.

Something shifted, as though two things jostling for space within a box suddenly slipped into place and fit snugly together. Except in this case, the box was my skull, and I was one of the items which now had to share space with something else.

But fit we did. It was huge, and vast, and only a small part of it was inside me, but I could taste its cold blackness, heavy as rancid oil on my tongue.

I straightened out of the crouch I'd fallen into. The dark corridor was bright as day to my eyes, and I heard Amelie give a little gasp. "Oh, your eyes! They're *beautiful*," she said, but the words were far away and meant almost nothing.

"Why aren't you a part of Zeiler's battery?" I asked Amelie. "You hear the dweller." I knew she did, knew it had reached for her just as it had sought me out.

"Because I haven't had the injection." She smiled guilelessly. "Dr. Zeiler says women's brains are too feeble to be of any use."

The fool. I laughed, but it didn't sound like me. It sounded like someone crueler, and for a moment, I was almost afraid. But the tides beat in my veins. I smelled the shore, and the power of the dweller surged through me. I no longer remembered fear. "Zeiler will notice his conduit missing, if he has not already. We should leave."

She led the way to the heavy iron door, but before we reached it, it was flung open from the other side. Judging by the group of sailors and attendants in the doorway, Zeiler must have realized the moment I escaped his psychic battery. Anger twisted their faces, and the one in the lead threateningly slapped his cudgel into his palm, promising violence.

They thought to stop me? How absurd. They should go down on bended knee and beg my forgiveness.

"Step away," I warned Amelie, clinging to a shred of myself. She darted behind me, even as the paltry creatures charged.

I needed a sigil to command the air, but the dweller had its own magic. So together we *sang* down the wind.

The wind screamed down the hall behind me, ruffling my hair and flapping the dressing gown about my knees. Gathering the flow of air, I snapped out my fist.

The men flew back with the crunch of breaking bone. The steel door tore loose, crashing into those who tried to flee, and now the ward once again echoed with screams and moans.

Good.

Amelie came to my side; if she feared me at all, it didn't show on her face or in her manner. She looked like something feral, her hair knotted about her shoulders, her eyes bright and wild. An odd feeling of familiarity caught at me, and I realized her willowy frame and large eyes reminded me of the shark-men statues at the undersea temple.

"I'll take their keys, and let the ones in the restraints go," Amelie said. "Then I won't get in trouble, because we'll all be out."

"Yes," I agreed. My voice sounded like something that had rotted on the seafloor for a thousand years.

I went down the stairs and into the ward below. I walked into the wide hall; the nurse fled, shrieking for help, so I simply kept walking. Every door I passed ripped open, clanging against the walls. The wind the dweller and I commanded howled and buffeted the furniture about. Loose clothing and papers scattered across the floor, and the inmates scrambled to flee my coming.

"Run," I told them. "Run from this place."

I passed from ward to ward, wending my way down, breaking open every door. Not all would flee, perhaps most wouldn't, but I could do nothing more for them than this. Those who glimpsed me began screaming. I fended off two who tried to attack me. As I passed by one of the nurse's stations, the glass windows caught my attention, and I paused.

My reflection stared back dimly, save for my eyes. Rather than their usual muddy shade, they'd paled to amber, and glowed as if a fire blazed behind them.

Something moved in the glass behind me. "Die, you devil!"

Kerr ran at me, clutching a splintered chair leg like a cudgel. I slapped it from his hand with a burst of wind.

"You dare attack me?" I asked. My voice sounded hollow, vast, ancient, reverberating in the hallway.

Kerr shrank back, his eyes wide with terror. This man had hurt Griffin, broken his heart, and now dared to call me a devil?

I'd show him what a devil truly was.

As I took a step toward him, however, chanting swelled up around me, calling me closer, twisting the dweller's song.

Damn Zeiler! I had discharged the psychic battery, but too late. The dweller was too close to land, close enough Zeiler and his followers could force it nearer with their chants and magic alone.

I would simply have to kill them.

Chapter 22

I left Kerr cringing on the ground. Zeiler had to be dealt with first; everything else could come later.

I walked down the stairs in front of the asylum and onto the wide lawn. Wind swirled around me, like a dog frolicking about its master, and the stunted trees shook and shivered. The air washed away the stench of human waste and madness, bringing with it an older, primal reek, of ancient mud and seaweed, of fish slime and barnacle-encrusted blocks of stone. A storm gathered on the horizon, conjured up by magic and the movement of something older than humanity itself, and my bones ached with its need for release.

We broke the surface. The clouds hid the hateful light of the moon, but still it hurt, the wash of air on our sleek skin. A ship made its way toward shore, trailing smoke, and we lashed out in our fury, smashing it with a titan tentacle, wrapping our self around it and dragging it down, while tiny creatures scuttled and screamed and rained down into the water.

The first spitting tongues of rain touched my face. Chanting echoed from the lawn behind the asylum, closest to the sea, and I followed the sound. The twisted chant snaked into my ears like a slimy tongue, and I shuddered at its touch. It was corrupt, vile, distorting the song of the dweller. I had to put a stop to it.

Torches leapt and guttered around a bonfire made from driftwood. Men dressed in the rough clothing of sailors, or in the simple suits of the asylum attendants, stood around the fire, the orange light revealing hideous looks of avarice on their faces.

As for Zeiler, he stood at their head, arms lifted high toward the sea, his strong, clear voice cutting the night and bending the chant to his will. A smile played around his lips, and his expression bordered on rapturous.

I thrashed through the sea/strode across the lawn. One of the ruffians on the outskirts of the gathering turned at the sound, swinging his torch so its light fell across me.

His eyes widened in incredulity—then he laughed.

"Hey," he said to one of his fellows. "Looks like one of the crazies got loose. Get a look at what he's—"

I dashed him aside with the wind of the storm. His scream cut off when he hit the asylum wall.

The chant fell silent. Zeiler turned from the sea to face me, his features dark with hate. "You. You think to put me in my place, just like your father. But you're the one who will suffer now."

This was the one who had distorted my/our song, this was the one who brought pain, and shame. Inhuman rage burst through me, like a tide of black filth, and I howled along with the wind that would strike him down.

Zeiler called out words in a language so old no human memory of it remained, and the cultists echoed him. Their voices crawled into my brain, like dirty fingers, prying, poking, intruding...

They'd taken the *oculares* injection as well. But instead of being drowned in dreams like the wretches Zeiler had experimented on, they used the connection with the dweller to enforce their will over it. No wonder they'd only needed the psychic battery to bring it to the surface.

I clawed at my ears, my skull, seeking to dislodge them, but the pain only distracted me and let them further inside. They had the dweller in their grip, and it and I were one.

The cultists continued their obscene chant, but Zeiler switched to ordinary English. "On your knees, Dr. Whyborne," he said with relish.

I tried to lock my muscles, but my body was beyond my control. My knee hit the damp grass.

Far below, the dweller surged into the cove. A nauseous odor, of dead fish and rotting bones, of black slime nourished by sulfurous water and a thousand years of decay, burst over the headland in a revolting wave.

"This is even better than what I'd planned," Zeiler went on. I wanted to scream defiance, but my jaw remained stubbornly shut. I was a slave to his will, free only in the confines of my mind.

And even that I shared with the dweller.

"Having Niles Whyborne's son leashed at my side will be a pleasure," he went on. His eyes glittered, not blown bright by the dweller's power like mine, but wild with hate and ecstasy. "You can take him apart with your sorcery while I watch. Perhaps I'll let my men have your mother first, while Niles looks on."

He turned to one of the sailors and motioned sharply. "Bind him."

A loud scream came from the direction of the asylum.

Zeiler looked up in surprise at the unholy storm of shrieks, rising even above the howl of the wind and the thunder of the ocean. What was happening?

I couldn't see, couldn't move, the chant pinning me in place along with the dweller.

The man who'd been ordered to bind me froze, eyes going wide, his voice falling out of the chant. "What the hell?"

"Keep on!" Zeiler cried. "The dweller will crush them—we will crush them—there is nothing to fear!"

The sailor seemed to take heart and started toward me. His skull disintegrated in a shower of blood and bone, the crack of a rifle echoing across the headland.

The chant faltered, putrid fingers slipping free of my brain. I regained enough control to turn my head and see what transpired behind me.

The patients of the asylum streamed out into the night, crying for vengeance. At their head ran Amelie, a garden hoe held high as a makeshift weapon. Griffin ran with them, his green eyes narrow with fury, and my heart surged for just an instant.

They closed with the cultists, and the chant fell into tatters, nothing remaining to hold me. A wave of anger roared through my body, washing away all other thought, driven by the dweller. Rage and pain, and fury that these crawling worms, these insubstantial creatures with their brief lives, would turn my own tools against me. The dryness of the air burned my skin, and I sang of my pain, the unearthly howl shattering the night.

I stretched out my arms, elation and power pouring through me. Cultists ran toward me, but I hurled them back with wind, or set them ablaze with a word. The air reeked of blood and I heard myself laughing above the roar of the tide.

A tentacle mimicked the motion of my human limbs, stretching for the sky. Titanic, it whipped into the air, towering above even the cliff. Bands of luminescent color rippled across its surface, stark white and furious red, interspersed with spots of black. A group of cultists attempting to flee froze at the sight, hypnotized.

The tentacle crashed down, smashing the wall into dust and crushing the cultists into a bloody pulp.

"And now the rest," I whispered.

A second gargantuan tentacle joined the first, then a whole writhing host of them, color strobing along their lengths and making them difficult to look at directly. They grasped the ground, the rocks, and even the walls of Stormhaven itself. One wrapped around the clock tower; a moment later, it toppled in a rain of masonry. The screams around us became a cacophony, cultists and patients alike fleeing before the coming of the dweller.

As it should be.

"Damn you!"

The wind whipped my dressing gown about my calves, power flooding my veins and hardening my cock. I turned slowly, leisurely, to face my tormenter.

Zeiler's face was distorted with a mixture of terror and frustrated rage.

"You're no better than me!" he screamed. "You have no right, you whoreson bastard! Just because your father—"

"I am my mother's son," I snarled, and reached out with fire and wind.

He screamed, blazing up in an inferno, a zephyr of flame spiraling off his flailing form. Wheeling and stumbling, he spun toward the edge of the cliff, but we flicked him back with a massive tentacle. He didn't deserve the quick death of a fall, or to pollute the ocean with his bones.

The charred shape which had been Zeiler collapsed onto the lawn, twitching feebly. But our vengeance remained unsated.

We were wrath and magic. These crawling ants would pay for hurting us, starting with the loss of their nest. I summoned the waves, the sea pounding against the base of the cliff. Stormhaven began to crumble, the entire headland collapsing, and I laughed as I strode ahead of the destruction. A great hand clutched the rock behind me, hauling its heavy body free from the sea. We'd strike out across the land, destroy these insects who dared imagine themselves our masters. They would pay. All of them.

"Whyborne!"

Another ant, crying out. I ignored it.

"Ival!"

The name snagged something deep inside, beneath the rush of power. A good memory. I wouldn't crush them all, perhaps. I'd take this one, take him again and again, make him scream for me even as I satisfied the lusts of a god. I'd…

He emerged from the smoke and dust of Stormhaven's destruction, his hair wild and his face streaked with blood. Our eyes met, and he froze, like a mouse in front of a viper.

"Zeiler is dead," he said. "Let the dweller go!"

His words made no sense. I wasn't keeping it here. We would bring suffering on those who deserved it, and those who did not would laugh and be free, reveling in the downfall of cruel men like Zeiler, and my father. Like Kerr and the damnable preachers who called my desire for men an abomination.

I tried to step around him, but he obstinately put himself in my path. A heavy tentacle curled around the jutting foundation of the asylum, not ten feet from us, its grip firming to haul a vast body further onto the land.

"Out of my way," I ordered, and my voice was made of wind and fire and wave.

His face had gone utterly white, but he shook his head. "No."

The wind rose around me, my every nerve burning to unleash against something, anything. "Out of my way!"

"Ival, please. Remember who you are. Come back to me." He swallowed convulsively. "I love you."

I was power and magic and rage, and by rights I should strike him aside. But something deep within me rebelled.

"You promised," he said, tears in his eyes. "You promised to stay with me forever. Don't you remember?"

Yes. I did. I remembered…something. A name.

My name. I was someone, wasn't I? Someone human.

Ival.

I was…

I was Percival Endicott Whyborne, and he was

"Griffin," I gasped, reaching for him.

The tether of rage snapped. Released, the dweller drew back, even as I tumbled forward, into Griffin's arms.

I blinked awake a few moments later, to the feel of someone frantically caressing me. "Whyborne? Whyborne!"

"Slap him," Christine suggested. "That will bring him around."

I dragged open dry eyelids as hastily as I could. "Please, don't," I croaked.

Christine and Griffin knelt over me, their faces drawn with worry. Seeing me awake, Griffin slumped back, putting his hand to his eyes. Christine, being more practical, extended her hand. "Can you sit up?"

"I think so." I let her haul me into a sitting position, and was vaguely pleased when I didn't topple over. "What on earth are the two of you doing here?"

"It took most of the day, but I managed to discover rumors of something important happening tonight," Griffin said, letting his hand fall to his lap. "The summoning, I assumed. I rushed back to the house and found you gone, and a frantic note from my mother, saying Pa had disappeared."

"They threatened to kill him if I didn't cooperate," I said. "I-I don't know what happened to him." God, if he'd been crushed by falling masonry, it would be my fault, as surely as if I'd killed him with my own hand.

"He escaped," Griffin said. "I encountered him on the lawn with the other patients. He tried to talk me into fleeing with him—he said something about you being a devil."

I shuddered, remembering what I had almost done to the man. "He had good reason to think so."

Griffin put a reassuring hand to my shoulder. "At any rate, I was wild with fear when I found you gone. I didn't know what had become of you, or Pa, or how to stop the dweller from coming. The only thing I could think to do was hurry to Stormhaven as quickly as possible and try to do something, anything, to disrupt the summoning. Everything else had to wait. Christine agreed, and we lingered only long enough to arm ourselves before rushing here. Even then, we were almost too late."

"But you weren't." A shiver ran through me. I hated to imagine what might have happened had he not been here to stop me.

"No." Griffin hesitated and tightened the hand on my shoulder. "Are you all right, my dear?"

Exhaustion settled over me like a heavy blanket. "I think so. Just scraped and bruised. And I lost my clothes."

He leaned back, concern on his face, and I realized what he really meant to ask. *"No,* Griffin. Nothing happened." Although perhaps I should be completely honest. "Well, almost. But I set him on fire."

He nodded, then kissed me on the mouth, heedless of the fact Christine sat three feet away. My face grew uncomfortably hot, but I returned his kiss anyway.

"Where is everyone?" I asked, when I could speak again.

"Run off," Christine said. She climbed to her feet, using her rifle like a cane. "The children and some adults like Kerr took off for the road even before the fighting started. I think most of the patients got away in the end. And a few of the cultists; I ran out of bullets, you see."

"We should follow their example and remove ourselves from the scene," Griffin said, rising to his feet and holding out his hand to me. "Someone will surely be along to investigate the disturbance, and I don't wish to answer any impossible questions. Better no one learn we were here at all."

I agreed whole-heartedly. "Did you bring a carriage?" I asked as Griffin hauled me to my feet.

"Horses. And they're bound to have run off," Christine said, taking one of the torches for light. "We'll have to travel by foot."

I wasn't certain how far I could walk wearing slippers, but leaving the immediate area seemed imperative, so I only fell in beside Griffin. As we walked through what looked more like a battlefield than the peaceful lawn it had been only hours before, I scanned the faces of the dead. I didn't see Amelie or Allan Tambling, and hoped they'd escaped unharmed.

The front wall still stood, the iron gates open wide. As we passed through them, a coach rumbled up. My heart sank—we hadn't escaped without notice after all. Perhaps Griffin could spin some wild tale which would allow us to slip away?

Then I saw the ornate crest painted on the side, and my heart sank even further.

The carriage came to a halt, and my father climbed out. He looked at us, at the ruins of Stormhaven, then back at us. "Well, Percival, I suppose this is your doing?"

"Yours, rather," I said shortly, too exhausted to tolerate his sniping.

He scowled at me. "What do you mean?"

"Zeiler carried rather a grudge against you and the rest of the Brotherhood. This was his means of settling the score. So congratulations, you've indirectly almost destroyed the world twice now."

"I accept no responsibility for—"

"Of course you don't." I waved a tired hand. "What are you even doing here?"

His lips pursed in the midst of his silvery beard. "Your mother roused the entire household, screaming in a nightmare. We had a devil of a time waking her from it. When she spoke of the sea, it seemed likely the Eyes were making their move. If Zeiler was involved, it must be here. And of course you were certain to be in the midst of it. Heliabel would never have forgiven me if I hadn't come straight away to make certain you were still breathing."

I exchanged a glance with Griffin. "Mrs. Whyborne heard the dweller's song?" he asked.

"I would put it down to a mother's intuition of her child's danger, but I suspect there was more to it." Father looked around again at the ruins and shook his head. "Well, get in the carriage. I might as well take you back into town with me."

He stood aside so Christine and Griffin could climb inside. As I waited my turn, he eyed my attire and let out a loud sigh. "Ah, well," he said, "a good thing Stanford is bound to come around in the end."

CHAPTER 23

A WEEK LATER, Griffin led the way across the rocky strand of a secluded beach to the south of Widdershins. We'd had quite a hike to get there, but the weather was fair, and my various bruises and cuts largely healed. As he had the day we rode to Stormhaven, Griffin carried a picnic basket. Unlike that day, this one held nothing but the expected contents.

We spread a blanket well above the water's reach. While I unpacked our meal, Griffin opened a bottle of wine and poured us each a glass. The sun cast the shadows of the cliffs over us, and turned the sea a strange shade of bronze. Only the crying of gulls and sigh of the waves met our ears, and I could almost fancy we were the last two humans on earth.

I held up my glass to make a toast. "To the anniversary of your arrival in Widdershins," I said.

Griffin clinked his glass against mine. "I must say, it proved a rather more eventful year than I'd ever imagined when I stepped off the train."

"And probably contained rather more monsters than you'd prefer."

He propped his chin on his fist and smiled at me. "Perhaps. But I wouldn't trade any of it for the world."

After we ate, we sat pressed together, his head resting against my shoulder. "It's beautiful, isn't it?" he asked, gazing out over the waves.

I looked down at our hands, intertwined on my knee. "Yes, it is."

"I can't help but think what's down there, though," he went on more quietly. "Beneath the waves. I'm not sure I'll ever feel entirely safe without solid earth under my feet."

The dreams had ceased—for me, at least, and the poor wretches Zeiler had experimented on. Allan Tambling had returned to work at the museum already.

His name hadn't been precisely cleared—after all, he had technically been the one to kill his uncle. But my testimony of Zeiler's mesmerism was enough to convince the authorities the doctor had been a dangerous madman, and the murder was blamed on him instead.

None of the papers had formed a coherent opinion of the destruction of the asylum, or the bodies of those who had fallen in battle outside of it. Officially, they had all died when a freak storm struck the area. For the most part, the police contented themselves with rounding up any troublesome escapees and sending them to the state hospital in Danvers. The rest were left to go on about their lives quietly.

As for Amelie, without the dweller's song pressing against her thoughts, she'd regained much of her sanity. She'd already written several letters to the newspaper exposing the abuses of the asylum, and there was talk she would be invited to address the legislature in their next session.

Her new role might not last, or it might become her calling, I didn't know. Either way, I hoped she would have a happy life. If not for her intervention, things would have gone very differently indeed, and the Eyes' plan might have succeeded.

"I heard from Ruth," Griffin said.

"I would have thought the family would have forbidden her to write you," I said.

"Either they didn't think to forbid it, assuming she wouldn't wish to, or she didn't care," he replied. "She said after meeting Miss Parkhurst and the other ladies, not to mention Christine, she has decided against remaining in Kansas and marrying immediately. She hopes to find employment in Baltimore. I wrote back and told her to contact me, should she find herself in any difficulty."

"That was very good of you."

"I thought you'd approve. As for Ruth, I think she'll be happier having experienced more of the world, even if she ultimately chooses to return home."

"No doubt." Assuming the rest of the family allowed her such a choice, at least. "And…your father? How is he?" It seemed impossible to believe I'd actually contemplated violence against the man. When I'd confessed the events to Griffin, he insisted the impulse had come solely from the dweller.

I did my best to believe him.

"Half the time he thinks the imagined the whole thing," Griffin said. "The other half, he swears to anyone who will listen that you're demon possessed, or a Satanist, or perhaps a black magician. Ruth says the family has convinced him not to talk about it in front of anyone else, at least."

"I'm sorry," I said unhappily. "I suppose there really is no chance of reconciliation now, if he believes me to be some unholy abomination."

"You're probably right," he agreed. Sadness tinged his expression, and I dropped my gaze to my shoes.

"Griffin…I'm sorry about what happened. About your family."

He was silent for a long time, staring out over the gently lapping waves, until I began to think the subject dropped. At last, however, he said, "I think some part of me believed if I convinced my parents my life was normal, if I saved Allan from the asylum, then everything would be like it was before my confinement. Time would turn back upon itself, and I could be whole again. Become the man I was before I went into the basement or spent months in the asylum. But the world doesn't work that way. Once something changes, it doesn't ever really go back."

"No." I turned my head and pressed a kiss into his hair. "I've given the matter some thought in the last week, and if you wish, we can have electricity run to the house."

Griffin laughed, sitting back in order to look at me. "I never know what is going to come out of that mouth of yours next, my dear. Your mind is a complete conundrum."

I stared down at my hands. "You've given up so many things for me. I can at least give this silly electric light a try."

Griffin laid his hand on top of mine. "I haven't 'given up' anything for you."

"Your family."

"They gave me up, not the other way around," Griffin said.

"But you had to choose."

"So did they." Griffin pulled away from me and drew a small parcel from his pocket. "I have something for you."

"A present?" I asked, taking it from him. "Whatever for?" Had I forgotten some special occasion? "My birthday isn't for over a month."

"Just open it."

I unwrapped the paper, revealing a small box. Inside the box lay a pocket watch. "Thank you," I said, although I wasn't certain why he thought I needed a new watch.

"Look inside the case."

I did so, and found it was of the type meant to hold a portrait or other memento. Griffin had fitted it with the photograph of the two of us from the pier.

Emotion tightened my throat, and I blinked rapidly against the burning sensation behind my eyes. "Thank you." I wished I had something to give him in return. "I'll keep it with me, always."

Griffin shifted closer and took my hands in his. "I may not be able to take you dancing, or bring an armful of flowers to your office, or hire a carriage for a romantic ride through the park, but I can at least do this," he said. "Give you something to carry with you, so you'll always have a reminder of how much I love you."

I tried to thank him again, but my voice broke, so I kissed him instead. I felt as if my heart had taken flight, skimming across the waves with the gulls. After, we sat together in silence, his head on my shoulder, our hands on his knee, until the stars came out.

Acknowledgements

Special thanks to Sarah, tour guide at the Trans-Allegheny Lunatic Asylum, for answering my many questions during the tour. Like Stormhaven, TALA was built in 1864 using the Kirkbride plan and, in fact, is the only remaining Kirkbride lunatic asylum that can be legally visited. You can learn more about TALA, Kirkbride buildings, and the history of treatment for the mentally ill at http://trans-alleghenylunaticasylum.com.

Extra-special thanks to my editor, Annetta Ribken, who put up with a great deal of whining and moaning from me during the editing phase of this book. Without her guidance, *Stormhaven* would have been far less than it could be. As always, any errors or disappointments are solely my responsibility.

Thanks also to Allan J, for providing the name for Uncle Victim, I mean Victor, via Twitter conversations during the writing of this book.

About the Author

Jordan L. Hawk is a trans author from North Carolina. Childhood tales of mountain ghosts and mysterious creatures gave him a life-long love of things that go bump in the night. When he isn't writing, he brews his own beer and tries to keep the cats from destroying the house. His best-selling Whyborne & Griffin series (beginning with Widdershins) can be found in print, ebook, and audiobook.

If you're interested in receiving Jordan's newsletter and being the first to know when new books are released, please sign up at his website: http://www.jordanlhawk.com. Or join his Facebook reader group, Widdershins Knows Its Own.

Printed in Great Britain
by Amazon